"There is a vivid rush of sea air and immediately you are immersed in this finely crafted historical novel, gripped by its world and characters until you reach the powerful, tragic conclusion. This book will stay with me for a long time." —**Adam Foulds**, author of *The Quickening Maze* and *Dream Sequence*

"*Far Cry* gives the best gift of fiction: a bracing, electrifying dive into another world, other lives. Period doesn't enter into it—this is reality. By exact and convincing detail, interior and exterior, York inhabits this fishing life. Not shrinking from pain or violence, she sends her line farther down to create an underlying elegy to the natural world, now so changed. The unstoppable tidal flow of the book's inevitable conclusion, the knotting and unknotting of the long net these people struggle within—that is true art." —**Marina Endicott**, author of *The Difference* and *Good to a Fault*

"*Far Cry* is a mystery set in a small west coast fishing village, wrapped tightly in kelp, unfolding to the rhythm of the sea. Not only did I become lost in a different time, but this novel brought my heart to a new place. I lived inside these characters; their impulses, their losses and their loves were mine. This is historical fiction meticulously crafted by one of our finest writers." —**Claire Cameron**, author of *The Bear* and *The Last Neanderthal*

"*Far Cry* is a mystery that only reveals the whole, shocking truth in the final pages, where the pieces come together with an almost audible snap." —**Gil Adamson**, author of *The Outlander* and *Ridgerunner*

FAR CRY

ALSO BY ALISSA YORK

The Naturalist
Fauna
Effigy
Mercy
Any Given Power

FAR CRY

a novel

ALISSA YORK

RANDOM HOUSE CANADA

PUBLISHED BY RANDOM HOUSE CANADA

www.penguinrandomhouse.ca

Library and Archives Canada Cataloguing in Publication

Title: Far cry / Alissa York.
Names: York, Alissa, author.
Identifiers: Canadiana (print) 20220235317 | Canadiana (ebook) 20220235449 |
ISBN 9781039002050 (hardcover) | ISBN 9781039002067 (EPUB)
Classification: LCC PS8597.O46 F37 2023 | DDC C813/.54—dc23

Text design: Kate Sinclair
Cover design: Kate Sinclair
Image credits: The Invading Surf by Frederick Judd Waugh / Artvee.com

Printed in Canada

10 9 8 7 6 5 4 3 2 1

Penguin
Random House
RANDOM HOUSE CANADA

for Anne Collins, the right card

and as always
for Clive

But what is the sound of the sea itself?
Waves that trickle over a beach or pound against
the cliffs and rocks of the weather-beaten
coasts? Yes, that's what the ocean sounds like
from land. Underwater it's a different story.

MORTEN STRØKSNES
Shark Drunk

Rivers Inlet, British Columbia

JUNE 1922

1

This morning the bay is green. Already the water has begun to stink—the yards-wide streak of the shithouse drift, the waste of a hundred incomers or more. In two days' time the cannery will come clanking to life. There will be blood on the waves, the sky wild with smoke and reeking steam, the wheeling white bodies of gulls.

Time to be getting on. Soon enough some fisherman who has not heard the news will come thudding down the boardwalk and halt to read my handwritten sign. *Death in the family.*

I have left the shutters closed at the store, and here at the cottage too. It is not always so convenient living next door to your place of work.

I ought to light the stove, warm the old dog lying by its iron feet. Dig out a decent shirt. I wonder, Kit, will you wear a dress? You would feel easier in your work clothes, and is that not what your father would wish?

I would have had his body here, you know that, but you wanted him carried home along the headland path—Knox, Willie and myself each gripping a corner of the oilskin while you insisted on taking the fourth. It was good of Ida to help you wash and dress him. Your father was not a large man, and you have always been strong for your size, but that is no job for a girl to manage alone. Young woman, I suppose I should say. I forget you are eighteen years old.

Burial, too, will be no easy task, especially in this country where the mountains lift up out of the sea. Any open ground is cross-hatched, roots over rock—you know the trouble your mother had scraping up enough soil for her garden. You are right, though, the lookout is a fitting spot. Your father and I walked that trail often enough, clearing deadfall and replacing pipe when the waterline broke. A fair view out over the inlet. And yes, he would never have found his rest at sea.

You are angry with me for how it happened—but, Kit, he would have been in the same state or worse on his own. I will be careful today. On my honour, only one drink before we troop up the mountainside with Frank in his box. Just enough to steady the soul.

◊

They're halfway to the lookout before Kit realizes she hasn't dressed for the occasion. Overalls dragged on over the shirt she slept in, boots. Not that it matters: hardly anyone has bothered to climb the waterline trail. The Pauls have come, of course, Willie and his two sons helping Uncle Anders lug the coffin. Mr. Knox walks behind them, then Ida Paul holding young Annie's hand. Kit brings up the rear.

It's no mean feat carving out the grave. They make a start at the base of a windthrown hemlock, the root mass torn up along with whatever foothold the great tree had managed to find. Ida stands alongside her daughter while her husband and sons take turns with Uncle Anders' spade. Knox gets out his pipe and fills it. Kit feels his glance—sympathy or something like—and steps back out of his fruit-scented smoke.

She's mostly quiet inside. Still, she feels something slip when Ida puts an arm around Annie and draws her close. A year ago, Kit would've had her own mother beside her. Who knows, if Bobbie hadn't left them, there might've been no burial to attend.

Once the men have torn out a scrubby yew, the box goes in. In minutes they've filled the shallow trough. Everyone helps drag dead-fall to cover the grave—one fair-sized log and a dozen mossy limbs.

When the last branch has been laid, Knox looks as though he might be about to say a few words. Uncle Anders beats him to it, speaking in his old language, something he rarely does. Kit understands nothing beyond her father's name.

When her uncle falls silent, Knox gives a sorry smile. "Rest in peace, Frank." He nods to Kit and turns to head back down.

While the others linger, Kit follows the cannery manager, catching up with him along the trail. Knox gives her a searching look before responding to her request. Yes, he can set her up with a fisherman's licence, if that will make her happy. If she's sure.

Standing at the end of the long dock, Kit stretches her gaze to the bay's far shore. Beyond Morden Point, the inlet opens wide. She could walk two docks over, crank up the *Dogfish*'s engine and steer her out over the deeps. Except that would mean standing where it happened—where she found him face down, floating between the dock and his own boat's hull.

Her hair flies up on a gust. She tucks the home-cut bob behind her ears. Forget the *Dogfish*, she needs to get the feel of a company skiff again, now that she'll be going out with the fleet. She's had three long years of rowing nothing bigger than the *Coot*, keeping close to shore. *I mean it, Kit, no more than a stone's throw.* Her father wasn't a rule-maker by nature, but neither was he one to be disobeyed.

Before that, she'd taken her uncle's rowboat out as far as she pleased. He's up there now, Uncle Anders, standing some thirty feet above her on the headland, hands on the railing of the storefront porch. She resists the urge to lift her eyes to him, lift her hand. It's a feeling she's known all her life, her uncle watching over her. Shame he didn't keep a closer eye on her dad.

Moving into the cannery's shadow, she makes her way along the wharf. Men hunker in their skiffs, checking their nets, patching their scrappy sails. A dozen or so kids roam the docks. Not a woman in sight—the fishermen's wives packing the week's grub boxes, the washers and packers scrubbing the cannery down. One turn of the clock until the fleet goes out, another until the collector boat steams into the bay with the season's first catch in her hold.

It's where Kit belongs, out there over the returning schools. Her father had long trusted her fish sense. *She knows how to find them, my girl. She's got the nose.* More like the ear. It was akin to listening, reaching a thought out to where they might be.

Third dock along, Knox said, skiff number forty-four. Kit looses the painter line from the cleat and steps aboard. Already she feels calmer, drifting back from the dock, settling herself on the thwart. Taking up the oars, she pulls a line of narrow strokes until she's clear of the other boats.

Rowing lets you watch what you leave. Far Cry Cannery and its quarter mile of town strung along the bay's eastern shore— boardwalk linking shacks to sheds, to proper little cottages with dark-green doors. Steep stairs cut up through the brush to where the cookhouse and the China House jut from the slope. Above it all, the slash of the waterline trail.

On the headland, Uncle Anders' cottage sits alongside the store. Nothing but boardwalk and scrub from there out to the manager's house on the point. She's passing it now, pulling round to come level with the mouth of the bay. A surprise to see the parlour windows open, curtains sucked out to flump on the wind. Of course—Mrs. Knox isn't there to keep them closed. She's stayed behind in the city this year, too sick to make the trip north.

And now another unexpected sight: the manager himself, home instead of holding forth at the wake. Stepping out his front door to stand among the flower tubs on the porch, he catches sight of her and waves. *Wave back, Kitty-cat*—her mother's voice in her ear, whether Kit wants it or not. *Never hurts to have a friend.* Kit raises her hand briefly before closing it again on the oar. Knox waves on, as though she's leaving for good rather than just out for a row. Shit for brains, her father would say if he could.

Kit rows out into the inlet, the mountains tipping up into view. This side of the headland is still mostly wild, her cabin just visible among the trees. She ought to be up there now, checking her gear, resting; a week of gillnetting in the skiff on your own is no joke. She could ask around for a boatpuller, but what man would agree to row for a girl? More to the point, whose company could she stand?

In open water now, she glides for a time, her oars suspended. Evening light, the sea all round her. She'll manage on her own.

◖

It was just as well you left before the wake, Kit. Ida was the only woman there, and she and Willie slipped away not long after the bottles came out. Fishermen crowded round the store counter as though it was any weekend night—Japanese and Finns, Scots and Irish, Greeks.

Hanevold and my other Norwegian countrymen were there, come down from Hagensborg on the Bella Coola River in their own skiffs. They joined the itinerant handliners in from every off-channel port, Oweekeenos from the village, city boys come up on the boat.

Talk turned to the coming run. Good signs out on the sound, not a big year, but bound to be better than '21. I wondered if I would have to remind them why they were there. You know your father was not one to surround himself with friends. Even so, there were men among those gathered who had admired him once, or at least envied him as the man who had married your mother. Drink flowed, and the stories followed. About the way Frank Starratt courted and caught his blue-eyed bride. The way he left Far Cry, and the way he returned.

"He was young to die," the Hungarian, Balko, put in.

I nodded. "Thirty-nine." Strange to think, Frank and I were like brothers, but he could have been my son.

Knox arrived in due time, his face arranged in a semblance of respect. One drink and he was ready to take over the talk.

"Oh, Starratt had a temper all right. I'd heard stories long before I set eyes on him. Thought twice about taking him on."

Yes, Kit, a good thing you were not there. A few more drinks and Knox had cleared the place like a seal come sliding through the school. He held on to the counter with one hand and turned to confront the empty store. After a moment he swung back to me. "Fancy a game of crib?"

It was the last thing I wanted—unless it was to walk next door and sit down at my table alone.

◊

The cabin is quiet, no one to feed but herself. Kit swallows a mouthful of salmon, sweet and rich. Nothing wrong with fish and porridge, especially when the potatoes have run out. She could save herself the trouble next time, eat at the cookhouse with the other bachelor fishermen. Is there a word for a girl bachelor? Uncle Anders would know.

The last of the porridge now, savoury with butter and salt. Her spoon rings in the bowl. She drinks down her tea, then stands to carry her few things to the basin along with the lamp. *Sooner you do them, sooner they're done.* Her mother standing at the kitchen work-bench, dark hair hanging down her back. Bobbie Starratt, small like her daughter, a presence in any room. Kit blinks the image away.

The kettle's still warm. She pours the water and wets the rag, rubbing it over the soap. Looks out into the night. Bobbie loved this window, gazing out over her garden of tubs. Frank and Uncle Anders left a scrim of trees to hold the cliff and manage the wind, but the water still sends its light up through the boughs. Step between the trunks and the world opens wide—the rocky climb down to the spill of sand at the stream mouth, the inlet stretching south before bending west to the sound.

Kit sets her mug and bowl in the basin, her fork and spoon. Lets her hands rest in the warm water. In the dark she can just make out the tubs, raggedy with self-seeding stragglers and weeds. There'd never been any question of digging beds in the rocky clearing. She and Bobbie would range over the headland, scrounging whatever dirt they could carry home.

One early summer morning when they returned with pails in hand, her mother knocked the bottom out of a shallow barrel, leaving a ring of staves secured by two iron hoops. This she set atop the potato tub, a few leaves peeking over its lip. While Kit held the ring in place, Bobbie wrapped the whole structure in sacking. They dumped in the hard-won soil, crowding it round the plants. It looked wrong, smothering the leaves like that, sparing only a handful of tips to gather the light.

"Don't worry," Bobbie said. "They like the dark." She packed down the dirt. "Why don't you make us some tea."

Kit would have been seven or so, trusted to feed the stove and boil the kettle herself. She made the tea with the same care she brought to any job—her mother's sweet and strong in the blue enamel mug, her own milky in the green.

Sitting with their knees drawn up, backs resting against the cabin wall, they caught the sun alongside Bobbie's plants. For a time they sipped in silence. Then Bobbie nodded toward the doubled tub.

"Trick of my mama's, that. She always planted a few things out back of the place. Pretty swampy on the Tar Flats, but she had a way of making things grow."

Kit looked at her mother. Bobbie never talked about her life before Far Cry.

"I was the only kid in the house," she went on. "The landlady's son, he was older, and there was a houseboy—well, we called him that, but he was a man." She smiled to herself. "He had this bicycle he used to ride to the greengrocer's. One time me and my mama were sitting out on the porch with some of the other women— I would've been about your age, I guess—and here comes Wing, pedalling up the road with his basket full of lilacs. All you could see of him was his hat. You should've heard my mama laugh."

Kit held her mug with both hands. She took a breath. "What was she called?"

"Huh? Oh. Jeannie." Bobbie glanced away. "Jeannie Holt."

It had been the wrong thing to ask. Her mother stood, tossing the last of her tea across the moss. "Not a word about this to Daddy."

Kit nodded. She was the child again.

They kept it up all summer. Every time the potato plants stretched into the light, they fitted another ring and filled it with earth. By harvest time, Bobbie had to stand on a chair with her watering can. The day they tore it all down, Kit saw her mother was right: potatoes did like the dark. There were pounds and pounds of them, clustered in their grubby skins. Enough to last the winter through.

◖

Knox stayed on for a second game. I suppose that will be the way, now that his wife is no longer waiting up for him down the end of the walk. Poor Orpha, left behind to dwindle in the city, a wraith in her brother's fine house.

I have propped the door open to clear out the sweet stink of Knox's pipe. Lys lies at my feet, attentive to night sounds, among them the whisper of pencil against page. It is my intention to keep a clear head while I write. That may prove difficult—I will admit, the drink at my left hand is not my first. Kit, I pray you do not inherit this fault. Your mother could take a drink or leave it. There were doubtless mornings when she rose with a groan, but she never knew the tidal round of it, the salt return. Your father had it in storms. It is thanks to me that he learned to drink steadily, day by day.

It used to fill him with light. You have witnessed it, seen him grow wilder, more handsome—more in love with your mother, that shine in his eye. There were times when drink had that effect on me. You will find that hard to believe, knowing me as a man who draws into himself a little more with every glass. *A livener*, my old boss Desmond Wells used to call it, drawing the whiskey from his coat pocket after we'd brought in the net. I would not allow myself to carry a flask in those days, but I watched as Desmond drank from his. I waited for him to pass it my way.

Livener, deadener—either way, it was something Frank and I shared. All those nights playing round after round until the cards began to swim. I told myself I was looking after him, but the truth is, it bound us to each other. It bound him to me.

Drink makes a man trusting. Drunk men tell you things.

I do not know how much you truly understand, Kit, but I know how much you see. Those eyes of yours—your father's eyes but darker, quieter. And you keep your ears open. Little wonder Lys took to you, and Skygge before her. It would not surprise me if you could smell a man's secrets too.

2

Where to begin? You have known me all your life, Kit, but what of the life that came before?

I was like you when I was small—from the first, I loved going out in the boat. On the day I am thinking of, my father rowed us out over the rocks at the end of our little bay. I knew to keep quiet when he beckoned me to him and pointed down over the side. Some two fathoms below, a blue-grey wolffish lay in wait. It was as big as I was, even allowing for the water's tricks.

My father took up the heavy little harpoon we call a *pik* and tested its line. He held it out over the side while he judged how the sea was bending the light. The *pik* dropped, its point sinking into the wolffish just behind its toothy head. I moved away to the bow— even a small wolffish can crush a clam in its jaws. The moment my father dragged the catch aboard, he brought down his club. One blow, followed by a quick stick with his knife to be sure.

He was a man of brief, disappearing smiles. *"Kom hit, min sønn."* Together we bent over the long blue body, and he showed me how the *pik* comes free.

———

He was not only a fisherman. We had land—not a large holding, but there were grouse among the aspen where the plot sloped up to the mountains, and good pasture leading down to a wedge of foreshore. White sand, the sea blue-green and clear.

Hvordan kan du vite vannet fra kysten? my mother would say. How can you know the water from the shore? My father was content to know it from the boat on all but the brightest midsummer days, but my mother met the sea every morning, light or dark, with a swim. I remember leaving my bed when I was small to find her coming in through the kitchen door with five new eggs in her basket and ice in her hair. "It wakes you up, *kjæreste*," she said. "I am a sleep-walker without my swim." *Søvngjenger*—she cannot have known how the word frightened me. The idea of your body going on with-out you, the thought of what it might do.

I was perhaps seven years old when I too began to rise early and make my way down to the sea. She would not wait for me—often I stepped out the door to see her partway across the yard, moving through starlight or, in summer, the glow of the night-long sun. Those times when I met her before she set out, she would give me a small nod I learned to return. It was not a time for talk.

We entered the water separately, taking care not to tread on the sea urchins where they gathered close to shore. To begin with, she stayed in longer than I could, but by the end of the first year we were walking back up the beach together, parting ways in the yard—I to the cows, she to her chickens in their roosts. We were more than mother and son on those mornings—or, if not more, then . . . other. *Sjøvenner*, my father came to call us. Sea friends.

Of course, a boy can only look to his mother for so long. By the time I was your age, there was more and more talk of the Laarsens who lived on the island's south shore. Mr. Laarsen took his living entirely from the sea, their holding being half the size of ours and nearly all rock and slope. Good people, my mother made clear, especially, it seemed, the eldest daughter, Marta. I knew her, of course, from the schoolhouse and from church. She was a good-looking girl—all three of the Laarsen children had large, sleepy-looking blue eyes—and she had recently grown tall. Almost as tall as her brother Nils, himself about to be married, my mother took the trouble to mention, to one of the Nyland girls, whose family ran a fishing station on Vestvågøy.

Marta's back had a look of strength about it, I noticed, sitting behind the Laarsens on a Sunday morning. In this too she resembled her brother, though his shoulders were broader, the seams of his good coat under strain. His mother would need to sew him a new one before the wedding. A married man must look the part.

"She will do nicely for you, Anders," my mother said at supper one evening, no longer content to let me find my own way. My father smiled into his potatoes, and the thought came to me like an echo, *She will do.*

I suppose my mother sent word to Mrs. Laarsen. Women manage these things. After the following week's service, my father turned the horse to the south road, and we took our coffee and cake at the Laarsens' table. Nils was gone to the Nyland Station by then, which left only my father and myself to rise when Mr. Laarsen suggested a look at his new keel. A smile on her face, my mother caught hold of my trouser leg beneath the table.

"Anders," Mrs. Laarsen said, "won't you have another piece of cake?"

Marta was smiling too, in her drowsy way. Her sister let out a chirp of a laugh.

"Yes," I said, sitting back down. "Thank you, Mrs. Laarsen, I will."

◖

Pre-dawn glimmering. Kit opens her eyes in the cabin's main room. She hasn't slept in her own room since they carried her father out. With no one left in the other bedroom, the place feels overburdened on the port side. One good swell and over she goes.

The chesterfield is easily as comfortable as her cot—a quality cast-off, proof positive that her mother had done the impossible and made a friend of the manager's wife. Kit runs a finger over the upholstery, tracing the raised pattern of roses. Bobbie had kept it covered with the plaid blanket; too fancy by half, she'd claimed, but Kit wondered if some part of her mother had wanted to keep the fabric nice. Frank never sat on it. Kit had half expected him to burn it last summer when he set fire to the few clothes Bobbie had left behind. The dresses were no great loss, but Kit might have liked a scarf. The blue one, maybe. She doesn't have her mother's eyes, and there's no need to hold back her chin-length hair. Still, she could have knotted it around her neck.

A shade more light—or maybe it's her vision, opening to the gloom. Her mother's net hangs on the wall above her, crowded with years of finds. Bobbie was always stooping to pick up a curl of birch-bark, a crab claw bleached by the sun. The abalone shell was one of Kit's contributions. She can remember spotting it half-buried in the sand; it came out whole, the biggest she'd ever seen.

She swings her feet down and stands. Drawing the blanket around her shoulders, she turns for a proper look. She was small when Bobbie nailed up the net, the memory glinting, deep. She watched while her mother wove in a piece of driftwood in the shape of a point-ing hand. Next came a dried kelp stem complete with holdfast, the stone still clutched in its grip. Skulls, two with beaks, another belong-ing to some small hunter with fur. A stray mooring ring crusted with barnacles—they'd called that one the fisherman's crown.

Her father was home from the grounds for most of a day before the net caught his eye. He rose from the table and went to stand before it. "What's all this?"

"Treasure," Bobbie said.

Frank turned to look at them both. Not much could measure up to his face when he was pleased. Kit couldn't help herself—she slid off her chair and went to him. His hand on her head, the heat of him. As though his belly were banked with coals.

Enough. She shrugs off the blanket, dropping it on the chesterfield in a heap. Crossing to the stove, she cranks open the door and shoves in the last piece of wood. She'll have to split some more—something else her father loved: a tool, a useful task. Both of them, really, Frank with his axe, his handline, Bobbie with her fry pan, her trowel.

Kit stands in the centre of the cabin, suddenly short of breath. Not a thing, *not one thing* in the place that doesn't speak of them. All right, she will cry. She'll sit down at the table, put her face in her hands. Then she'll get up and make some tea.

◖

Thank God Sunday is a half day in the store—yesterday was a trial without your help. You have always been a good worker, Kit. A picture of you comes to me now, six years old, dragging the mid-season mailbag up from the docks. I cannot fault your stock-taking, and if you do not set things out as prettily as your mother did, you never leave a shelf in disarray. But you know what I will say now—you have a way of shrinking in a crowd. The only time you ever went wrong with your sums was in the heat of the Saturday crush.

In any case, I must learn to manage on my own, now that you will be going out with the fleet. Yes, I have heard the talk. Slip of a girl, some of the men are saying, won't last the first week. They do not know you like I do.

I suppose you will not be coming for Sunday lunch. I am not very hungry myself. I will pour a glass, though. Put the cap back on the bottle, the bottle on the shelf.

My mother would not have drink in the house—her own father had had a taste for it. Even so, she never spoke against my father taking the trap into town on Saturday evening. For his part, he never drank more than one pint. Neither did I when I began to go with him—though I remember watching men approach the bar for another round as my father stood up to go.

There was a pattern to those gatherings. The talkers schooled around a central table, the quieter men taking to the corners with their rustling copies of the *Nordlandsposten* and their pipes. My father landed somewhere between, finding a chair at the edge of the group, now and then putting in an opinion, a joke. He did not have to raise his voice to be heard.

"Those who leave, leave because they must," he said one evening. The talk had turned to the latest young man to give up fishing on another man's boat for the New World dream of a farm to call his own. "They are still *nordmenn*," my father added. "They go with our blessing, I think."

There was little the others could do but agree, though some might have thought, *Easy for you, Elias Viken, with your good patch of land and your freshly painted boat and only one son to make a place for in this world.* Meanwhile, that son was listening with different ears. I could not name what I was feeling—I could scarcely locate it within myself. I knew only that when I looked ahead to years in the shape of my father's life, my heart thudded inside me and grew cold.

My father and I returned from the tavern one Saturday to find my mother sitting with the *Nordlandsposten* open before her on the kitchen table. Often she would greet us with a story from its pages— *Listen, now, what do you think of this.* Not that night.

"Sit down," she told me.

I sat, a little loose in the body from the beer.

"You like her?" my mother said.

I did like her, yes. Did I not? I could not seem to make myself nod.

My father dragged his chair out and sat. "If he doesn't want her, there's the sister—"

"Hush, Elias."

He was unaccustomed to her taking such a tone with him. After a moment he took off his cap and folded it in his hands.

"You like her," she said again. When I did not reply, she ran a hand across the newspaper as if wiping away the words. She looked at me. "Anders, there is only one road in this life."

The way she held my gaze—a thousand times I have asked myself how much she understood. In those days even I had only the evidence of my dreams. Alone in my bed I told myself they were nightmares, the shape a boy's fears might take as he became a man.

She was right, though, Kit—the track we had driven home on led back to church and schoolhouse, market and tavern, everyone we knew. One road. I lowered my eyes. But there was also the sea.

Strange to think how many of the great turns in my life began by stepping into a boat. I suppose it is only natural for a Lofoten boy, particularly one who waited for high tide on a calm, clear night to push his father's boat off the sand. Only the little *reska*—I would not think of taking the *Lunde*, his pride.

I remember holding my breath at the sound of the oars rubbing in their locks. Three hours to Nyland Station, I reasoned, four at most, so long as the sea kept quiet. I had heard talk in the tavern that a man could work for his passage on one of the cargo ships bound for Kristiania. If not, there was the shameful purse in my pocket, *kroner* I had taken from my mother's sideboard drawer.

I reached the fishing station at sun-up. I soon learned that Marta's brother Nils was out on one of the boats—in any case, what did I imagine he and I would have to say to each other? In a few hours I had work loading crates of dried *skrei* onto the square-rigger that would take me south.

Two months' work on the Kristiania docks, and I had my fare. I sent the sideboard money home before I set foot on the ship to Quebec, every *krone*, wrapped in a scarf that had caught my eye in the harbour market. I remember, it was white with an embroidered pattern of *multer*. You know them, Kit, cloudberries. There is that patch on the way up to Violet Lake.

They brought the taste of my mother's preserves to my mouth. Even now I can see her unwinding the scarf, letting the *kroner* fall to the floor as she searched for the letter that wasn't there.

3

Time foundered on the passage from the Old World to the New. On days when we were not confined below by heavy seas, I circled the deck, pushing through the hours. I had never been so long without a chore.

As always where men gather, there was drink, there were cards. Knowing the evenings I have spent at the cribbage board with your father, you might wonder at how little satisfaction I took from those games. Youth, I suppose. My mind would stray, and there was always one man at the table who took a lack of concentration as a slight. Besides, most men lost, and I had a better use for my coins. Two months out of my mother's house, I had come to value a daily drink or three.

We were a week at sea before I found another way to pass the time. I had laid down my cards and was wandering among the tables, making a show of interest in the other games. In one corner of the ship's saloon, a trunk stood open, showing the leather backs of books. I knelt for a closer look.

There was *En glad Gut*, a book I knew from the schoolhouse, and there was a history of Nord-Trøndelag I recognized from my mother's little shelf. The rest were new to me. I recall an illustrated treatise on Norway's native plants, the flower heads so familiar they caused me to close the book. At the bottom of the trunk I came upon two titles in English, a water-stained copy of the Bible and a dictionary. These had been carried on board by an old Irishman, I later learned. You have seen his name, Kit—*Neville Barry* in brown ink, a careful hand on the inside leaf. On his way home after decades of work, he had slipped and cracked his skull on the gangway, leaving his books behind.

I let the Bible lie. The other, I carried back to my berth.

Sums had come easily to me as a boy, but it was the puzzle of language that had occupied my mind on the long walk home from school. Those early lessons were my first roads in—Good day, Norway is a fine country, Good night. I found my way to those words that were in league with the *Norsk*—*kniv*, *egg*, *fisk*, *katt*. From there, *båt* taught me "boat," *hjerte* gave me "heart." Hour upon hour I lay in my berth, touching the thread of one word to another, fashioning webs. "Honey" connected to "comb," to "cell," to "swarm." "Estuary" was a word I heard often as we entered the St. Lawrence's muddy reaches. *The mouth of a river in which the tide reciprocates*. And "reciprocate"? I looked that one up too.

Nord Amerika. My notion of the continent's span came from the map on the schoolhouse wall—three, four times as wide as my own country was long. It took me months to work my way across to the west coast. Do not imagine the city as you saw it four years ago, Kit—it was 1879 when I arrived. Granville, it was called then, another seven years before they would set the name Vancouver in stone.

There was work to be found clearing land, even though some of the crew bosses were starting to hire Chinese at half the wage. It was not the first time I had taken up my end of a saw—my father chose one or two of the older aspens each year to take down and sell. The tallest of those old home trees was an infant compared with the giants I came up against here. *Den nye verden*. People were always speaking of the New World on the passage over, but standing among those great cedars and firs, all I could ever think was "old."

I had never known labour like it. In the main we worked a nine-pin method, weakening a couple dozen of what I came to think of as smaller trees by cutting across their backs, then sawing one of the monsters clean through, aiming it to take everything down.

You will remember the crowds, Kit, the sidewalks and ware-houses, the great stone faces of the banks. Picture instead acres of felled trees and tangled brush. Miles. At times you had to climb up out of it to know where you were.

It went on for years, the city greedy for land, but after a few seasons I had had enough. I found work as a dock hand for a time, then as an oiler at the Hastings Mill. That was a filthy job, oiling the saws and winches with dogfish grease, the pistons, chains and gears. The stink of it settled in your skin. If you were not on your guard, stray dogs would follow you on your rounds, licking away the grease. The job came with a shotgun, but I threw offcuts of lumber instead—only to scare them, though at times that meant hitting the mark. Better than a muzzle full of shot, I reasoned. You did not dare chase them off with a torch, especially not in the summer of '86.

With no rain for weeks on end, it was only a matter of time before one of the clearing fires ran wild. The wind came up, and in less than an hour a thousand buildings were gone. Every man had a bucket of sea water in his hand, but the fire made steam of whatever we threw its way. It kept on until it found the forest and burned itself out in the deep-green damp.

I thought it was finished, the city, it had to be. By sun-up there came the sound of sawing and hammering. The mill had survived, but I was done with that job. There was work to be had building, and I took it. It is what we do, Kit—most of us, anyway, most of the time. Even when it makes more sense to lie down and die.

〇

Never mind the looks from the men in the other skiffs—it's a joy riding out with the fleet, one of fifty or more tied onto the towboat's line. When the view opens up past Squid Island, Kit gazes down over the side. It's been that way since she was big enough to grip the gunwale, Bobbie or Frank or Uncle Anders holding the back of her shirt. She can't see far: the ocean's surface is just that, so much beneath it she'll never know.

She takes the tow all the way down through Schooner's Pass. It's deep where she finally drops off the line, the Pacific itself curling round Calvert Island into the sound. A sense of the ocean floor falling away as she rows. How is it, then, that her mind, her memory, climbs?

Violet Lake. When she first heard the name, she wondered if there could be a whole lake the same shade as Mama's best blouse. It was a five-mile hike inland, all of it uphill. The first leg followed the waterline to where it met the stream. They rested then, the four of them taking damp seats on a rotting nurse log, tucked between the saplings grown up in a line along its trunk. Mama took a swig from the water flask before handing it to Kit. Kit drank and passed it to Daddy, who likewise drank and passed it on. Uncle Anders sat with the rifle propped beside him—the berry bushes that grow along a cleared path bring the bears. He looked back the way they'd come, the inlet wide and grey below. Finally he tipped the flask to his mouth. "Skygge, come," he said, and the dog pushed out through the ferns.

From there they followed the stream. Birdsong changed around them as they climbed. It was the same going down into the sea, barnacles giving way to mussels giving way to starfish. The world was alive in layers.

Daddy led the way, then Mama, her hair swaying under the white triangle of her scarf. Behind Kit, the shush of her uncle's stride. Skygge wove through the ranks, slipping into and out of the brush. Kit's legs were a child's, feral in their strength, then weak. She didn't complain. Daddy or Uncle Anders would carry her if she asked.

She was on the point of doing so when the ground began to even out. The stream broadened, its rocky banks turning soft. The mineral smell was gentler, too, mossier. Together they wound through the trees. The lake was there in flashes—Kit felt its light in her limbs and ran.

She'd never seen anything so clear. Mountain runoff, the snow-caps dazzling, close. The lake was wider than the bay, waveless. At the water's edge, she sat down on the pebbles and freed herself from her boots. Skygge lowered his muzzle to drink, but stopped short of wading in. She soon realized why. Pushing her socks into her boots, she stood and stepped into the water. Cold shut like a trap on her foot. She leapt back, letting out a cry.

Behind her, the grown-ups laughed. Kit felt foolish until Mama called, "Is it freezing?" and she could look over her shoulder and nod.

When the dog moved off to join them, Kit looked down at her own bare feet. Moss ruched up along the shore. Bedded in that plush green were wild white violets—thousands of them strung around the lake. She crouched for a closer look: each plant a circle of heart-shaped leaves, each flower striped purple at its heart.

There came the sound of Daddy's tread displacing stones. "Hungry?" he said.

She nodded again, rising.

He held three beers against his chest with a folded arm; in his hand, a bottle of blackcurrant cordial. He stooped to rest them in the water's cold.

"C'mon." His hand on her shoulder, they walked to the stretch of sand where Mama and Uncle Anders were laying out the food. Mama's scarf was as bright as the snowcaps, her dark hair slipping forward over her shoulder.

There were hard-boiled eggs and thick slices of buttered bread, a can of jellied ham. Before long, Daddy returned to the water to retrieve the drinks. Kit's cordial was dark in its bottle, icy to the touch.

The sun was strong. Daddy soon had his head in Mama's lap, so Kit settled for leaning against her arm. She was dozing off when her uncle brushed the crumbs from his trousers and stood. Skygge followed him as far as the water's edge, sitting back on his haunches when Uncle Anders began to unbutton his shirt. Daddy rose up on one elbow, his hand on Mama's thigh.

"Christ, Andy, you're not going in."

Uncle Anders smiled back at them. "Best thing for the heart."

Kit was wide awake now. You were meant to wait after eating— Uncle Anders had told her that. It hadn't been anything like an hour.

"You should try it," her uncle added.

"No thanks," Daddy said. "I like my balls where they are."

Mama laughed. "Me too."

It was the voice she usually kept for Daddy alone. Kit stood and went to join Skygge at Uncle Anders' side.

"Nuh-uh, Kitty-cat," Mama said behind her.

Kit trained her eyes on the water: blue-green, brilliant. "I know."

Uncle Anders was down to his trunks. As always, he didn't hesitate, striding in without so much as a gasp. One day she would learn to dive in the way he did, fingertips parting the water like a sockeye's nose.

He swam a straight line out into the cold. Of course, his limbs wouldn't fail him, even if fresh water didn't hold you up the way the ocean did—he'd told her that too. Still, she kept an eye on him as he swam, far and farther, a disturbance on the face of the lake. Beside her, Skygge whined out his nose. Kit stole a look back at her parents. They were anything but worried, both of them lying down now, wrapped in each other's arms.

◖

It is strange, Kit, but there is nothing like a fire to bring on the growth. Vancouver might have been a forest itself, buildings pushing up through the ashes as if they were fighting for the light. Water mains and electrics, rattling trams. Suddenly there was hard road underfoot where there had been dust or mud.

I lost my room on Powell Street when they knocked the house down to build a hotel. The move landed me several blocks south, around where the fire had first run out of control. It was rough in those parts. The railway had moved its maintenance station down from the Fraser Canyon, bringing a saloon town of workers along. I was the odd man out in my row of bachelor sheds, every one of my neighbours a CPR man, tied to the new roundhouse and surrounding yards.

For a time I worked as a hunter for one of the butcher shops in town. I found a .32 up for pawn and bought it. It was a long row out to Bowen Island in a borrowed skiff, but the woods out there were crowded with deer. These days the sight of a man shouldering a carcass down Cordova Street would draw comment, but back then no one gave me a second look. Not even when I walked back to the docks in my bloodied shirt and trousers. There were quiet spots where a man could ease out of his boots and dive in. Treading water among the pilings, I would slip off my clothes and rub out the stains. That close in, there was nothing more worrisome than dogfish— though sometimes a harbour seal caught the scent of blood and bobbed up nearby. When I had got my clothes clean, I tossed them up onto the dock and swam.

It wakes you up, my mother had said, yet as the days passed into months, I began to feel like a man making the rounds in his sleep. More than once I found myself standing where the edge of the city met the retreating line of the woods, my clothing stiff with salt, the itch of it in my skin. What was a man to do with himself? Stare into the wilds. Turn back in search of a bar.

You might think I would seek the company of my fellow country-men, but the longer I was away from home, the more the sound of men speaking Norwegian caused me to pick up my drink and move away. So many who came over were from the North. They would know me for a Lofoten man by my way of speaking, and then the talk would turn to islands, to families, until they pinned me to my own. To this day I am ill at ease in the old tongue. Well, you have seen me when Hanevold and the others come into the store.

By then I had more than enough English to put in an opinion or two at the bar, but I had never learned my father's trick of joining halfway. Instead, I listened, building on the game I had begun with Neville's dictionary. In the schoolhouse we had spoken poems aloud until we knew them in the blood. I can still see Nils Laarsen standing by the teacher's desk, his neck flushed, mumbling a passage from Wergeland's great epic. *Nu kjende vore Hjerter vi: vi vide, at deres Fordring Sandhed er og Frihed* . . . the heart's claim to freedom, to truth. And so I began to repeat lines I overheard—in my head to begin with, but by the third or fourth whiskey I would catch myself moving my lips.

She was worth every penny.

Lonely country up that way, a man could go spare.

Swear to God, the bugger stood up on its hind legs.

I see now the picture it makes, a man standing to one side, muttering under his breath. I can say only that there was some-thing in the English that comforted me. It was as if I knew that one day I would have your father and mother to talk to. And you, Kit. I would have things to say to you.

4

The bachelor sheds were never truly quiet. Even when the trains slept, men sang and shouted, and there was always a dog or a rooster—or a nearby railway wife's baby—awake and proclaiming in the night. It suited me—a door with a bolt, my coat on a nail, my boots at the end of my cot. Muscles aching from the day's work, I slept.

From my mother I had learned the habit of reading the newspaper right through. It took patience in English, sounding out words and searching out meanings in Neville's dictionary, but every page held clues to how the world around me turned. Much of it was for sale—syrup of figs and flood-damaged pyjamas, ladies' buttoned boots. China-made sugar was full of bugs—only home-refined was safe. Boys were wanted for office work, girls for housework. A great whale had washed ashore in New Jersey. The Irish nationalist Parnell was dead, peasants were being sent to Siberia and an Austrian dynamite fiend was no longer on the loose.

The more my thoughts came to me in English, the easier I was in my mind. If the morning was fine, I would boil coffee on the camp stove, take my tin cup and *Daily World* out onto the step.

Whiskey, I drank sitting up in bed. The men on the row had noses for an open bottle—no matter how softly you poured, a door would open to spill lamplight into the road. Either way, I read. Even words that were strangers, I could often grasp from their surrounds, just as my father had taught me to spot a flounder by the way it shaped the sand.

On summer nights, my shed filled with the rotten breath of False Creek. Come winter, I would lie on my cot and crack patterns in the ice forming on the wall. I could not always bear to stay home.

The night I am thinking of was warm, toward the end of May. As ever, there was life to be found at the Colonial Hotel. I could hear laughter long before I dragged open the door.

I positioned myself where I did in every such place, at the end of the bar nearest the door. The old fellow beside me had hair that stood up thick and cream-coloured, like a pony's close-cut mane. He kept his coat on despite the fug. Fish scales sparkled on the sleeves.

He glanced at me and nodded. Said nothing until I ordered my second drink.

"Norwegian, are you, son?"

I nodded. "Anders Viken."

"Wells," he said, shaking my hand. "Desmond Wells." He drained his whiskey and signalled for two more. When they came, he raised his glass. *"Sláinte."*

I held up my drink. *"Skål."*

"Got one or two of your boys where I've just come from."

"Oh yes? Where is that?"

"Steveston. South arm of the Fraser."

I nodded. "Salmon."

"That's right."

There was quiet while we drank. Then Desmond Wells said, "Been working with a young fella, my boatpuller. He's only gone and taken himself off to Colorado. After the gold, you know. I told him, we'll have silver running right here on the Fraser, going to be a good year." He looked at me. "Done much rowing yourself?"

For a moment my father was before me, cutting the oars down through the surface, leaning back to pull. I held up my hands. "You say it yourself, I am Norwegian."

He laughed—a rough, sudden sound I would come to know.

Desmond Wells had not been lying—'93 was a good year at the Fraser's mouth. Hard work, but I was used to that, and rowing always woke in me the feeling of being a boy. I was not yet thirty-five and as strong as I have ever been.

Five days a week, we were aboard Desmond's *Kerry Maid* before dawn. The breeze blew inland, but Desmond favoured the salt water of the outer drifts, so I would row for three, four hours to reach the set. It is hard to believe now, with all the dog salmon Far Cry handled during the war, but in those days sockeye was the only fish the canneries would touch. How many pinks and cohos did we chuck overboard to the sharks? How many of the big fighting springs?

The liveliest fish, we knocked on the head. Some came up stunned and gulping, still others smothered under the weight of their own kind. The *Kerry Maid* sat low in the water, even after we had thrown everything but the red fish away. That was when you hoped the wind would be with you so you could hoist the sail. You did not want to be late back to the cannery dock. The pitchers worked without rest, jabbing the fish through the head or the tail and flinging them into the bins, but you could still end up bobbing in line with the sun beating down on your catch.

Kit, Rivers Inlet is all the life you have known—eight or nine canneries scattered over thirty miles or more, a weekly tow out to the grounds and the collector boat coming round for your haul. Steveston was a whole town of canneries. Imagine forty vast clapboard sheds built out over the brown and bloodied flood. Thousands of gulls screaming, circling in the smoke and steam.

You can get used to the smell up here. Even when the fog traps it in, there are the trees to sweeten the air and, sooner or later, there is the breath of the sea. The tides draw out the worst of the waste, the rest of it sinks away. On the Fraser, the mess washed up on shore. The incoming tide carried it upriver, marking the banks with stretches of grey, reeking rot. Not just the offal, heads and tails. On the heaviest days of the run, when the fish piled up on the cannery floors, the order came to lift the hatches and shovel the catch away.

I thought the waste was bad that first season. It was nothing to what would come.

◗

Kit lies in the bow, the skiff drifting on the falling tide. Last time she looked, the jacklight at the far end of the net showed the set following, good and taut. You couldn't help but marvel at the reach of it: twenty feet deep, nine hundred long. Now and then the slightest tug—not even that, more of a *tick*. The sound of another sockeye catching itself by the gills.

When she was small, she would play fisherman in the stockroom while Mama worked the weekend rush with Uncle Anders in the store. For a net, she stretched a length of sacking across the floor. The old zinc washtub served as a skiff, but she wouldn't climb aboard until she'd laid out a whole box of spoon lures, each one a homing sockeye headed for its end. What was it about guiding those glinting shapes across the boards? Skygge rested his chin on his paws and watched, a great grey island. For an occasional thrill, Kit made a shark of her arm and drove it through the school.

Meantime, fishermen crowded into the store. All lineup and no letup, Mama used to say—the sound of them relentless, the

week-without-washing animal smell. Mama's voice, bright and lilt-
ing, rose above it all. From time to time she remembered Kit and
swept back through the stockroom curtain with a cup of canned
milk or a slice of buttered bread. *How's my girl?* If too long passed
between visits, Kit could always catch sight of her through the curtain's gap.

Daddy would be in to fetch her later on; she was big enough now
to walk beside him down to the docks. There was real work to be
done on the skiff. He'd sit her down on the forward thwart while he
checked the net, testing every lead weight along the bottom edge,
every cork float along the top.

It was easy to tell when he arrived at the store: the men made
sounds as he pushed his way through the line. *Easy, boys, I'm not
buying.* Why not come in through the side door the way Kit and
Mama did? Kit came to stand by the curtain. Mama was laughing,
standing alongside Uncle Anders behind the counter, the dust cloth
in her hand. Uncle Anders had the register open. Daddy came up
beside the man who had his hand out waiting for change.

"Hi, Frank," Mama said.

"Hi yourself." Daddy looked from her to the man and back.
Behind him, the lineup quieted. "What's the joke?"

"Huh? Oh, nothing."

"Just Carson here," Uncle Anders said. "Telling tales."

"Nothing new there," Daddy said. He was smiling—Kit could see
his teeth from where she stood. Mama smiled too, but Kit witnessed
the dimming. Like a gull on the wing, flaring then folding, becoming
a gull on the dock.

◗

That first summer in Steveston set the pattern. Come early June,
I would drop whatever work I had taken in the city and ride the

carriage twenty miles or so out to the Fraser's mouth. Then came days of labour with Desmond in the boat, off-hours in the bar of the Tolmie Hotel, the stumble back to the bunkhouse along the boards. On Sundays, the long walk out around Garry Point, a breath of clean air if the wind was willing, and a swim.

Steveston dies at the close of season—the boarded-up hulks of the canneries, not a soul in the streets—but while the fish ran, the town was alive all hours of the day and night. People sorted themselves out along the familiar lines—Indian shacks down one end, bunkhouses for the unmarried fishermen, cottages for the family men. The Chinese slitters kept to themselves, except for those white men who gambled alongside them in the China House. There were Norwegians, just as Desmond had said, but I found ways to keep my distance from them, among all the Japanese and Irish, Greeks and Swedes. At times a group of Yugoslavs came in from the surrounding farms, bringing the homey smell of cow shit from the fields. And all that was without a ship in port.

The sight of a square-rigger's sails always brought the children down to the docks—there was sure to be a monkey or parrot on board. The crews made the most of their time ashore before loading up with cans for the return trip to Liverpool around the Horn. Those nights, the Tolmie felt like a hold full of horses—half-fed and barely watered, penned in the dark for months.

On the night the *Godwit* came in, Steveston was already over-full—four years after the run of '93 and everyone calling for another big year. I might have turned round and gone back to my bunk when I saw the crowd, but it was a long time since I had fallen asleep without a drink. I pushed my way forward until a space opened up at the bar.

I was used to having an inch or two over most men, but the sailor beside me was taller by at least a hand. My own age, or was he older?

I remember his earring, not far from my eye. The weight of it dragging down his earlobe. The yellow gleam.

He held up a hand and made his order understood. A pair of whiskeys, a pair of beers.

"Fisherman?" he said, pushing his coins across in exchange for the drinks. I nodded. "Thought as much." He made a show of pinching his nose.

"You think you smell so sweet?"

He laughed. "Not sweet, no. Let's say strong." An Englishman, the accent rough. It was loud in there, men shouting each other down, but when he met my eye, I felt my head go quiet. Together we drank our shots and took up our beers. He told me what I had already guessed, he had come in on the *Godwit*.

"Just dumped our ballast, whole load of sand from Valparaíso. You think sand is sand, but I've shovelled up all sorts—pink, black, some of it fine as flour. Port Elizabeth, Sydney Harbour. Ever think of that? All them countries lying down there on the riverbed?"

"—No, I never did."

He took a long swallow, draining his beer. "Christ, how many is that now?" He glanced at me. "There a backhouse?"

"There will be a lineup," I said. "You can go behind the forge."

He nodded, waiting. My heart hammered.

"Or there are the warehouses." I gestured westward with my chin. "Right."

Can I really be telling you, Kit? I console myself with a thought— I can always tear out these pages and drop them in the stove.

I kept my eyes forward when he left. The silence in my head filled with the sound of my own blood. I drank down my beer. I turned and made a path through all those men.

Outside the Tolmie, the crowd carried on, the boards sticky underfoot with tobacco juice. As I left the lantern light behind, I could hear someone retching, then a woman's laughter from one of the upstairs rooms. I made myself walk slowly. At the alley between two warehouses, I steadied myself as though drunk, looked behind me and slipped into the gap.

Soon I was feeling my way forward. When the thought of myself rose up before me, I shouldered it aside.

I heard him first, the rush of his piss hitting the warehouse wall. I smelled him. As the sound trailed off, I strained my eyes to see. The glint of the earring, him turning, still holding himself in his hand.

If he had spoken, I might have run. As it was, I let him back me up against the wall. My God, the shock of his mouth on mine. I felt as though my lips had been sewed shut, as though he had cut his way in with his tongue.

I drew back, gasping. "I never—"

"What?" He laughed, his fingers at my trouser buttons. "At your age?"

I said nothing, fighting for air.

"You poor love." His hand was inside my smalls. "Did you think you were the only one?"

How I made my way back to my bunk, I cannot tell. I know I did not sleep. I stared into the dark of the bunk above, my body humming so I could almost hear it.

You did not mean it. You were drunk.

Drunk? On a shot and a beer?

The fellow above me snored. From across the room there came the low sounds of a man seeing to his own needs. Familiar sounds— bunkhouse and boarding house, tent and clapboard shed. Even all the way back to the crossing from Kristiania, the below-decks berths for single men. On occasion I had joined in silently from a distance, taking the other man's groans for my own. That night in Steveston, I lay with my arms stiff and buzzing at my sides.

Late became early, and when I could no longer bear to lie there in my own skin, I dressed and went down to the *Kerry Maid*. Over at the long dock, the masts of the *Godwit* stood up black in the gloom. How many crates of good red fish to fill her hold? How many hours before she was ready to set sail?

Before long, Desmond came swinging his jacklight. "What's this," he said, "up with the shark?" He slipped the line off the cleat and stepped aboard. "Jesus, son, you look like death himself."

Staring past him, I bent to the oars.

We felt the change in the run long before we reached the set. I had heard fish hit the hull before, but never at such a rate. Soon I was striking them with each pull of the oars. The water was silty a long way out, but their backs broke the brown surface, so many they changed the light. We all knew stories of the old days, early traders afraid to enter the river for fear the homing schools would capsize their boats. Desmond reached over the side to touch them. For a moment the night and all I had done left me, and the two of us sat grinning at each other like dogs.

It took all our strength to wind in the net. A single set and we were full to the gunwales. The cannery quota was two hundred sockeye per fisherman's licence—we picked over nine hundred that day. While Desmond hoisted the sail, I pushed back to my place and sat packed around with fish.

One rough swell and we would have been swamped. There were a dozen other boats in view, no doubt wrestling with their own hauls. Trained by my mother, I could swim for the nearest skiff— though not if I had to drag Desmond along. The fins of the salmon sharks were cutting all around. They would not normally take interest in a man, but in a school like that, there was no telling where a bite might land.

"Lean on those oars, Norway!" Desmond shouted. "Gotta beat the boys closer in!"

But by the time we made it back, the wharves and cannery floors were already piled high. We were under contract to South Arm Cannery. Desmond was amazed when they took our entire haul, the pitchers tossing the fish onto a nearby scow. The next morning they shovelled those same salmon overboard.

Over the coming days, the price per fish dropped from eight cents to two. Soon you could not give the over-catch away. Those of us in the boats had less work—no sense rowing out to a favourite drift when men were dragging up the day's quota by dropping a net off the end of the dock. Desmond drank more and spoke less. Around us the wonder began to sour.

The Big Run lasted for three weeks. The cannery workers saw no rest. There was talk of accidents—all that blood and fish slime, you can imagine the cracked skulls, the broken limbs. A spill of solder, a stumble against the boiling retort. Fillers cut themselves on cans. One of the slitters took two fingers off his own hand. All day, all night the machines ran, and still they lifted the floorboards to let piles of best Pacific sockeye drop away.

5

It may be that the fish sense gets into your blood, the homing. I cannot say why else I returned to Steveston the year after the Big Run—Desmond and every other man who knew the river mouth were calling for '98 to be an off year.

You will not have forgotten the sailor, Kit. Nor had I. My heart kicked every time I came down to the boat before sunrise to find the great shadow of a square-rigger alongside the dock. Fear, yes, in part. But it was never the *Godwit*, never him.

As a rule, boatpullers did not spend time inside the canneries— no one without cause did. On the day I am thinking of, though, Desmond had business with the net boss.

"Come on," he said. "I'll do the talking, you just puff up big."

I do not recall the meat of the argument, only that I stood silent in the office doorway until the shouting was done. I remember the difference as Desmond and I walked out across the cannery floor, a let-down in my shoulders where there had been an electric strain.

You know the air in a cannery—half-light at midday, the dripping, stinking heat. The noise. Wailing belts and clattering cans, the beat of the knives, the always-running water piped down over the washers' raw hands. Underneath it all, the terrible quiet of no one talking—slitters and washers, fillers and packers, all of them lost in keeping up.

Our boots sounded on the plank floor, then again in the echoing drop to the river below. Passing the slitters' workbench, I could not help but watch. You grew up with the machine, but in those days men did all the cutting—lopping off head, tail and fins before opening the belly to slip out the guts. Whistle three quick notes and it was done.

I followed Desmond past a long line of their backs. In the heat, the men had stripped to the waist. Thin black queues lay along spines, muscles twisting against bone—I doubt they ever got enough to eat. At the end of the bench in the light of the open door, a back younger than the rest. This man wore no braid—his hair was cropped short, shaved up around the ears. The bare bend of his neck. Did he feel my gaze? Was that why he looked back at me over his shoulder, the knife gone still in his hand?

The week turned much as it does here—the nets brought ashore on Friday evening to be mended and cleaned, then whatever work the boat and gear required, then a wash and the week's supplies. After that, every bachelor and most of the family men were drunk or asleep until they could set their nets again. I was no different, except in one regard. On Sunday mornings, I swam.

If I met anyone on my walk around Garry Point, it would be one of the Tsawwassen women returning with a basket of salmonberries or, later in the season, crabapples from the twisted trees. On the flats the seagrass was full of fish heads and fins, the mud littered with guts. I had a long way to go to reach water that was any way clean. I did not mind the walk. You are too young to know the binding a fisherman's legs can suffer in the boat, but I was thirty-eight that summer, and my knees gave me trouble when I stood up after a day at the oars.

I had been following the beach for an hour or more on the morning I saw him. The sun was just up, the new light hurting my drinker's head. For a second I thought it was a dream. He was sitting on a log at the high-tide line, straight-backed, looking out to sea. Pure chance, or had he noticed me setting out the week before? I glanced behind me. Not a soul. I stood with my heart pounding, watching him from a distance of a hundred yards. Again he turned his face to me. This time he did not look away.

It was the natural thing to approach and pass the time of day— or it would have been, if the two of us had been of a kind. I had no cause to expect much English. I bid him good morning all the same.

He nodded. "Morning."

I stood there not knowing what to do. Finally I sat down on the log.

He looked back at the water, sea light moving on his face. "Air good here."

"Yes," I said. "It is bad in town. Some nights a man can hardly breathe."

He gave a snort. "You try China House."

"Yes, I am sure."

It was difficult not to stare. His hair was a shining cap, lit up rosy at the back. That strip of bare scalp showing above his neck.

"Chinatown bad too," he said.

"Yes?"

He turned to me, holding his hands up to show a space the width of his own shoulders. "I have bed in room. Half bed," he added. "Nighttime mine, daytime other man."

"Ah, yes." I looked down at my hands, the palms ridged to the shape of the oars. Always some beggar worse off than you.

The beggar beside me gave a sharp laugh. "Okay if he no have bug."

"Yes." The only word I could seem to find. I could not stop myself looking at him again.

He met my gaze. "What your bed like?"

"Narrow." I closed my eyes. "Lonely."

I thought he would not speak. "Lonely," he said. "I know this word."

Again, like a thief, I looked behind me. I looked all around. My fingers moved. The coarse fabric of his trouser leg and, beneath it, the muscle of his thigh. He held perfectly still. Then he lifted my hand to his mouth.

Afterwards, when he sat up to tie his trousers, I said, "Sometimes I walk early, when it is still dark." But he was already squatting on his heels, peering out of the high grass. He stepped out, climbing down over the jumble of beached logs. I rose up on my knees to watch him hurry away—his dark trousers and loose blue blouse the cannery standard, the naked base of his skull a shape I knew.

◗

A decent catch for her first night out. Kit watches the collector boat carry it away, steaming on to a distant skiff. Tired or not, she sluices the boards and bails, sea water buzzing in the cracks of her hands. At last she sits down.

Movement on shore, a murrelet leaving the trees to skim out over the waves. Catch a sand lance, maybe. Carry it back to its chick.

She should eat breakfast, but the stove seems like too much work. Cracking the grub box lid, she feels for the damp loaf of bread and tears off a chunk. The sky is dark for this hour of the morning, the clouds swollen. Sure enough, rain.

Crawling in under the canvas at the bow, Kit turns over on her back. Her legs stick out, dry enough in oilskin apron and boots. She eats her bread, the downpour shuddering above her, spilling a thin curtain from the shelter's peaked hem. It's all right, the light is taking on a pearly cast; the rain won't last long enough to sweeten the surface, drive the salmon below the net.

The bread gone, she turns on her side, ear to the boards. Beneath her, who knows how many fathoms. She closes her eyes.

Nearly ready, Kitty-cat.

They were going for salal berries—late summer, then, or maybe September. Pail in hand, Kit waited by the door. Mama was taking her time, standing where the mirror hung on its nail. Hair like hers took looking after: brush the oils through before bed, comb the strays out in the morning. Whale tooth, the comb was made of, carved with a schooner under sail. Mama let her hold it sometimes.

Daddy was watching too. Still sitting at the table though breakfast was done, his hand on the grey mug he liked best. Not lifting it to his lips, though. Letting the coffee cool.

"Bad luck on a boat," he said.

"What is?"

"Scrimshaw."

Mama turned from her reflection. "Yeah, I never got that. Sailors make them, don't they?"

"Bad luck on a *fishing* boat." A shift then, a sound that wasn't quite there. "That who made yours, a sailor?"

Mama lifted the comb back to her part. "How do I know? It was a present."

"Yeah? Who from?"

"—You know who from. My mother."

Is it only now that Kit hears the hesitation? The lie?

Daddy nodded. "Christmas, was it?"

"Birthday, actually." The comb returning to the part, other side now, head tilting. "Couple of months before she died."

Daddy's face slackened—was he sorry now? Mama must've seen it too. Quick as a cat, she stepped in close and dug the comb into his beard. He caught her hand—but wouldn't it hurt, her fingers closed like that around the bony teeth? No, it was all right. He was bringing her wrist to his lips.

"Kitty-cat," Mama said, "you go on ahead. You know that patch by the beach. Any bear mess and you come straight back." She was on Daddy's lap now, where Kit sometimes sat. She had her eyes half-shut. "Go on." She gave Kit one of her shimmery smiles. "I won't be long."

◖

A man cannot always rely on reason, Kit. One week after I had met my young man on the beach, I set out in the small hours again. I had been in the bar, but I had been careful, sticking to beer and letting the glass sit empty before ordering again. A crescent moon lit the way past the westernmost cannery to where the boardwalk gave onto the path. It was foolish to hope, but a fool is what I was. I hastened my stride the moment I imagined myself out of sight.

The trail around the point was packed hard, so it was not until I reached sand that I saw the footprints—a single set, the sole smooth. I longed to break into a run, but if I could see tracks, someone else could too. I placed my steps over his. Only one man had come this way, a man alone.

The tide was out, the mud flat reeking. An hour's walk never felt so far. But then, the same log, the same strong, straight back. This time it was the moon that shone on his cap of hair. This time he stood up as I drew near.

—

It was different out on the sand, better. Afterwards we sat smoking a cigarette I rolled by feel. The moon had gone down. In the darkness I leaned back against the log. Beside me, the soft sound of him moving his fingers through the sand.

"It is from all over the world," I said. "The sand."

The shadow of his profile shifted—he was looking my way.

"Ships take it on for ballast—weight—when they unload in other ports. They dump it here before loading up with cans."

He reached for the smoke and drew on it, lighting the coal. "Huh."

"It is true," I said. "A sailor told me."

"Sailor." He nodded to himself. "You have wife?"

"No, no wife." I hesitated. "Do you?"

"No. My brother, he have wife."

"Your brother? Is he in China?"

"I have brother in China. This brother here."

"Here?" I felt a pinch of fear. Somehow I had imagined us alone together in the world. "In Steveston?"

"No, Chinatown. He cook in restaurant. I work sometime too, wash dish. He come seven year before me, work and work. Need money for wife, even wife like my brother find."

"What's wrong with her?"

"Not wrong, only . . . poor."

"Ah."

"Chinatown, many men no woman." He paused. "Some men . . . lonely together."

My heart gave a kick. "Yes."

"Some men only lonely."

"Yes."

"Some men . . . want."

Kit, I will burn these pages, I swear I will. But let me write it. I groaned when he spoke those words. I grabbed for him in the dark.

It was not until our third meeting that he said to me, "My name Lo Yim."

We were lying in the V of two logs, hidden from all but the sea. The dark was giving way to morning. He should have been gone.

I rolled on my side to face him. "I am Anders Viken."

He smiled. I stopped myself from touching his cheek, the skin there so smooth. Was he nineteen years old? Twenty?

"You have good English," he said.

"You also."

"They teach at church. You here long time?"

"Nearly"—I thought for a moment—"twenty years."

He raised his eyebrows. "Old man."

"Not so old."

He touched my arm, felt it. I let myself think he would kiss me, start everything over again.

"How old?" he said.

"Thirty-nine. How old are you?"

"Twenty-nine year."

It came as a relief somehow, only a decade between us. Then the thought, like a bitter little joke—*Yes, Anders, now nobody will mind.*

Lo Yim. His name was in my head when I lay down to stare at the bunk above me, and when I opened my eyes in the morning dark. I pictured him lying wakeful in the fire trap of the China House, every part of him slender, strong. I thought about him—about the two of us together—while I worked. I remember the kick of a salmon in my hand, the rush of desire so powerful I had to sit down.

"Break time, is it?" Desmond said, winding in a length of net, but then he looked again. "All right?"

I made myself nod and stand.

Later, when Desmond and I bobbed alongside the wharf while the pitchers stuck into our catch, I let my eyes travel the weathered boards of the cannery wall. *There,* I told myself. *He is standing there.*

More than once I found myself passing the cannery's high, wide-open doors. How did they work all day in that brownish light? No matter. It was enough to see by—his back, the back of his neck. It was enough.

When Saturday came again, I left the bar before midnight. Cat's-eye moon, the tide falling by the time I reached our beach. I imagined I was alone until he heard me and sat up from behind our log. This time I let myself run.

We came together in the open, as though we could never be found. Finally we came apart. For a time he seemed to sleep, and then somehow I did too. I woke to find him watching me. "Where you come from?"

I sat up. *"Norge,"* I said, the old language breaking through. "Norway," I added, but neither appeared to make a picture in his mind.

With a glance down the empty beach, I stood and pulled a stick from a mess of kelp. "This," I said, scratching a rough outline, "is North America." Beside me, Lo Yim rose up onto his heels. I cut a line inland from the west coast. "Fraser River." Then dug the point in twice. "Vancouver. Steveston."

I had thought to draw Europe next, but it came to me that the Pacific route made more sense. I guessed at the size of his homeland. "This is China."

He glanced at me, nodding.

I dragged a great oval with the stick. "Russia." And now the shape I knew from the schoolroom wall—the great ball-sack of Finland and, hanging down beside it, the doubled cock of Sweden and Norway.

High up in the Norwegian sea, I poked a handful of dots. "Lofoten islands," I said. "I come from there."

Lo Yim looked over my drawing. "North," he said.

"Yes."

"Cold."

"Not as bad as you might think. The ocean helps."

Again he nodded. "Hot in Guangdong." He held out a hand for the stick. On the south coast of his country he drew the wedge of a bay. "This Zhu Jiang, Pearl River." He stood the stick up to make a mark. "This my village."

I do not know why it made me want to touch him. Of course I do. He looked at me and let the stick fall from his hand.

It was past time we were going. Lo Yim kept a little pouch tied inside his trousers—I had felt it there before. In the morning twilight, he untied its bow. The object he produced was the colour of calf's liver. He hooked it on his finger and held it up—silken string knotted to form a small, neat mat. Its tail was a swaying bundle of threads.

"For good fortune, good . . . life." He handed it to me. "My mother give."

I nodded, and for a moment my own mother stood before me, wringing the sea from her hair. What parting gift would she have offered if I had told her I was going? What would she have pressed into my hand?

"You keep." Lo Yim stood suddenly, pulling on his blouse.

"What?" I looked up. "No, Lo Yim—"

"You keep." He stepped past me, and like a memory of that first bright morning, he walked quickly away.

———

A love gift. You know the charm of the thing, Kit—I remember you holding it in your little hands. At night I took it into my bunk. At the bar or on the boat I reached into my pocket to gather and hold the tail. Once, when Desmond was busy with the net, I took it out for the quickest of looks. Under full sun, it was a brilliant red.

By the end of the week I was having trouble thinking straight. Again and again a picture came to me, the two of us walking side by side. *There must be somewhere*, the thought would begin, *somehow . . .*

In the Tolmie on Friday night I drank and floated, setting the glass down and raising a finger, watching the pour. Time was passing. I would sleep, and then it would be only hours until we were together, not days.

I was not listening to the men at the nearest table, not until one of them said loudly, "Fucking Chinks."

The room tilted when I looked round. The speaker was John Appleby, manager of the South Arm Cannery—Apple Boy, he was called, for his fat red cheeks. The other had the look of the office about him too. "Can't fault 'em for knifework," he said.

"You needn't tell me. One of mine—young, you know, keen—just packed up his knife and buggered off."

"Just like that."

"Had word from his brother, if you please. Had to go Saltwater City chop-chop."

"Where the hell is Saltwater City?"

"You never heard that?" Appleby grinned. "That's pigtail for the city. Guess they can't say Vancouver."

I looked away from the sight of them laughing. I steadied myself against the bar. *It is not him.* I walked to the door. *It does not have to be him.* Board by board, I got myself back to the bunkhouse. I had had enough whiskey to sleep.

The following night I was careful again at the bar, watching myself, keeping count. The moon was thin, but I was getting practised at walking in the dark. Lo Yim did not come. When I tired of sitting on the log, I lay down on the sand. When first light woke me, I walked back. There was still time for a swim, but I did not trust myself to go in.

6

When the season ended, I returned to Vancouver and took a
room in a house on Seymour Street. Mrs. McClintock ran
the place, no mention of a Mr. McClintock and no need of one either.
I remember meeting her coming down Beattie Street with a sack of
turnips on her shoulder—she only snorted when I offered to help.
You might be picturing a big woman, Kit, but the bones showed like
blades beneath her skin. Her hair was pigeon-coloured, forever pulled
back in a knot. Every night, after she had fed as many men as came to
the table, she carried a bottle of gin to her chair in the front room.
She was no housekeeper, but the rent was cheap and she never minded
a man coming home drunk.

"Just so long as you're not a brawler," she said, the day I came to
ask about a room.

It was not a word I knew, but her meaning was clear. "No, ma'am,"
I told her. "I keep to myself."

———

I was careful to skirt round Chinatown in my wanderings. What else to do, stand in the middle of Pender Street and call his name? The thing was finished. My work was to forget, to remember how I had lived before. Walk and work, drink and sleep, swim. The *søvngjenger* helped. When summer returned, I sleepwalked back to Steveston, where Desmond was waiting in the *Kerry Maid*.

I could find no excuse to enter the South Arm Cannery, but like any man, I happened to pass by its doors. The slitters stood along their workbench. His back was not one I could mistake for another, and his back was not there. All right, I reasoned, Appleby might not welcome a man who had left in mid-season, but there were other operations, every one of them standing open to the street.

It was the natural thing, a man with boat-cramp walking the length of the town. No matter what name hung over the open doors, the scene inside each cannery was the same—scores of Chinese, slitters and packers, lined up either side of the women at the washing tables. Not one of them was Lo Yim.

That should have been the end of it, and for a time it was. The fish ran until they did not, then it was back to a different room in Mrs. McClintock's house. Most evenings I drank just enough, but then there would come a night when there was no such thing. Drinking through to daylight makes a man unsure. It was early November, a rare morning without rain, when I stood up from the chair by my window, leaving the bottle on the sill. My feet found their boots. My boots carried me along Seymour Street. At Pender they turned me east.

Stumbling down off the boardwalk, I joined the drays in the road. Three blocks along I began to feel uneasy, prey to a rumbling sensation in my bones. The bend at Cambie set me straight—the disturbance was rising up through my boot soles. Cattle. Thirty, forty head driven up from the rail yard to thunder through the city streets. Their lowing was not the sound I knew from my youth—a moaned reminder if ever I was late to the milking shed. These cows were fearful, on their way from the boxcar to the end.

I followed at a little distance behind the drovers with their sticks. In Chinatown the old men came out to watch like children—a few actual children too, but only a few. *Chinatown, many men no woman.* A boy of five or six years pointed, not at the herd, but at me. I saw myself then, straggling like the calf the wolf's eye follows, the one on shaky legs. *Lo Yim.* I did not let myself call his name, but I let myself look. He could be standing at a window, watching the brown river of cattle push through. He could step out from a doorway into the light.

Somehow, I knew to keep moving. The herd carried on for more than a mile through Strathcona, down to Burns Slaughterhouse at the foot of Woodland Drive. I was beginning to feel hollow the way a drinker does, as though he has been eating fog. The air was foul, and I knew the inlet would be too—all that blood and manure. I turned west as the cattle crowded into the yard.

On my way past the Rogers Refinery I breathed the sugary stink. Finally I came to a row of closed-up warehouses, a stretch of cleaner sea. The rain started not long after I dropped off the end of the dock. I swam out among the ships at anchor, farther than I had ever dared.

In those days I did not look much beyond the coming season. Desmond was thinner every year, slower hauling and picking the net. The century turned.

The year 1900 saw a poor run on the Fraser, made worse by a strike. There had been ugliness before—there always is where men live and work and drink together while the owners keep watch— but those weeks on strike made me long for the days of ordinary strife. The canneries tried to break us by sending out tugs as escorts for men desperate enough to scab. I shouted along with the others when a picket boat towed an unlucky pair to shore—at least until the boatpuller was thrown like a straw man across the crowd.

The violence gave the bosses their wish—a mob calls for a militia. The union stuck at twenty cents a fish, but the Japanese had their own association, and when the offer of nineteen cents came down, they got back in their boats. The rest of us followed to chase what was left of a poor run.

It was no surprise when the trouble carried over to the following year. By then the men on the union boats were armed. While Desmond and I worked a picket post on the wharf, our brothers boarded vessels, cut up nets and put the frightened fishermen ashore, setting their boats adrift. Never a town for a quiet drink, Steveston went mad. There were fights in the bars and along the boardwalks, the bright smash of bottles on skulls. Not Appleby and his kind, or the cannery men who were their masters. Always the workers, brawling, beating each other down. Mrs. McClintock would not have approved.

In the end that strike faltered too. This time it was another big year, the river mouth once again choking with fish. A feast to drive down prices at the market and on the wharf.

"Only thing worse than a bad year is a good one." I had heard Desmond say it before, but never in a voice like that. We were on our way in with our catch over quota. "A man gets fed up, Norway," he said. "Right to the back teeth."

I nodded and hauled on the oars.

◗

Yesterday afternoon in the skiff was hot; today, merciful cloud cover, high and white. Adrift on the open inlet, Kit grips the whetstone's hilt. Laying her knife against the grit, she guides it forward and back.

Watch your fingers, Kitty-cat.

Eyes on the job.

Her mother and father, looking on. It was what Kit wanted when she was a kid, the pair of them together, close at hand. The best was when they sang—usually at Uncle Anders' cottage, after supper when Kit was curled up with the dog on the rug. Daddy's boot thudded time, her uncle's beat gentler, though he was the bigger man. He only ever sang at Christmas, and then only the one hymn. The lonely stream of his home language, the quiet when he was done.

Mama's singing voice had a lift in it, Daddy's, a crystalline depth. Sometimes Kit hummed along. There was the one about the black sheep—*Don't be angry with me, Dad*—and the one in the pines, and Clementine. Kit's favourite was "Molly Malone." "Fishmonger" was a word she had to learn. Of course, she knew "cockles"—they always dug a few up with the clams—and "mussels," the bright, chewy meat in its blue-black shell. The line she liked best came halfway through— "For so were her father and mother before"—the notes in their sweet, overlapping descent.

Parts of the song shone a clear picture, others lay dark. "She wheeled her wheelbarrow" was plain enough, "through streets broad and narrow" less so. At Far Cry there were docks and boardwalks, two paths across the headland, the uphill cut of the waterline trail. Kit knew not to ask Mama about her life before Far Cry, at least not when Daddy was home. She waited until he was out on the grounds.

"How many streets in the city? Geez, Kitty-cat, there must be hundreds."

"Didn't you get lost?"

Mama shook her head. "We never got that far."

The song took a twist at the end. She died of a fever and no one could save 'er and that was the end of sweet Molly Malone. Daddy held his tongue after that, leaving the last lines for Mama to carry alone. "But her ghost wheels her barrow . . ." It was all right. Even when her voice turned spooky, Mama smiled as she sang.

——

A splash to portside. Kit turns her head in time to see the salmon's tail. She holds the knife up, gauging its glint. Feathers the edge with her thumb before turning the other side to the stone.

Of course, it wasn't all singing. When the season was under way, there were always children at Far Cry who bore the mark of their father's hand, and sometimes a woman with a split lip or a bruise around her eye. So far as Kit knew, Frank never hit Bobbie. There were words he used, though—never sober, and never when Kit was in the room. As if that made a difference. When he and Uncle Anders had built the cabin, they'd used planks to separate the two bedrooms, saving the logs for the outside walls.

Words. Not every night, not even every week. Her mother's voice quiet until it wasn't. *You shut your filthy mouth, Frank Starratt!* Or, *You knew damn well when you married me!* He could go stick it in a knothole for all she cared because he sure as shit wasn't getting anywhere near her. There might be the sounds of a scuffle. There were. Other noises too, some ugly, some just secret. All of them raw.

How old was Kit when the idea came to her—six? Standing up on her cot, the window was an easy reach. She knew how to open it, she was a big girl. She knew how to climb. The drop wasn't far, the moss spongy with the coming of spring. No lantern—she wasn't allowed to light one on her own. The trees creaked as they always did—there were lives smaller than her own among the roots and boughs. The night was not all blackness. In the starlight she found her eyes.

Uncle Anders tended to leave things unlocked during the off-season. She could reach the side-door handle. The hinges gave a little cry. She knew her way around the store, too—licorice sticks in the jar, but it was wrong to take things without asking. She borrowed a blanket from the pile.

The stockroom smelled of wood and burlap, rope and iron. A comforting waft of grain. In the back corner, she pushed over a sack of oats and settled against it, drawing the blanket up over her head.

It helped, knowing there was somewhere to go. It was quiet in the stockroom—mouse claws sometimes, and once the scrabbling of a red squirrel that had gnawed its way in—but quiet in Kit's head, her chest. There was moonlight through the back window on lucky nights, and always the early grey light to wake her so she was back in her cot before Mama and Daddy began to stir. The night path would be changing by then, cedar perfume and the flutter of bats flying home to roost. One time, a sound above her like a breath, the pale square of a flying squirrel floating from tree to tree.

When Uncle Anders found out, she feared he would give her away. Instead, he asked what the trouble was. He walked her back to the cabin at dawn, letting her in softly by the front door when she could easily have climbed the log wall to her window. After that, she could pass by his cottage, open the door and whisper for Skygge to come out. The two of them padding back past the darkened storefront, round the corner to the side door. She never slept cold again.

◗

"You looking to the future?" Desmond asked me during that last season, but whenever I tried, it was like staring down into a bunker of coal.

Steveston emptied out when the run was over, and this time I found myself in the narrowest room at Mrs. McClintock's, with a view out over the privy and the air to match. For all the trouble at the start of the season, the run had paid out. My share—minus the tithe paid across the bar at the Tolmie—was sufficient to keep me idle for a time.

One morning I had the idea to walk the False Creek waterfront. It was the tide that forced me inland, the foot of Carrall Street swamped, water foul with horse muck and machine oil. Logs that had slipped their booms bobbed in the shallows. I splashed up to Pender, my trousers soaked to the knees.

I could have turned right, heading east as I had when I'd followed the cows to their end. Chinatown lay to my left. *He cook in restaurant. I work sometime too, wash dish.* Three years had passed, but his voice in my head was clear.

I chose a restaurant with an empty table in the window. I could sit there like a picture in a frame, my eyes on every face that happened past. The place was as good as empty. Down the far end, two people sat at a table beside a red door—a pretty young woman and an old man who turned in his seat to survey me when he saw the look on her face. She stood and hurried to meet me. When I looked to the window table, she nodded, then turned and padded back to the old man. A quiet word between them before he rose from his chair and walked slowly to stand beside mine.

"Yes, sir."

"You have coffee?"

He shook his head. "Only tea."

"Yes, all right, tea."

He paused. "This Chinese food. You want café?" He pointed across the street to a shopfront with signs in English among the characters. *Pork Chop. Steak and Egg.* Restaurant, Lo Yim had said, not café. Because that was the true, secret story I was telling myself—not that I would spot him passing, but that he was already there, behind the red door, bent over the pots in the sink. He would hear about the white man sitting in the window. He would feel compelled to steal a look.

"You have beef?" I asked the old man.

"Best beef."

"Yes," I said. "Fine."

Of course, there were other restaurants—many on Pender, let alone down the side alleys. Still, I tracked the old man with my gaze as he shuffled back and pushed through the door. A glimpse of grey apron, black stove. I waited, heart hammering, for the door to swing back my way.

The girl brought my tea without a word—a pot with a cane handle and a soft blue painting of a tree. The cup made paws of my hands. The tea tasted of earth and smoke.

The girl did not sit back down. Instead, she took a cloth to a line of figurines on a shelf, bending her head to each one as though listening. When the old man backed out through the door, his body blocked any view. *Fool, Anders. Eat your meal and move on.*

I had seen men working their little sticks out front of the China House in Steveston, bowls held up to their chins, but the old man had mercy on me, laying a flat-bottomed spoon down alongside my plate. No knife, but the meat was already cut up in a stew, the slices thin and slippery on the tongue. No carrots or potatoes either, just a mound of snowy rice in a bowl. The gravy was salty, good. A flavour there I already knew—some root or seed I had tasted on Lo Yim's skin.

I ate it all. Dumped the rice out onto the plate, shoved the mix into the spoon with my thumb. I glanced again at the kitchen door, then poured out the rest of the tea. I could sit a little longer. I was doing no harm.

When the old man came for my plate, he stood holding it, looking me in the eye. "You want extra?"

"Extra?"

He looked back at the young woman, still polishing the little people on the shelf. "She good girl, clean."

I cannot say why I was surprised. It was the common thing, nice girls, clean girls, friendly. You found them at work camps and newsstands, cafés and bars—anywhere men gathered without their wives.

I stood up. "How much?" I said, reaching into my pocket. "For the food. How much for the food."

I paid what he asked and more, unwilling to wait for the change. Outside, I stood with the world moving around me—until it shuddered to a stop. Two doors down on the far side of the street, Lo Yim was standing out front of a shop, talking to one of the many men of Chinatown. At his side stood a woman, plainly dressed in trousers and a padded jacket. Plain.

In Lo Yim's arms, held up for the other man to admire, was a child. Three years he had been gone, and yes, here was a child two years of age—as near as an unmarried man such as myself could guess. The *søvngjenger* took over. *Turn and duck your head, Anders. Run.*

My heart was labouring by the time I reached Cordova Street with its string of bars. You know my thinking on the subject of Prohibition, Kit, but the wives and ministers are right about saloons that never close. I am ashamed to tell you, I lost days.

There were men—two that come to me in flashes, but a feeling even after all these years that there were more. The first was a logger with a great dark beard. The *Cassiar* was in at the Union Wharf, Water Street wild with men down from the camps. I remember him dropping to his knees, moaning and shouldering me as I worked my trousers down.

The other was a Swede, starlight in his hair and his language terribly close to home. *Kom igen*, he kept saying as I followed him into the dark, *Kom igen!* There was a smell of hay and horse dung, a muffled neigh when he turned me round and shoved me up against the splintery boards. *Hora*, he said in my ear, an unkind word in his tongue and mine, but the familiarity of it made my heart twist. I turned to face him when he was done, bringing my mouth to his. He struck me down. I held a hand out to break my fall, and there came a pop like a great cork being pulled. I felt his boot then, but it was the agony in my shoulder that put me out.

It was first light when the pain brought me back. I was lying on my bad side—rolling off it made me shout. If there was anyone at work in the stables, they didn't appear. The horses would have heard me. I had an idea of them standing ears-up in their stalls.

My left arm was useless. I held it against me as I struggled to stand. I could see the water then—False Creek by the colour and smell. Logs groaned in their booms. In time, I made sense of the landmark that was the Granville Street Bridge. Walking was a torment. When I bent at the roadside to be sick, the violence of it brought me to my knees.

I cannot say how long it took me to reach the house on Seymour Street, only that I feared I never would. A smell of porridge met me at the door. Then its maker, stepping out from the kitchen to regard me down the dim length of the hall.

Mrs. McClintock shook her head. "For shame, Mr. Viken."

I managed a bitter smile.

"Shoulder, is it?"

I nodded, the movement causing me to yelp.

She sniffed. "Best go into the front room."

The curtains were still drawn, the light a muddy green. She came to stand before me, bringing her smell of juniper and kitchen rags. Without a word, she undid my shirt buttons. I held the left arm folded close while she tugged the shirt down over my right arm, then walked it around behind me to hang from my bent elbow by the sleeve. The bruise was dark. I looked down over the dent in my shoulder, my arm angled as though it had been nailed on in haste.

"Lay down," my landlady said. And when I moved toward the settee, "Not there! On the floor."

While she stood watching with crossed arms, I went down on one knee, worked my legs around to the side and rolled backward, letting out a cry. The rug puffed out dust and mould. My eyes were streaming. Mrs. McClintock stood by my head in the knitted slippers she wore indoors and out. I never saw them without thinking of the over-catch salmon washed up along the Fraser's banks.

"Stick your arm out beside you," she said. "The bad one. Straight out."

What choice did I have? I whimpered and did as she said.

"Nei!" I heard myself shout when she took hold of my wrist.

"Quiet," she said. "Lay still!"

She braced her feet in their ragged slippers against my ribs. A new smell now from beneath her housedress, parts of her untended, unwashed. I thought she would be brutal. Instead, she leaned back slow and steady. The pain was like sound now, a scream from inside my bones.

"Vennligst!" I howled. "Please!"

"My Thomas was a brawler," she said, staring straight ahead. "You want to watch out or you'll end up like he did. Even the thickest skull can crack." She glanced down at me. "Easy now, it won't go in with you laying there stiff as a corpse."

I took a breath. Then another. That was when I heard it—not a pop this time, but a clunk. Afterwards, a quiet that was unbearably sweet. Forgive me, Kit, but I can only compare it to the ebb that follows the rush of love.

I felt Mrs. McClintock rise and stalk out to the kitchen. I knew the slosh of liquor in a bottle when she returned. She set the gin down by my hand.

I looked up at her. "Thank you."

"Add it onto next week's rent."

I closed my eyes.

"Up you get," she said. "Go on, get to bed."

7

It took a week or more for the strength to come back into my shoulder. Meantime, I thought of little but leaving—my room, that house, the city itself. I took the first chance I saw. After all those years of giving my countrymen a wide berth, I signed on to the *Skarv*, a Norwegian-owned halibut boat heading north.

Hearing the old language all day, I began to dream of Lofoten, asleep and then awake. The jagged shadows of Stormolla and Litlmolla overlaid the islands we passed. Then there was the other trouble. More than their voices, there were the men themselves—bare forearms and broad-knuckled hands, trouser buttons undone at the rail. Below decks, the sound of them turning in their bunks. The dreams grew bolder, men now, not islands. Men covering men.

The halibut is a strange fish to look on day in and day out—the cut and colour of the sea floor, both eyes twisting round to heaven, the true one and the wanderer. We passed all manner of vessels under steam and sail. Along the rocky shores, lone men in little rowboats fished the kelp beds. *Krabber* was the name the crew had for these handliners. It was no compliment, to be sure—the meat of a crab may be sweet, but he makes it crawling over the refuse of the sea.

In truth, many on board knew well enough the feel of a handline. It was the best way for a man on his own—or a boy with his father—to catch the Atlantic cod we call *skrei*. Do you know, Kit, that cod home as salmon do? Just not so far. They breed in the open sea, swimming alongside each other, stirring egg and seed together with their tails. Every winter my father rowed us out into Vestfjorden over the great returning schools. You dropped your hook twenty fathoms or so. Even when they didn't strike, you hooked them in the flank, the eye.

One morning I stood at the stern of the *Skarv* watching one of the *krabber* ride the swell where it washed back off a cliff. He had a fish on the line. Hand over hand he hauled it in—then came the flash as he whipped it aboard. The slippery struggle and the club coming down, the fight going out of them both. I stood with one foot on the transom, staring across the waves, until the captain bellowed, "Viken! *Våkne opp!*"

Not long after that, we put in at Alert Bay. My eye caught on a rowboat lying on the stony beach with her hull to the sky. Someone had slopped *For Sale* in whitewash across the keel. Up close I found her name in small black letters—the *Coot*. I walked her length, ten feet. A proper *reska*. She looked in good repair.

It put the *Skarv*'s captain in a bad temper to lose a man midseason, but I saw no sense in trying to explain. I held a hand out for what I was owed. Added to what was left from the salmon run, it stretched to buy the *Coot* and any supplies a handliner might require. A doubled blanket and an oilskin sheet, bacon, flour and beans. Pan and kettle, hammer and hatchet, a knife to stick and skin. Hooks and line. A number-five brass spoon lure to twist in the current, catching the salmon's eye.

The storekeeper at Alert Bay had the look of a man once stocky, now softening to fat. Edging out from behind the counter, he led me to where the traps hung in dark bunches on the wall. "Salmon don't run all year, you'll need to earn a crust." He glanced at me. "Not to mention something to do with your days." He took down six small traps, each one trailing its chain. "Newhouse 1½, best thing for mink. These are second-hand, but I've oiled them up good as new."

"Yes, all right."

He reached down a Number 3. "Case you come across any beaver."

I nodded. For anything larger than that, I still had my .32.

The *Coot* felt even more like a one-man vessel by the time I had everything stowed. Two decades after I had dragged my father's *reska* down the sand, I rowed again into a life I could not know.

Reading over this last passage, I see the hole I left in my list of supplies. The storekeeper had whiskey in stock, but my money went further on Hudson's Bay rum in the jug. After those lost days in the city, I had a plan of rationing in mind. I wrapped the jugs in my blanket like newborn triplets come into my care.

There was a lightness to pushing off in my little boat. Island to island I rowed across the strait. From Echo Bay I crept north along the mainland coast to where the top of Vancouver Island gives way to the Pacific in all its force. Rounding Cape Caution, I felt the drag in my bad shoulder. I had gone just about far enough.

I made camp in a cove some way up Smith Inlet. It gave fair shelter from the worst of the storms, which is to say the wind never quite lifted me off my feet. I thought I knew rain from the city—running down the windows and beating on the roof, the drop, drop, drop of it coming in—but that November I learned to long for snow. I suppose you never think of it, Kit, having been born to the rainforest. The roar of it. It made an animal of me, backed me into my lean-to beneath the trees.

When the sea allowed, I rowed out to drop a line down into the kelp. Not every fish is a welcome catch, you know that. Back home, only the poorest of men dropped his hook into a school of mackerel. They are marked, you see—a skeleton on the back to show they have eaten the drowned. Foolishness, my mother said, but when I hauled one up by accident as a boy, my father worked it from the hook in seconds and flung it back.

Along this coast, a man can always bring up a rockfish or a kelp greenling. Ling cod, too—not a true cod, I could not help thinking whenever I swung one over the gunwale, not *skrei*. Early one morning I dragged up a greenling that a ling cod had taken as bait. The moment I lifted the doubled catch from the sea, the ling cod let go. In my surprise I let the wide-eyed greenling drop and dangle on the line, only to see the hole of the ling cod's mouth rush up from below and bite again. This time I got the gaff into it before letting it feel the air.

A big fish like that could go half to waste that time of year. The sun never cut through long enough to dry the flesh. I tried and failed at my mother's method—opening each body like a butterfly and tying it by the tail to a pole. I can see her *skrei* now, wings hanging down to lift a little in the wind. In the end I fixed strips to pointed sticks and smoked them in a cedar-branch hut. Some of the flesh still spoiled, but it spoiled more slowly. Most of the time I had enough.

You know what winter is in these parts. There were days, weeks, when the wind raged up the inlet, and I dragged my *reska* into the brush where the tide could not snatch it away. The rain became a second lashing sea, turning the branches into great green fins. On heavy nights, I crawled beneath the *Coot*'s overturned hull to sleep. Neville's dictionary stayed wrapped in its square of oilskin. By then I had a proper habit of muttering, remembering my English to myself.

A man needs shelter. I had noticed the ruin of a sawmill near the inlet's mouth. On the first clear day, I rowed back to scavenge boards. Salmonberry and salal had grown in over the place—I tied up to a tilting remnant of dock and hacked a path in. It was worth the work, some decent planks to be found among the rot. A zinc washtub caught my eye, but when I took it up by the handles, I found the bottom had rusted through. A man in company would have cast it aside. I held it up like a picture frame and looked out through the crusted circle to sea.

They are lonely, those places where men have lived and left their wreckage behind. I had spent a month or more on the inlet with ravens for company, watching the tall fins of the blackfish as they passed the cove. Coming back from that old sawmill marked the first time I drank over my daily share.

That night I held a parley with myself, ask and answer by the spitting fire.

Well, Anders, you have come to this place.

I have.

And will you stay?

I will.

Alone?

A pause while the questioned man drinks. *How else?*

The fire was dying, the rain starting in the branches high above. I closed my eyes and gazed on him. Lo Yim.

The light was grey when I woke with a jay calling *shooka-shooka* overhead. Morning? Midday? My head lay on a sopping sponge of moss, red roots snaking round. A man could die, letting himself lie through a winter's night in wet clothes. I got myself upright, leaned on the shaggy bulk of a cedar until the sparks cleared from my eyes. It was not far to my camp. A thinking man would have dug out the less-wet wood and started a fire to get warm. Instead, I stumbled down to the beach.

The tide was falling, the cove iron-coloured with a swaying swell. A fair chop on the inlet. I dropped the weight of my coat on the stones, worked out of my boots and trousers, dragged the wet sweater over my head. Fumbling at the buttons of my long underwear, I peeled the mess away. The wind cut into me as I walked into the surf. I dove as soon as I had the depth. Soon I could feel my heart, the circling beat of my blood. *It wakes you up.*

Out past the headland I met the inlet's sweep, *out to sea, out to sea.* I stroked along, slipping inside its pull. Swimming is not walking, Kit. To stop is to begin to let go. What was there to lose—the cove? The camp? But the body would have its way. Warm now with trying, it turned into the current and came clawing back.

◖

Kit's arms are burning, her shoulders howling with every turn of the oars. She heads for quiet water, her skiff loaded with an impressive catch. Wednesday morning, the week only half-done. No complaints— she wanted to be out on the grounds, and now she is. Of course, the dream had never been to do it alone. Sons went out as young as fifteen, boatpullers on paper, but fishing alongside their fathers all the same. Why not a girl?

The war opened the door a crack for her. There were fewer fishermen about—her father one of many who had gone—and the price was up for any salmon you could catch. Mr. Knox came into the store as he often did mid-week. Uncle Anders closed his order book, but Kit noticed he didn't reach for his stool. *If you get too comfortable, they will too.*

She was in the lead with the broom, her mother following with the mop and pail. The manager gave a sigh. His wife was poorly—well, come to that, when was she not? Kit stole a look at his face: part have-a-laugh, part poor-old-me.

Bobbie dunked the mop, plunging it up and down. "I'll look in on her when I finish up here."

"You're a gem, Mrs. Starratt." Mr. Knox wiped his thin hair back. "Isn't she a gem."

"She is," Uncle Anders said.

Bobbie bent to twist the water from the mop.

"And a hard worker to boot."

Uncle Anders gave a nod.

"Not like these buggers I have to deal with. Beg pardon, Missus."

Her mother smiled. "Don't mind me."

"Only, they wear a man out. This one little— Thompson, his name is. He tells me he's worked as a pitcher before—*Oh yes, Mr. Knox, I got experience*—but you should see him. Jabs his pew into the fish any old where. I tell him, the meat's no good to me full of holes."

Kit stood still. Could Bobbie feel it? The wish in Kit's hands—gripping the broom handle but feeling the haft of the pew. Their eyes met, and her mother spoke.

"You ought to give Kit a try. She's a demon with the pew."

Kit looked down at the broom head.

"A little young, isn't she?" said Mr. Knox.

"She's fourteen," Bobbie said, a lie of one year—something the manager might easily have worked out himself. "Older than some you got working down there."

"On the floor, maybe," he said. "Pitching's skilled work."

"I'm telling you, she's a demon."

"It is true," Uncle Anders said. "You will not find better."

And so Thompson was demoted to the cannery floor—cleaning round the feet of the slitters, catching the empty cans that rolled down the chute and lugging them to the packing line—and Kit got her chance.

There was a trick to pitching—stick and fling, a kind of flying figure eight. You had to stay calm to keep your footing knee-deep in fish. The pew had a single tooth, and you knew by feel when it slipped and bit into the good red flesh—something Kit hadn't felt for a long time. Frank had taught her when she was seven or eight, letting her pitch the catch ashore every time they went out—even if it was only a few greenlings or a single weighty spring. You had to trust the pew. Her father never said that. He said, "Head's good, or the tail. Just look where you want it to go."

She liked the work. Keeping an ear out for the collector boat, pelting down to the fish ladder to meet it, pew in hand. Mr. Knox watched her pitch, and the following year, when a spot came up on the collector, the job was hers. Now she was out in the clean air among the fleet, hopping down into skiff after skiff to pitch the fish up into the collector's hold. When Frank returned, she would be ready to labour beside him, setting and picking the net.

That was the idea. But when the man himself finally came home, he was no use in a boat. The sea-scare, Uncle Anders called it. He said it once in his own language, and it sounded even worse.

God, she's tired. The catch twitches about her boots. The sun is hot on her crown, blinding off the swollen waves. She can't seem to let go of the oars.

Her father's gone. The truth of it just about swamps her. Both of them now, gone from her days. Not from the world, though, not Bobbie. Her mother could still come back. *Foolish.* Kit has no idea where Bobbie is—not a word before she left and not so much as a postcard since. Uncle Anders won't speak her name aloud; like Kit, he bowed his head whenever Frank talked poison about his faithless wife. Still, Kit lets herself picture it: Bobbie walking back to her down the *Camosun*'s gangplank, *a mistake, Kitty-cat, all of it, a mistake.*

Kit curls forward, resting her forehead on her knees. Somehow she releases her grip, letting the oars dangle in their locks. Blades trailing, the faintest drag. Where the hell is the collector? She needs to off-load her catch. She needs to row in close to shore, drop anchor and lie down.

$$\phi$$

It troubled me, that slip I had made with the rum. I tried to make up for it by cutting back, but even half an ounce under ration brought on a sick chill and shaking hands. Such careful accounts the blood keeps. I am up to double that daily measure now.

I made three trips to the abandoned sawmill all told. The last had to wait for a quiet sea. I had torn the corrugated roof off a four-seat privy—the length of it made the *Coot* unsure. Soft snow came dropping, dissolving. I wore my arms out rowing back, fighting the outgoing tide. A following sea could have swamped her on a single swell.

For a time my days were full—a swim when storms allowed, a trip out to the kelp beds in the rowboat, work on the shack. You know how night comes down in these fjords. More than once I found myself hammering a nail I could no longer see.

Heavy weather often kept me ashore, the surf dangerous even in my little cove. The longer I went without pulling boat or body through the waves, the heavier my limbs became. The storekeeper at Alert Bay had been right—I came to value the long wander along the creek to check my traps.

The hardware had come with advice. "Thing is to figure out where they go," the storekeeper told me. "I used to roll a log right up to the riverbank, leave a skinny path, see, dig down in the mud for the set." He nodded to himself. "Look out for hidey-holes under the bank or round the roots of a tree. You find one with a heap of shit full of fish scales, you've got your mink."

I smoked my traps as he had suggested, laying them out beneath the dangling strips of fish. I made sure to handle them with gloves.

Having rolled a log up alongside the creek, I crouched on it to make the set, leaving little sign. The first animal I took there was a good size. The trap held him by the hind leg—he had made a wallow with his thrashing and drowned. I can still see my hands turning red with cold as I washed the mud from his fur. I shook the water from his pelt, the death rigor already going out of him so he snapped like a rag.

Over time I took ten mink at that single spot. One had chewed through two of his toes and was working on a third. Standing just out of his reach, I gripped my gun by the barrel, raising the heavy butt. "Trust me," I told him, "it will be a relief."

Of course, I was handy with a knife—I had gutted thousands of fish, field-dressed scores of deer. The meat of a mink is slim and foul with musk. I was only hungry enough to eat it once. "Tack the skin out as soon as you can," the storekeeper had told me. "Stretch it, sure, but only a bit. That way you keep a good dense pelt without selling yourself short."

Nights when the rain held off, I unwrapped Neville's dictionary and opened it by the fire. "Fire" was *the igneous element.* But also *the passion of love* and *the punishment of the damned.* A little way up the page, "finny" meant *furnished with fins, formed for the element of water.* I looked for "mink" but did not find it. I spoke the word any-way, in case one was hiding nearby, waiting to hear its name.

By the end of January I had baled up a few dozen pelts, enough to be thinking of a trip to the Fortunes' floathouse store. And yes, I was thinking about those Hudson's Bay jugs, the last one making a hollow sound now when I tipped it to pour. I had suffered no more slips since the first—I was making myself steady, a man at his own helm. There was a pride in it, work and weather, mea-sured reward.

Tom and Grace Fortune. If the man in Alert Bay had set some unknown compass in me, pointing the way to the storekeeper's life, then the Fortunes tapped on its housing, bringing the needle true. I thought I had lost all taste for company, but when they offered supper and a bunk, some part of me I had hoped I was rid of sat up eager as a dog.

Grace was a big woman, but she skimmed around their kitchen, each hand on its own errand, so she seemed to be both cook and kitchen maid. A good-looking woman, I suppose, a great mass of rust-coloured hair tied back, a light in her eye whenever she glanced at Tom.

While she cooked, Tom got out his board and cards. Cribbage is a baffling game to begin, but he was a patient teacher. If you have ever minded the hours your father and I spent playing, you have Tom Fortune to blame.

He was older than his wife by a decade or more, with a cured look to his skin that I recognized. After months of rum, the first shot of whiskey was a happy breath of fire. The smoky taste followed to soothe the tongue. Grace cut her rye with cordial, but she kept up well enough once she had the loaf in the oven and the stew simmering on top.

Later, when we had wiped our bowls clean with that good, dense bread, I found myself talking without end. Grace nodded from her post at the washing-up basin, Tom looking past his grip on the glass into the lamp's bright flame. The sawed-off nails in the cribbage board glinted, Tom's well ahead.

It was about the mink, my sermon, and about myself. How the mink hunted and fished, and I hunted and fished, using the fish I had caught for bait. Did it stay in the flesh, all that fish? In my flesh and the mink's? "Flesh" was a slippery word, one Neville's diction-ary had afforded several lines. *Animal nature. Near relation. The body distinguished from the soul.*

"I never thought," Grace said. "What do you reckon, Tom?"

"Couldn't say."

They were being kind—I could see it, looking in on the three of us floating there. How many solitary trappers, handliners and hand-loggers had they welcomed and let babble on? Surely there was no shame in it. Even so, when I woke in my clothes on the stockroom cot, I sat up sweating like a man disgraced.

I was as quiet as a half-sober man can be, feeling his way out through a home he doesn't know. On the dock I found the dark beginning to thin. The rain was steady, almost gentle, the sea no threat. Tom had lined up my gallon jugs and other supplies just inside the shop door. The pelts had covered my bill with credit besides—all the same, I crept back and forth to the *Coot* like a thief, stowing everything under my oilskin. No sign of life in the float-house as I pushed off. They would wake to find their home returned to them. I do not know if the relief I imagined was theirs or my own.

It was not as though I never saw another soul. Indians travelled the inlet—not Oweekeenos but another group Tom and Grace called Gwasalas. You saw them rowing or paddling, the odd one-lunger putt-putting through the fog. Like the blackfish, they passed the mouth of the cove but did not trouble to turn toward shore. I suppose they knew the beach was too steep for clamming, and the rocks hid only small, sinewy crabs. Or perhaps they had lived a lesson or two in how white men make friends.

In late spring the fresh-fish collectors steamed through to buy up the piecemeal catch, and by summer the lone cannery on the inlet was sending a boat around. The fair-weather handliners rowed out from whatever town they had been haunting during the winter months. I raised a hand to any man I passed on the inlet. Those who strayed into the cove I greeted with crossed arms.

As ever, the Fortunes' store was only a day's row away. I needed supplies like any man, and they often had a copy of the *World*. The news was weeks old but fresh to me—an orphan girl's suicide, Chinese exclusion renewed in the US. Reading in my little shack on the cove was not so different from turning the pages in a room at Mrs. McClintock's, or back at the old bachelor's shed. Even in a city coming up like mushrooms, I had been a man on his own.

The cove was warm on sunny afternoons, or so it seemed to a winter swimmer—the water green with plankton, strong-smelling and soft. On the day I am thinking of, I had swum out around the eastern headland and followed the coast for perhaps a mile. I turned back at the sight of two rowboats bobbing by the little island I called the Gem. If the fishermen spotted my head, they probably thought sea lion, *thief,* and were glad to see me go.

Back in the cove, I floated, feeling the depth well beneath me, the sun press down on my chest. I would say I caught sight of it in the corner of my eye, but I remember the red light through my eyelids, so they must have been closed. I suppose I heard it—the great tail swishing at the surface, driving the lead-grey bulk. I rolled to see the fin not ten yards away—a ragged triangle, darker than those of other sharks. Darker and larger by far.

You have seen baskers, Kit, out with your father in the boat. Imagine no hull, just your body in the water as one of them makes a lazy turn your way. The black lobe of the nose cuts a wake. Sunlight finds the white-ribbed gills in the cavernous mouth. *Filter-feeder,* the brain tells the heart, *nothing to fear.* But the heart hears little over its own wild sound.

It would have seen me and shifted course—I am certain it would. As it was, I backstroked out of its path. Passing close, the basking shark showed its length to be five times my own. I could have stood up inside its open mouth.

I cycled in the water as it crossed the cove—three, four times, a slow patrol between my body and the shore. I was sure it had spotted me on that first narrow pass, I had marked the dark beach-stone of its eye. There was no harm in the thing, only that it made such a portrait of hunger. Treading water over the deeps, I closed my eyes and wished it away. A last slow pass. The fin rounded the headland and was gone.

8

Were the storms worse that second winter in my camp? I only know that I slept through much of the dirtiest weather the first time around, and then somehow I could not.

Night after night spent staring into the blackness of a waste-wood shack, rain hammering, wind snatching at the planks. I knew weather, coming from Lofoten, but the house I had grown up in was solid. It anchored the land around it, the way a child, or even a good dog dozing by the stove, anchors a home.

A dream would come to me as I lay awake in the din—though I suppose a wakeful dream might be called a wish. It was simple enough. That the shack would tear away from this world and take me with it. That sleep—or to say the truth, waking—would no longer be my concern.

Dark days. I walked my trapline, cleared and remade my sets. In the shack, the finished pelts lay in a pile, others still stretched on their boards. Their musk made a kind of company in the night.

The first calm day in a dozen, I dragged the *Coot* down through a gap in the logs and floated her on a lapping high tide. I was down to a few foul strips of smoked rockfish, my insides crying for something fresh. A cold fog sat on the water, rubbing out both headlands so the cove went on and on. No matter, I told myself, the oars will remember the way.

You know how sound skips and dies in a fog, how your ears reach into the stillness like hands? Anything. *Anything?* The oars croaked in their locks, cutting softly into the swell. From time to time a patch of shoreline came clear, fluttering like a sheet on my mother's line. It was my nose that told me the Gem was close. I could smell the little forest on its back, the larger one swishing around it in the sea.

Making the most of the quiet water, I fished in tight against the rocks. The fog deepened, draping wet, woollen layers over the island's bristle of trees. Still the fish made me wait. By the time the line yanked where I had wound it around my boot, I had floated to a grey patch in my brain.

A greenling of four pounds or more—it had passed some years in the inlet's depths. I dragged it up gasping, stared into its flexing mouth. It spilled against the planks, fins the colour of whiskey in the soft, strange light. Golden freckles on a body of brown, a tricky eye-spot by the tail. *Here is the end of me, here is the start.* I came back to myself and took up the club.

With the greenling dead, my work was to drop the line again. Instead, I bailed the midline puddle and lay down.

What kind of fisherman lets himself drift off in a fog? When I opened my eyes, night was rising, as it sometimes does, from the sea. I lay there listening—the sound wider now. Had the *Coot* found her way to the inlet's mouth?

I would have dozed again if not for the sound of something tearing—something wet and soft. I raised my head. A gull was standing over the greenling in the stern, holding me in its gaze. Its beak caught the last of the light, yellow scissors marked with a blood spot to guide the chicks. It was ripping into my catch.

A true fisherman would have shouted, kicked out with his boot. Propped against the thwart, I spoke. "Where have you come from?" And when the gull did not fly off, "Where are we?"

The longer I listened, the more certain I was that we had departed the inlet for the open sound. The appearance of a distant light did not move me. The gull had to show me how. Stepping back from the fish, it folded open its wings, pumped and lifted away. Bereft of its white head and back, the dark doubled. The light wavered, a good way off. I dragged myself onto the thwart and took up the oars.

You know the story, Kit, at least in part.

"Who's that?" came Tom Fortune's voice.

It took me a moment to answer. "Anders Viken."

"Andy? I'll be damned."

I could make out the shape of him now, a narrow man thinning with age and drink. Still, he was quick to catch the line and wind it round the cleat. A second boat was moored alongside the floathouse runabout, longer by a few feet and broad of beam, in need of a coat of paint. The lantern light fell over the rusting bulk of its engine, an Easthope one-lunger that might have been the poor cousin of Tom's well-oiled pride and joy.

"You're just in time," he said.

I had thought to offer up the greenling, but a glance at the picked-over head changed my mind. I stepped up empty-handed onto the dock. "For what?"

"You joking, boy? Christmas supper is what." Tom clapped a hand on my back. "Come on in."

◗

The wind behind her, Kit hoists the simple sail. Up-inlet now in pursuit of the fish, a couple dozen skiffs scattered within view. A grey glimpse in the distance—whale back, is it? Maybe just a wave.

When was it? Before the war, certainly—she must have been eight or nine. Out with her father in the *Dogfish*, a decent chop, cool but not properly cold. Headed for some handlining in Scandinavia Bay, they came round Stone Point to the sight of a humpback waving its fluke. Next came a tail, too soon to belong to the same beast. One then the other poked a head up, eyeing the boat. The first was the larger; the other wore a great lump of barnacle on its brow.

Kit looked round at her father, and he shook his head— something in the manner of "here we go." He cut the engine, even though starting it had given him trouble that morning.

With the Easthope gone quiet, the whales showed more of themselves. The long curve of a back punctuated by the stubby hump. The hovering span of a tail. The surface would mend for a time, until one or the other broke it with a lazy roll—flashing the white underside of a fluke, bringing it down with a resounding clap. A hundred yards, no more, from where Kit and her father sat.

After a time she turned to him again. "What are they doing?"

"What's it look like?"

"—Playing?"

"Sounds about right. Talking too, like as not."

"Talking?"

"You never heard of that?" He gestured with a tip of his head. "Have a listen."

An inch of wash sloshed along the hull's midline, but she knelt down anyway—getting in a boat meant getting wet. At a point below the water line, she laid her ear to the planks.

To begin with, there was nothing beyond the slap of the waves, the ocean's great empty that she knew in fact to be full. Then she heard it: a door moaning open, a hinge that had never been oiled.

Quiet again . . . and then a word. *Hey. Hey, hey, hey*—stuttered and somehow funny, because it sped up to become *hahahahaha*. Her father too seemed amused, smiling to himself and then to her. Leaning forward, he pressed a hand flat to the hull and listened through the skin of his palm.

It was a thing that only happened in the boat. On land he never seemed at ease; even glassy-eyed with drink, he gave off a feel as though he might jump up at any moment, grab at something or someone, let out a sound. In the boat he could be even. Light seas or heavy, he could be calm.

◊

That Christmas night, I followed the sway of Tom's lantern through the store, light glinting off the hanging pans and ladles, a smell of iron and wool. The side door opened into the kitchen's warmth. Now I could smell spruce—boughs laid along the windowsill and hung on nails. Meat and gravy. Best of all, baking bread.

"Look who's here, Gracie."

Grace turned, wooden spoon in hand, hugging an enamel bowl to her chest. She smiled at the sight of me. "Well, if it isn't the wild man of Borneo."

That raised a laugh. The two men at the table were strangers to me, plainly father and son. Dark-eyed, handsome men—thick black hair, heavy lashes and brows, sharp little beards. I will admit to the feeling that welled up in me. I stood motionless, willing it to pass.

The father's looks were partway lost, his nose not only broken but crushed. The likeness was further strained when they stood, the older man taller by a head—my own height but broader by far. Here was the owner of the unloved boat.

"Who's this, then?" he said, and I heard for the first time the airy whistle of his ruined nose.

"Anders Viken." I held out my hand. He took it in his grip.

"Frank Starratt. This is Frank Jr."

He was nineteen then, your father—a man, of course, but also a boy. His face like a dream of his father's before life's violence had left its mark.

"Hope that stew'll stretch," Frank Sr. said, seating himself.

"Not to worry, plenty for everyone." Grace set down her mixing bowl. "Here, Anders, give me your coat."

My eye caught on the whiskey bottle. A three-man game of cribbage was under way—not Tom's plain pegging board but a handsome block of wood stained almost black, the track set out in metal plates.

Tom took his seat. "Your deal, Frank."

"That it is," Frank Sr. said, reaching for the pack.

Meantime, Grace arranged basin, soap and flannel down one end of the kitchen workbench, along with scissors and a looking glass. She lifted the kettle from the back of the stove and poured. I stood with my back to the rest of them, washing away the greenling's scales before propping the mirror against Grace's bread bin.

You have never seen me with a beard, Kit, and you never will. I was used to meeting a stranger in the glass, but that night I got a shock. Hair down to my shoulders, beard resting on my chest. I was forty-two years old, and the grey had come creeping in. My eyes glittered like a crab's.

Being a swimmer, I was cleaner than most men in my situation would have been. Still, I could smell fish and mink and my own sour smell as the warmth worked into my fog-dampened clothes. I washed my face, then took the scissors and trimmed the beard close, dropping skeins into the fatty suds. My hair was crisp with salt. I had cut away the mess about my face and was reaching around back when Grace slapped the flour off her hands. She held one out for the scissors.

"Careful, Missus," Frank Sr. called over. "Christ only knows what he's got living in there."

Grace stood behind me, snipping. "Don't mind the joker." She was done in minutes and reaching for the broom.

Out back there was a little apron of deck where Grace dumped her scraps. I carried the basin out, shutting the door after me to keep in the warm. The fog lay close against the floathouse. In the light of the kitchen window I tipped the bristly soup away. Crouching down to rinse the basin, I felt a sudden urge to tip forward into the sea. But there was the bottle inside, and the supper to come.

"I don't take that kind of crap from any man," Frank Sr. was saying as I stepped back inside. "Crew boss, manager, first mate, makes no odds. I learned that on the *Anna May*, first whaler I served on. Man eats shit in this life, it's shit he gets served." He tossed a card to the crib, glancing up. "Andy, m'boy, you're a new man." He pushed out the chair opposite with his boot. "Sit yourself down."

If Tom minded his guest playing the host, he gave no sign. I took a seat and Grace set a glass down by my elbow. I reached for the whiskey.

"That's the spirit," she said. "You got some catching up to do."

With three already playing, there was no place for me in the game. I was just as glad to sit and watch, nodding whenever one of them tipped the bottle over my glass. Tom was a thoughtful player by nature—the drink made him labour over every hand. Frank Jr. had a boy's way about him, grinning to show a good hand, skipping his peg along from hole to hole. His father kept a hard eye on the proceedings. Round after round he drew ahead of the others, breath whistling between his words.

It was not the first time father and son had stopped in at the Fortunes' store—it seemed they were up and down the coast after all manner of work. Just lately they had left the logging camp at Grief Point, Frank Sr. unwilling to eat the shit on offer there.

"Makes no odds," the son said, looking to his father. "Always work for a man who knows what he's about."

Frank Sr. gave a nod, flipping over the starter card. "Heard they're looking for a winter watchman at one of the canneries on Rivers Inlet."

Tom looked up. "You talking about Far Cry?"

"That's the one."

"Not just a watchman," said Grace. "Storekeeper, too." She knocked a fresh loaf out of the pan and carried it over on the board. "Now clear all this away, or it'll be midnight before we eat."

Frank Sr. sat back while the rest of us rose to shift the game to the corner armchair. "Even better," he said.

"What is?" Grace said, bringing over the bowls.

"Storekeeper. My boy here's got a head for figures."

Frank Jr. looked surprised at that.

"Get another bottle down, will you, Tommy?" Grace was piling scraps onto a tin plate. The sound brought a small surprise—a lead-grey puppy left its box in the corner to cry at her feet. She ladled gravy over the mess, blew on it before setting it down on the floor.

I sat down in front of my bowl. The white backs of dumplings rose from a golden stew. Suddenly alive to the pickled length of my own innards, I suffered a flood of hunger painfully close to fear.

"Christ almighty," Frank Sr. said. "I don't know when I last tasted chicken."

Grace took her seat. "It's only our last old layer. A few hours in the pot will have softened her down."

"I said it before, Tommy, and I'll say it again. You're a lucky man."

Tom looked up, not at Frank Sr. but at his wife. He gave a solemn little nod.

There was quiet then, only the strange singing of Frank Sr.'s nose, and the sounds of four men and a woman eating. Down below, the tinny hint of the puppy nosing its plate across the planks.

Frank Sr. was wiping his bread around the bowl before the rest of us were halfway done. Grace rose to get him a second helping, and just as if she was his own wife, he gave a sound rather than a word when she set it down. A few mouthfuls in, he gestured to his son. "This one's mother couldn't cook worth a damn."

The spoon in Frank Jr.'s hand went still.

"Don't know what I was thinking, marrying a woman that thin. And she only came up to here." He cut a hand in over his heart. "Case you're wondering how a man like me fathers such a runt."

"Oh, now." Grace winked at the son. "Good things in small packages, isn't that what they say?"

"They can say it all they like," the father answered. "It's the big packages get talked about."

Tom yipped a laugh.

"Ha! Still with us, eh, Tommy?" Frank Sr. took the bottle by the neck to fill his host's glass. Tom was coughing by then, turning red. Grace got up to rub his back. He settled, and, like a breath released, Frank Jr.'s spoon started up again.

At the sound of it scraping bottom, Grace stood and held her hand out for the bowl. "You'll have some more. You too, Andy."

Frank Sr.'s eyes followed her to the stove. "Yessir, skin and bones she was, always sickening with something." He turned back to his son. "Finally gave up the ghost when you were, what, thirteen?"

Frank Jr. blinked. "Fourteen."

"Fourteen. No more mama's boy. Got him out working with his dad." He took another mouthful, then seemed to hear the silence around the table.

Grace set my refilled bowl down, then Frank Jr.'s. Her gaze rested on him, the motherless boy.

"Thank you," I said.

"Yes," the son echoed, "thank you."

We bent to our stew again.

"I'll tell you what those dumplings put me in mind of," Frank Sr. said.

Grace rose to clear. "What's that?"

"Doughnuts. Cook on the *Anna May* used to knot up the dough for us when we were rendering the blubber. We'd drop 'em in the cauldrons."

"You never."

He laughed. "Tasted like whale oil, too. Funny what passes for a treat when there's no woman aboard."

Tom fumbled with his pipe while Frank Jr. rolled up smokes for his father and himself. He noticed I had none with me and passed the pouch.

"Humpbacks was mostly what we were after," Frank Sr. said. "Down through Georgia Strait."

Grace nodded. "Whenabouts would this have been?"

"Well, I was fifteen when I started, so that's, what, '65, '66. I stuck it for five years or so before heading south. San Francisco, now there's a town. Too many Chinamen, mind you, and not enough skirts. Still, I could tell you stories. Not for a lady's ears." He grinned. "The strait was about whaled out by then, and anyhow, humpbacks are a bugger to bring in. You can lower and make fast all right, but then they run. Big bull towed a boat I was in for miles in a fog, and then didn't the bastard give up and sink. Took the ship the best part of a day and night to find us. No fun, is it, Andy?" He slapped the table in front of me. "I say it's no fun, getting lost in the brume."

I shook my head, the smoke wagging at my lip.

"Don't say much, does he?"

"Depends," said Grace.

"Hey," said Frank Jr., "what about the game?"

His father's eyes shifted.

"Hang on," said Grace. "Wouldn't be Christmas supper without mince tarts." She was up again, shuffling to keep from stepping on the dog. "No, pup, you've had your supper. Go on, back to your bed."

"You're not keeping that mongrel, I hope," Frank Sr. said. "Wolves at heart, every one."

"Oh, now." She found the tarts and carried them back at a dangerous tilt. "Tommy's mum's recipe, isn't that right?"

Tom squinted up at her.

"Your mother's tarts."

"Best," he said. "You make 'em best."

"Charmer." She set the plate down and laid her hand to the back of his neck, a gesture that brought a dull pain to my chest. I reached for a tart. It was the first time I tasted mincemeat, and the fatty tang of it caught me off guard. I took another bite. Filling my glass, I swilled the spice over my tongue.

"Bowhead," Frank Sr. said, swallowing. "Now there's a whale you want to hunt. Lazy and full of oil. Baleen too, good long plates." He swung his head Grace's way. "You ladies gotta have your whalebone."

She laughed. "Not much call for corsets round here."

"No," he said. "I dare say."

"Bowhead's the same as a right whale?" Frank Jr. said.

"Close, not the same. Why you think they give them different names."

The son gave a sheep's grin. "I don't know."

"Don't think, more like. No, there were still a few rights up around the Aleutians—we'd lower for them while we waited for the ice to draw back. Hardly worth it. The ones that were left were nervous of men. Slap an oar on the water and they were off." He took a second tart and pushed it into his mouth.

Grace looked pleased. "Better than a whale-oil doughnut."

"Damn right, Missus." Frank Sr. wiped a knuckle across his lips. "Tell you what, though, you gotta watch your step around those cauldrons. Whole ship gets greasy when they're lit."

He turned his forearm in the light of the lamp. Among the coarse black hairs, a hundred shiny freckles gleamed—a pattern of spatter burns. Grace clucked her tongue. Beside her, Tom gave a delayed shake of his head. For my part, I could think only of the speckled greenling—not the lifeless body but the life before.

"My last season on the *Anna May*," Frank Sr. went on, "this dumb bugger of an oarsman is fishing scrap out of the cauldron when he goes in ass over ears."

Grace's hand went to her mouth. *"No."*

Frank Sr. nodded. "I ought to know, I'm the one who pulled him out. Got this for my trouble." Leaning back, he dug both hands down the front of his trousers and dragged up his shirt. Grace obliged with a wincing breath. Across his chest he wore a glassy scar, as though the hair there had been polished away. Plenty of hair below it, though. Black curls swirling under his nipples, a dark arrow down his belly's midline.

The son was sitting forward in his chair, watching a show he had doubtless seen before. "He lived, though," Grace said.

"Oh, he lived all right." Frank Sr.'s expression darkened as he drew down his shirt. "I shouldn't've bothered."

"Don't say that," said Grace. "You saved his life."

"Damn right," Tom said to his lap.

"Dobbs was his name." Frank Sr. made a sound in his throat, and I saw the puppy stir in its box. Beside me, the son lowered his face to his drink.

"What?" said Grace. "What happened?"

"What happened, Missus, is that we laid this Dobbs out screaming on deck and doused him with sea water. By then the cook had caught wind, so up he comes from the galley with a can of molasses—"

"Molasses?" said Grace.

Tom nodded. "Hell yes, molasses."

"I took a smear of it myself." Frank Sr. patted his chest. "But the cook painted Dobbs all over, and when the bugger looked like a black boy crying for his ma, he dusted him down with flour and made him white again." His grin flared. "That kept his skin on for the sail down to the doc."

How long had it been since I had spoken? I took a drink. "So what was the trouble?"

Frank Sr. looked at me. They were your father's eyes, Kit, your eyes—and they were not. All the spark but not a flicker of the warmth.

"The trouble was that Dobbs was a liar." He swept his gaze around the table. "I was the one pulled him out of there, right?"

"Right," Frank Jr. said.

"You seen the evidence. Risked my own skin."

The son nodded vigorously, and the others along with him. My own head, heavy with drink and the hour, somehow bobbed along.

"That Dobbs, that sonofabitch." He shook his head. "He said I was the one who pushed him in."

It was the smallest of movements, a split-second cut of those eyes. What had Dobbs done, I wondered, to single himself out in Frank Sr.'s gaze?

Tom broke the quiet, scraping his chair back and standing, hands spread on the table until he located what sense there was left in his legs.

Grace looked up at him. "All right, love?"

He felt out beside him for the wall. "All right."

He was wise to take his leave—we had all drunk more than enough. Frank Sr. lifted his glass. "Happy Christmas, Tommy!"

And Frank Jr., like a magpie, "Happy Christmas!"

"Good night, Tom," I said, reaching for the bottle.

"Christmas," he said, lurching off through the doorway. "Night."

9

It was late when the singing began. I remember Grace doing a hymn on her own, the puppy whining when she hit the high notes, making her laugh. And I remember "God Rest Ye Merry Gentlemen," fast the way your father always sang it, with Grace taking the sweet line and Frank Sr. shouting along down low. I kept time banging on the table, but Grace felt sorry for me not knowing the words, and she pressed for a song in my own tongue. You know the one, Kit, you have heard it every Christmas of your life. I was surprised the first time your father asked for it. I thought he would wish to forget that year at the Fortunes', but it seemed he wanted to paint over parts of it, making a picture he could keep.

I had not heard "Mitt Hjerte Alltid Vanker" for more than twenty years, but when I opened my mouth, it was there. It was eerie, hearing my voice carry the tune alone, my mother and father mouthing along like phantoms. I managed the first verse only, up to *Jeg kan deg aldri glemme, Velsignet Julenatt!*

Frank Jr.'s eyes were shiny when I fell quiet. Grace too looked as though she might cry.

"Oh, now," she said. "Wasn't that pretty?"

"I'll say." The father gave a dark smile. "You hit some notes there, Andy-boy. Thought you were gonna strain yourself."

"What's it mean?" said the son.

I looked at him. He was beautiful, Kit, you know he was—but it was his spirit, the life he carried inside himself, in spite of the father he served. "My heart," I said, "my heart always wanders."

He nodded. "What else? What about the end?"

"The end? The end says I cannot forget you. And Happy Christmas. Happy Christmas night."

I do not know how I found my way to the cot in the stockroom. I can only thank heaven for that long doze in the *Coot*—even though it was a fool's rest that might have delivered me to my death. Without it, who can say how deeply I would have slept after all that good food and drink.

My eyes blinked open in the dark, but I shut them again, thinking the sound was a gull mistaking night for day. Grace told me later how she bit the hand he closed over her mouth. Had she not, I would have rolled over beneath my blanket and sunk back into sleep.

Tom did not wake to the sound of his wife crying out. Her second scream brought me stumbling from my bed. I ran a hand along sacks until I found the door. Lamplight showed the way to the kitchen, and the source of what was now a scuffling, breathless sound. Frank Sr. was jammed up against Grace, bending her back against the kitchen workbench. And yes, his hand was clamped over her mouth.

A single lamp, the wick down low, yet I could see her wide-open eyes. At Frank Sr.'s feet a shadow moved. The puppy was tearing at his trouser leg, and now, given the sudden shout, the needle teeth found flesh. Frank Sr. kicked the animal to the wall, its yowl cut short when it hit.

"Jævel!" I shouted, for a devil he appeared in that light. "Let her go!"

Or was it the son who yelled those words from the door behind me? Or perhaps the two of us bellowing as one?

I reached his father first. As a boy I had clung to my own father's mare as she ran—that was the feeling of Frank Sr.'s neck in the crook of my arm. His elbow hammered back, driving the breath from my chest, almost knocking me off my feet. He whirled to face me, and Grace slipped like something spilling to the floor. The hand she had bitten was dark with blood. I saw it curl and come hurtling toward my jaw.

"Dad! Leave him!" Frank Jr. grabbed his father's arm, but Frank Sr. shook him off, kicking out sideways to drop him to his knees.

Grace was up on all fours now, crawling away. The father drew into himself and seemed to grow. I had heard men laugh in the course of their violence, but I had never seen the like of his wordless grin. My body remembered the beating it had taken behind the stables, the raging Swede. I gulped for air. I leapt. We went down in a thrashing pile.

"Enough! Enough now!" I shouted, wrestling free.

"Dad!" Frank Jr. was on his feet again, and for a second I feared a son's loyal boot in my side. Until I saw what he was seeing—his father no longer moving, that grin filled up with dark.

"Dad?" This time the son came to his knees on his own.

Grace let out a sound. I scuttled across to help her out from under the table, propping her against the wall.

"I'm all right," she said, her hands feeling up and down her crossed arms. Her dress was torn at the shoulder. Glancing across at Frank Sr., I saw his trouser buttons were undone. Nothing showed at the flap of his long johns—was that not a hopeful sign?

Frank Jr. had picked up one of his father's hands. He held it as though testing its weight. "He sent me out to the boat," he said. "He sent me."

Grace took a shaky breath. "Is he dead?"

"Yes," I said. "His heart, maybe."

She nodded, and I helped her up onto a chair. Frank Jr. took one of the blankets she had put out for them, and covered his father head to boots. I opened the stove door and shoved in a log, then filled the kettle and set it to boil. It was then that I heard the whimper. Grace glanced toward the sound. Her eyes had emptied out—she sat under the blessing of shock. I crossed to crouch down where the puppy lay. If anything was broken, I would take care of it. Carry the poor creature outside and swing its skull against the dock.

I showed the puppy my hand, then felt along the small, soft form for any sign of pain. Instead, there came the touch of its tongue. *Skygge*, I thought, and so he had a name. Shaggy, you called him when you were small, mistaking the sound, *She-geh*. It was a good fit for a beast in a ragged grey coat, but *skygge* means shadow, you know that, Kit. I named him for where he lay that night, and for all he had witnessed. For the shade he might have become.

◖

Last morning on the grounds, and the bacon and bread are all gone. With the coffee coming to a boil, Kit guts the small sockeye she kept back. Her finger hooked under the jaw, she rinses the fish over the side. Laying it beside her on the thwart, she lops off the back fin, turns the blade against the head and runs it down along the spine. Lifting the fillet away, she slices up under the ribs, freeing them in a ribbon of flesh.

That's the way. Her father, seated by the tiller, letting her learn with his knife. She rests in the memory until it twists, taking her back to the dock. Again she approaches the *Dogfish* at its mooring. Again she finds him floating, drowned alongside his own boat.

Kit shakes her head to clear it. Another quick rinse, and she takes her blade to the salmon's second flank. How many fish has she cleaned in her life? Come to that, how many has she eaten? Just about every supper, give or take the odd worn-out chicken or hash of bully beef, the annual stretch of venison while they worked their way through an autumn buck.

Even Christmas called for fish. They celebrated on the twenty-fourth, the way Uncle Anders had done it back home. It started weeks before that, though, when he rowed out to bait his line for a fat ling cod. It was not *skrei*, he never failed to mention, but it would have to do. Drying the fish was a trick amid winter storms; often he would carry it inside to hang alongside the stove. A stink in the cottage, but nothing they weren't used to. Nothing to what would come.

When the hinged fillets had the look of two grey boot soles, her uncle would soak them in water for days. Then in lye. Finally, to save poisoning them all, a bath in fresh water again. Kit could look but not touch. The swollen, jellied *lutefisk* required handling with care.

Meantime, she and Bobbie walked the headland to gather boughs snapped off by snow or rain. They laid them along shelves and window-sills in the cabin and the cottage. They wound two fragrant wreaths. Kit thought up the crowns—smaller wreaths, really, sized to their four skulls. Only the softest cedar tips would do.

She helped her mother on the twenty-third too. Bobbie would catch the chicken and pull its neck, but Kit had the touch for pluck-ing. On the day itself, she was always the first one over to the cottage. Uncle Anders would cook the *lutefisk* when it was time, but before that there were *lefse* to be made. "No lumps," he said as she stood over the pot of steaming potatoes, masher in hand. He was strict about it, running a fork through her work before letting her whip in the butter and cream. She had always been allowed to form the warm little balls, and there came a time when he trusted her with the rolling pin too. He manned the fry pan, though, and that was fine. She could decorate the table with sprigs of spruce. She could spread butter and sugar on the finished pancakes, roll and stack them for the feast.

By then her parents would have arrived, Frank setting down the pickled beans and onions before tramping back out for wood, Bobbie unwrapping the roast bird she'd swaddled like a newborn against the cold. Skygge and later Lys moved between them all, leaning up against a leg, touching a nose to the back of a hand.

Lutefisk in the pan made a smell like an alarm. Frank wouldn't touch the stuff, but Bobbie always forced down a bite for kindness' sake. Like her uncle, Kit had grown up with the reeking treat. Soft like so many of the sea's bodies, slippery. No chewing required. And the taste—not ocean so much as ocean floor, a flavour she longed to know.

Year after year, her father ate both drumsticks off the chicken, leaving the thighs for his wife. With plenty of meat still on the bird, he broke open each leg bone and sucked the marrow. He twisted the neck off at its root and went over it like a cob of corn. There seemed no end to the number of *lefse* he could pack away.

There was whiskey, of course, and for Kit there was cordial and milky tea. As many chocolate drops and gingersnaps and sugared almonds as they could manage—and more to be had from the store next door. There was singing, and once the hymns had opened their throats, there were stories. What was it about Christmas that got Frank onto whaling? His own father had ranged all over the Nor'west Ground, even hunting sperm whales in the waters off San Francisco Bay. Kit knew the shape of that coastline; Uncle Anders had set her a lesson to trace the continent's western edge.

"Now that was a hunt." Her father was wearing the crown she'd made him, a branchlet drooping down over one eye. "Right down to the bottom those buggers go, you know that? After the squid. Not squid like you seen, Kit, more like the size of a skiff." He held up his plate, a cracked bone rolling onto the table. "Leave a sucker mark this big."

Bobbie laughed, the window behind her a picture of a winter's night. "Geez, Frank, you'll never get her back in a boat."

"You kidding?" Frank reached for Kit, pulling her by the arm to sit on his knee. "She's made of sterner stuff than that, aren't you, Kit?"

She nodded, her mind still on the sperm whale, the headlong descent into the squid's pale tangle of arms. Not sweet stories—not *Christmas stories*—but she wanted them. And what did it matter if her father told them as though they were his own?

Up in the crow's nest on the lookout, the scramble to lower the boats. No time to waste once a carcass was tied alongside—it was all hands on deck to strip the blubber, or the sharks would have the lot. It seemed an impossible feat, even for a ship full of men. Of course, there were times when it was. The eighty-foot blue they lost to a pod of blackfish. The right whale they had to cut free when it stove in one of the boats. The humpback that towed them deep into a fog before it gave up the ghost and sank.

There had been no stories last Christmas. Everything was different with Bobbie gone. When the first week of December passed without Uncle Anders dropping his line, Kit rowed along the shoreline and spent a cold morning pulling up rockfish, waiting for a ling cod to strike. The one she finally caught was on the small side. She left it in a bucket outside Uncle Anders' door. The next day it lay in tatters where something had dragged it, near the top of the boardwalk stairs.

She could still pick up a few boughs on her way back and forth. No cedar crowns, though, not anymore. She caught the chicken herself, held it longer than strictly necessary before yanking its neck. She sat alone in the cabin while it roasted, then wrapped it up warm for the walk. She had planned to make *lefse* once she arrived at the cottage, but finding Lys asleep and her father and Uncle Anders bent over a game, she hadn't the heart. The pancakes would taste all wrong anyhow, with no *lutefisk* to clear the way.

◖

Boat day yesterday, Kit—I wonder, did you catch sight of the *Camosun* from your skiff? When I failed to notice Lys waiting by the door, she gave a breathy woof. I let her out to hobble down to the dock. Not long afterwards, I followed. If the storekeeper does not see to the order, who will?

Not even a week into the season and I am accustomed to the juddering cannery, the screaming gulls. The tide swilled about the pilings, a bloody broth. Sunlight caught the skim of scales. When the *Camosun* docked, I made my way to the forward side doors, order book in hand. My pencil travelled the columns, a check for every barrel, every sack.

I cannot say why my eyes strayed to the gangplank, the passenger coming ashore. I believe I let out a sound. For a moment I lost track of myself in time.

Stepping down onto the dock, the young man stood uncertain, as though he might turn around and reboard. I lowered my eyes, intent on the swimming figures in my book. At the edge of my vision, he seemed to decide. His rucksack swung at his side as he headed for the other Chinese on the dock—Jung Lee Long and a couple of line workers Knox had loaned him to help carry the cookhouse order up the hill.

I turned my back. Sacks of oats and crates of whiskey, leaden spools of chain. When I allowed myself another glance, the newcomer was making himself useful, shouldering a quarter of beef for the long walk up the cookhouse stairs.

With you and your mother both gone, I had the Johnson boys for help, also on loan from Knox. They worked like men, and when the order was packed away in the stockroom, I paid them more than we had agreed. Money has never meant much to me, you know that. These days it matters even less.

By the close of day, I had almost convinced myself I was mistaken. The shop bell rang as I was about to step out from behind the counter and lock the door. Had he been watching from the boardwalk, waiting for the last of the wives to fetch her mail? He drew the door closed behind him. Again, time slipped out from beneath me. Is the resemblance really so keen, or did my mind touch at his features with a wishful brush?

I cleared my throat. "Can I help you?"

"I hope so," he said. "I'm looking for someone."

"Your father."

"You knew him?"

I gave no reply.

"Jung Lee Long said he was here last year."

I nodded.

"He said he used to row out to that island."

"—That is so."

He watched me. "The men . . . I heard talk of a woman, a Mrs. Starratt?"

A trembling ran down my arms. I gripped my hands to quiet them.

"Did he leave with her?" the young man said. "Do you know where they went?"

My body moved out from behind the counter. Measured steps to the door, the bell a bright jangle as I drew it open wide. "There is nothing I can tell you."

Up close, I saw the line in his forehead, a half inch of vertical worry his father had never worn. "Please," he said. "All he told me was he was going north."

You will think me hard, Kit, but it pained me to meet his gaze. I looked out over the bay. "If there is nothing else, I am closing up."

———

But you must be wondering what happened at the Fortunes' float-house. Frank Sr. was your grandfather, after all.

Tom was set on doing things by the book. It would take a couple of days for Dr. Pollock to make it down from Namu to sign a certificate of death. In the meantime, we kept the body in the cool of the stockroom, laid out on a platform of crates. As a witness I was obliged to stay on, though in truth I had given little thought to my abandoned camp. I slept by the stove now, on a second pallet not far from Frank. He and I kept busy scrounging deadfall along the shore, dragging it back to split and stack. Already we had a way of working side by side.

Frank would not hear of us digging a grave. "It's good of you, Mr. Fortune, but I think he'd rather go at sea."

We took Tom's boat. Who knows how much Grace had told her husband. I cannot be certain if he was helping out as any man does on the coast, or if he was walking an extra mile—for the dead man's son, perhaps, to show him what a decent fellow might look like. Or for Grace, to see the bastard off the place.

We motored a good way out into the sound, looking across at the idea of Asia, the ocean's lead-coloured truth. Tom stood up, his knees bending with the swell. "Anyone want to say a few words?"

Frank had that boy's look on his face again. His eyes met mine, so I stood up by the body Grace had been good enough to stitch into a blanket. "We give Frank Starratt—"

"Francis," Frank said. "That's his proper name, our name. That's what my mother called him."

I nodded. "We give Francis Starratt Sr. to the sea. May he rest in peace."

Tom took the legs while I got hold of the shoulders, Frank struggling to get a grip midway. The body would have been heavy enough without the lead sinkers. "Worth the waste," Grace had said when I walked in on her winding them around his ankles. "Make sure the devil stays down."

"Right," said Tom. "One, two—*heave.*"

The splash seemed slight for such a big man. Down he went, dark into darker. The three of us watched him go.

While Tom and Frank worked over the engine on the boat that was now Frank's, I gave Grace a hand stock-taking in the store. At the time I wondered at her tackling the job so soon. That was before I knew the calm taking a tally can bring.

She spoke of Frank Sr. only once more in my hearing, and then she did not say his name. "Storekeeper? Some hope." She stood with her back to me, straightening a line of tins. "Can you see that sonofabitch keeping a place in order? Never mind serving folks." She looked round. "Ever think of it yourself?"

"Me?"

"Why not? Helps to have a place in this world."

A picture came to me, my hands on the counter, steady and clean. I saw myself from the waist up, half a man and better for it. And yes, I pictured your father too. I was not foolish enough to let myself love him—not in that way. Much as I had laboured to keep to myself over the years, I could recognize the spark of want in a man's eye. The only longing Frank ever turned my way was a boy's.

He offered to come with me to collect my things, but already my little life up the inlet had become a source of shame. I was not too proud, however, to accept the loan of his boat. It was one of those strangely still days that lie either side of a storm. The Easthope's *t-t-t-t-t-t* multiplied as I turned into the cove. Everything seemed wretched—it was like clearing up a dead man's camp. I left a note for any poor soul who happened upon the shack before the forest reclaimed it. *You are welcome here.*

Frank changed during that week at the floathouse. On New Year's Eve his voice came out for "Auld Lang Syne." You know his face when he sang, Kit, he and your mother doing the one about the Irish girl, *alive alive-o!* Yes, he was beautiful. I felt the stab of it from time to time.

The day we were due to leave, I found Grace sitting on the little back deck, gutting the morning's catch. She folded forward to rinse her hands. "About set?"

"We are."

Standing up, she edged a mess of innards off the planking with her boot. "You'll take the dog."

I had not known it was what I wanted. I looked at her.

"I'm too old for babies." She gestured with her chin. Skygge had come padding out to stand beside me. "Besides, he's sweet on you."

So there were three of us who left the Fortunes' store in Frank's boat—the *Dogfish*, of all names. Its one-lunger kept a steady rhythm as we motored north, the *Coot* tied up and wagging in our wake.

◗

Friday afternoon on the tow back in, Kit forces herself to sit up straight. The sea is whale-coloured, crusted with waves—a chop she feels in her teeth. She dips a nod to any man who looks round from the skiffs before her, shows her back to those behind. She's done it: five nights setting and picking the net, five mornings off-loading a respectable catch. Two days on dry land now to recover her strength.

At last, the shaggy rise of Squid Island, kelp crowns thrashing off the point. There are sea lions in Deep Cut Cove, several heads in the water, a big male hauled up and swaying on the beach. A string of bluffs and lesser coves before the island draws aside, revealing the shoreline she knows best. Evening light on the little beach, the twist and glimmer of the stream. On the headland, her cabin shows in glimpses. No smoke from the stovepipe. Why would there be?

At the mouth of the bay, a solitary figure in a cannery rowboat. Headed the other way, he passes them at a distance, his progress smooth in spite of the chop. Black hair, blue jacket—Archie Paul? No, slimmer shoulders, longer arms. Nobody she knows.

Kit closes her eyes. Lys will be waiting—on the dock or, if her joints are bad, on the boardwalk at the top of the stairs. Uncle Anders, too. Having stepped out of the store, he'll be standing at the porch rail, watching over the fleet's return. Of course, he's sorry; he needn't say it out loud. She'll let herself look for him. She might even answer his wave.

10

You cannot know how it comforted me, Kit, you stopping by the store after your first week out. Not much to say for yourself, but that was nothing so strange. I had the crowd to see to—scores of grubby, wound-up fishermen in need of a drink—and you were plainly tired.

I had hoped to sleep well myself tonight, knowing we are friends again. That was before I caught sight of my pad and pencil on the bedside crate.

Far Cry Cannery. Your father and I asked the way at Duncanby Landing and caught the incoming tide up-inlet to the bay. It was clear even before we tied up that no one had been looking after the place. Knox was here on his own, acting the part of winter watchman until he could find a man to take on the job.

I told Skygge to stay in the boat—even as a pup, there never was such a good dog for overcoming his want in the face of a command. Over the years I let him have his head, knowing he would come when called. Except the once, but you know all about that. A tale for another time.

Alone for too long, Knox could not help hurrying down to the dock. He straightened his smile when he heard we had come about work. Man of business, he led the way inside the cannery—colder somehow than the out-of-doors. We crowded into the office at the top of the stairs, and Knox got himself in behind the desk, leaving your father and myself to stand. He took up a pen. "Frank Starratt, you say?"

Frank stepped forward. "That's right."

Knox clucked his tongue. "Seems to me I've heard that name before. Maybe a story or two."

"My father, sir," Frank said. "He passed on."

Knox looked at him. "I run a tight operation here, Starratt."

"Yes, sir."

"No time for troublemakers."

"No, sir."

"Frank is his own man," I said. "He is a hard worker, steady."

"That so." Knox watched me for a moment. "And you fancy yourself for storekeeper."

I nodded.

"Got any experience?"

Tell him you helped out here, Grace had said. Tell him you've got a head for figures.

"Oh, yes?" said Knox. "What's seven times nine?"

"Sixty-three."

He nodded. "How about people?"

"People?"

"Storekeeper does more than keep accounts. We get all sorts coming through when the run is on. How are you at managing folks?"

It was Frank's turn to speak up. "Andy gets along with everyone." He shot me a grin. "Doesn't take any crap, but he gets along."

"That so," Knox said again. He scratched a long note to himself. Finally he looked up. "I'll try you out, the pair of you. See what you can do."

◗

Kit opens her eyes to the cabin's blackness. A sound? If so, it doesn't come again. A silence then, emanating from behind the curtain to her parents' room.

Touching her feet to the floorboards, she pushes the blanket aside. Finds the lamp and matchbox by feel. Light helps, but she can still hear it, the bedroom's hum.

She stands and crosses to the curtain, pulling it roughly aside. Nothing. His clothes on their hooks, the trunk beneath them. The bed is dark, a painted crate for a table on either side. Above the headboard, the shining shadow of the pelt.

A mink is a vicious thing, her father said. Hungry, was Uncle Anders' word, a great hunter for its size. At nine years old, Kit was used to being keeper of the chickens, cleaner of the coop. On a bright March morning she opened the little door to find one of the hens cowering in its box. The second bird lay bloodied and the third flopped around squawking. The mink registered at the edge of her eye, a twist of darkness at the tear in the wire. She'd seen one before, up on its hind legs by the stream.

She ducked into the coop. Catching up the broken hen, she tucked it beneath her arm and pulled its neck. Quiet, then—until the one in the box let out a cry.

The mink would be back, Uncle Anders said, it would not forget its kill—even though both birds were already plucked and quartered, softening in Bobbie's pot. The trap was heavier than it looked. It smelled faintly of smoke. Kit and Uncle Anders wore gloves when he showed her how to make the set. The next morning, the mink lay lifeless. Her uncle was good at many things. She watched him skin the animal, helped him tack the pelt out on a board.

"Ought to fetch a buck or two," Frank said when the skin was dry.

Uncle Anders had stopped by on his way back from a swim. He stayed when Bobbie got down the fourth mug.

"You keep it," he said. "He was your visitor."

"Yeah?" Frank said, reaching for the pelt. "Thanks." He draped it over his wife's shoulders, against her dark-brown hair. "Look at that, willya? Perfect match." He touched the back of his hand to her throat.

"Well." Uncle Anders drained his coffee and stood. "What do you think, Kit? Will we see what is biting out there?"

All right, she's looked. The pelt is lifeless. The bed is— The bed is marked, squiggles of white on the grey blanket, like the chalk on Uncle Anders' slate. It takes her a moment to understand that it's salt. Of course. He was wringing wet when they carried him home. She got a good look at him then, her father. She and Ida rolled him carefully to one side then the other, tugging off his soaking clothes.

Kit backs away from the bed, the touch of the curtain making her jump. It's all right, the main room flickers around her now. She turns to the window. How long until dawn?

◗

We were alone together, your father and I, those early months at Far Cry. Knox stayed on for the first few days, watching from the office while we sawed the rotten planking out of the cannery floor. Satisfied we knew what we were doing, he boarded the southbound steamer, leaving the two of us to work through the daylight hours and settle in over the cribbage board by dark.

We drank enough to sleep untroubled, rarely more. The store-keeper's cottage had a proper stove, so we dragged a second bed up from the bachelor sheds. I was often the first to wake. If I lay watching Frank for too long, Skygge would let out a whine. I learned to look briefly and rise.

Knox had left us a list of jobs twelve pages long. When we got on to patching the cannery roof, Frank clambered over it like an ape. It took us the better part of a month to right the pilings and set the long dock true. From there we moved on to the bachelor sheds. There was no note about the China House and the Indian shacks, but we could see the sorry state they were in. Knox would not have stood for us wasting new lumber on them, so we took a tour up-inlet to the wreck of Glenelg Cannery on Shotbolt Bay. Scavenging was not nearly so dark a task with a friend.

All through the winter, I swam—as far out as Squid Island when the sea wasn't too rough. When the weather turned fine, Frank carried his few things down to claim the best of the bachelor sheds at the near end of the row. He had a plan to cut a window in the wall. I told him he would let the wind in along with the light, but his mind was made up. On our next trip to Shotbolt Bay, we found a frame with four good panes.

When Knox came back on the steamer in mid-May, your father and I gained a third at the cribbage board—a careless player who hated to lose. There was that pipe tobacco of his, like fruitcake left in the oven to burn. Worse, there was his way of sucking his knuckle then smelling it. Have you marked the habit, Kit? I know you have heard your father's name for him—*Knuckles Knox*.

Far Cry eased me into the storekeeper's trade. There was plenty of time for stock-taking and looking over the books. Shortfalls, overages—it was all clear enough once I got used to the previous storekeeper's scrawl. Customers came by the handful to begin. By the time the season was under way, I was just about equal to the lineup Friday night and all through Saturday, not to mention Sunday morning's sore heads and last-minute supplies. There were often fights, especially when it was raining and the line stretched out past the overhang. Strange that I should find myself at home in the heart of it all. What was it Grace had said? A place in this world.

◗

Kit sits at the table, the lamp hissing beside her, doubled in the window's dark. A cup of milky tea inside her and she's still wide awake. She stares at the kitchen shelves. Bobbie would've been the one to paint the crates; Frank must have held them up where she told him, scratching the log wall with his knife to mark where he'd nail them in place.

Her eye takes inventory: Plates and bowls, mugs and a few short glasses, spools of line. The jars hold coffee and tea, dried peas and sugar, assorted bolts and screws. Cans of milk and beef and even a couple of salmon. Woodley's catalogues, bottles and jugs, the whiskey maybe one-third full. Light shivers in the liquor, a tiny flame. She could, couldn't she? It used to help her mother sleep. A wave of fearful sickness washes over her at the idea.

Bobbie never could drink like the men. The same stuff that fuelled them late into the night only slowed her down. Sooner or later she would drift off in the armchair, only to startle awake and notice Kit sleeping or playing quietly with Skygge on the rug. *Better get this one home.*

From time to time she drank enough to change her voice, one word shunting up against another, her breath both sour and sweet. Those nights, Kit led the way down the headland path, carrying the lantern and keeping hold of her mother's hand. Safe in the cabin, she cleaned her teeth even when Bobbie forgot to tell her. Changed into her nightdress and lay down.

The stories were best on those nights. Instead of just bending to touch her lips to Kit's brow, Bobbie would sit at the edge of the cot. Sometimes she would even lie down. There was room enough if Kit held still.

"I was like you, Kitty-cat, I liked to help. My mama would feed the chickens, but getting the eggs was my job."

Jeannie, Kit's grandmother had been called. The first mention of her was like the breaking of a seal—the lid went back on, but never quite as tight.

"I helped in the kitchen too," Bobbie continued. "Mostly fetch and carry, down to the cellar to bring up a jar of gherkins or fish a lump of butter out of the salt water in the crock. That was my favourite. I could pinch off a bit for Barnacle and get him to lick my hand."

The tomcat was a recurring character, one Bobbie knew Kit liked. Jeannie had named him for his white-and-grey coat.

"He was always down there after the rats. Mice too, and beetles. I even saw him eat a spider once." Bobbie smiled in the lamplight. "On patrol, my mama used to say. Barnacle's on patrol."

There was another name Kit listened out for.

"Mama?"

"Yes, Kitty-cat."

"Your friend, Jasmine . . ."

Her mother made a sound—Kit was almost sure it was a laugh. "That was just something she called herself. Her real name was Kath. Katherine."

Kit was quiet. Katherine was her name too, though no one ever said it out loud.

Bobbie felt for her hand. "Don't tell Daddy. He didn't like her much."

"How come?"

"Jealous, I expect. Wanted me all to himself."

There was something sly about talking to her mother when she was like this, something not quite fair. Kit rose up on her elbow to watch Bobbie's face. "What was she like?"

"Kath? She was . . . fun." Her mother's mouth gave a twitch. "This one night when I wasn't feeling too good, in she comes to my room. 'Get up, Bobcat.'"

"But you were sick."

"Huh? Oh, no, not really. More, a little sad."

"Because of Grandma dying?"

Bobbie glanced at her. "In a way." She paused, and Kit held her breath. "I guess everybody else in the house was asleep. Anyhow, we snuck out. Kath had this bicycle, a real beauty, and there was Wing's old rattler. Kath said where was the harm in me borrowing it, he wouldn't be riding to the market in the middle of the night. I knew how to ride, just about. I had to work to keep up, though. Geez, we were flying. Past all those houses with their curtains drawn, all those warehouses loaded up with God knows what. 'Where we going?' I kept calling after her, but she'd just grin back at me over her shoulder. 'You'll see.'

"Of course, I knew about the park. I'd just never been that far west. All the way to the end of Georgia—you had to watch you didn't catch your tire in the tracks. Oh, and there was this massive fir, big as any of the trees you get up here. We rode over a little bridge—there were swans there on the lagoon, or geese, I don't know, something big. And there was this road." She turned her face Kit's way. "You know when the moon's on the water?"

Kit nodded.

"It was like that, this shining white road. They made it out of shells, Kath said. There were Indians living there from way back, and I guess they had some kind of buried dump, every clam and oyster they ever ate. Think of that, eh? Enough for a road to reach all the

way round the park." She looked back to the rafters. "We never got
that far, though. The first point we came to, Kath jumped off and let
her bike fall. There was a fence there, and a field right down to the
water, all these tree stumps in the stubbly grass. At first I thought
there was a clump of brush over by the edge, but then Kath tore up a
handful of grass and jumped up on the fence, and that brush started
to move." Bobbie wriggled onto her side to face her. "Can you guess?"

"What?" Kit said. "What was it?"

Her mother's eyes were bright. "Buffaloes."

"—What?"

"Buffaloes, a herd of them right there in the park. Kath was
waving that grass around, and they were coming for it. I don't know
how many, a dozen maybe? Anyhow, they were huge. I'm not kidding, way bigger than cows, and every one of them had a pointy set
of horns. The first one took that handful of grass, and Kath stuck
her hand back, so I laid Wing's bike down and started ripping up
more. Handful after handful, Kath keeps passing it on, and pretty
soon the whole lot of them are pressing up against the fence. She's
talking to them now—'Hello. Hello there. You hungry?'—shifting
along the fence rails to reach another one, holding her hand back for
more. I'm bent over tearing up grass, so I don't see it happen. She's
over the fence that fast.

"'Kath!' I shout, and she shushes me. She's right, of course, it's
no time to be raising your voice. I can see where she is—her hair
was glowing in the moonlight along with all those horns. They're
taller than she is, too. If a couple of them rubbed shoulders, she'd
be crushed.

"'Well?' she says to me. 'You coming in?'"

Kit stared at her mother. "Did you?"

"Are you nuts? I climbed up on the fence, though. God, they
smelled good."

"The buffaloes?"

Bobbie nodded. "Like cow shit, but that's a good smell, you know, clean—well, cleaner than us. I don't know, they smelled like . . . leather. And wool. They had these shaggy coats. Kath kept at me, teasing me until I touched one of them, just there on the neck. I'm telling you, you never felt anything so soft." She lay back, closing her eyes. "You could hear them breathing. You could smell it too, a green smell. Grass."

Bobbie's own breath was audible now, soft and slow. Soon Kit would have to wake her, lead her back to the big bed. "What happened?" she said.

"Hm?"

"To Kath."

"Oh, she climbed out of there when she was good and ready. She was fine."

○

The year 1903 brought a good run to the inlet, the sockeye steady and a decent size. You have heard how your mother and her friend came north to work in the cannery. Perhaps you have imagined them boarding the crowded steamer at the Union Wharf, walking down the gangplank at Far Cry. I am sorry, Kit, but it did not happen that way.

It was late afternoon, a week into the season, when a tugboat steamed into the bay. I stepped out to look down on the scene. The man at the helm was a poor pilot—the long dock shuddered when he brought her alongside. But it was the crew that held the eye, two girls, one pale-haired, the other dark. The blonde sat in the bow, the brunette busy on deck. It was she who threw the line to the dazzled boy on the dock—Richie Johnson, I think it was. The man who ducked out of the wheelhouse was the nearest I have seen to a giant. Well, you met him that day in the city. Not a figure to forget.

Kit, there is no way to tell the story without telling it. There is only one reason a man brings two girls like that to a place like Far Cry.

Knox hurried down to meet them. Much nodding and smiling, shaking hands all round. The blonde stood close while the men talked terms, but the dark-haired girl wandered over to Richie. Soon the two of them were sitting on the dock's edge like kids. I took myself back inside. Like all incomers, they would make their way soon enough to the store.

Within half an hour, the bell jangled as though the door was being torn free. The giant held the door open for the girls before ducking inside himself. He nodded my way, but the blonde was the first to speak.

"Afternoon."

"Good afternoon."

She would have stood out in the city. At Far Cry she was hard to believe. Her shape was unmistakable in a pale-green dress, the bodice cut low. Her hair, more silver than gold, was swept up to show a slender neck. Your mother wore hers long down her back, tied with a ribbon like a schoolgirl's. Her dress was softer, simpler. She stepped up beside her friend and smiled. That little mouth of hers, those blue, blue eyes. There would be mayhem when the boats came in.

Girls, I have called them, but they were young women. Somehow I had not thought of it before, your mother being the same age you are now when she arrived.

"How can I help you?" I said.

The giant moved up alongside them. "Couple of gallons," he said, gesturing with his chin to the row of jugs behind my head.

The blonde laid a hand on his arm. "I'm sick of rum."

"You got any whiskey?"

"The good stuff," she added.

He glanced at her, and I caught a glimpse of something in the look she gave back—a dark little wriggle, like an ant disappearing down a bloom.

"Yeah, okay."

I took the key from my waistcoat pocket and bent to the cabinet. "How many bottles?"

She laughed then, the blonde. "How many you got?"

"Half a dozen will do," the giant said. Then, to the girls, "What else?"

Your mother's eyes were on the candy jars.

"Bobbie wants peppermint sticks, don't you, Bobs."

"Mind reader."

"Peppermint sticks," he repeated as I set the last two bottles on the counter. And when I twisted the lid off the jar, "Give me the lot."

The blonde spun away, crossing to the lead sinkers on the far wall. "Look, Bobcat."

Your mother went to her.

"Shut your eyes."

Again, Bobbie obeyed.

The other took hold of her hand and set a weight on her palm. "How heavy?"

"What? I don't know."

"Come on, how heavy?"

"—Half a pound?"

The blonde clapped her hands. "Sharp girl. What about this one?"

I tore a length of paper from the roll. Emptying the jar, I tidied the red-and-white sticks and folded the package closed.

The giant showed a wedge of bills when he paid. "Stanley Swift," he said when I gave him his change.

"Anders Viken." I shook the hand he held out, my own two-thirds the size.

"That's Jasmine in the green dress. And Bobbie." The girls came back to him as though called. "Here." He gave each of them two bottles to carry. Tucking the package of candy under his arm, he took the last two by their necks. "We'll be staying a few weeks."

"We got the tug done up nice." The one he had called Jasmine backed up against the door and nudged it open. "You ought to come out and see."

Bobbie gave me a smile and followed her friend, leaving Swift the final word. "I'll do you a deal," he said. "Seeing as we're friends."

Word must have got out on the fishing grounds, Lem Turcotte or one of his pitchers on the collector boat spreading the news. Swift had anchored his tug in the middle of the bay. Several of the men rowed straight for it when they dropped off the towboat's line.

All night the lineup of boats ran out like a tail from the tug's low stern. Swift stood outside the cabin, a human door. I cannot think what it was like inside. I suppose there were two berths, perhaps a curtain between. I hope there was a curtain. Did your mother and her friend have time to exchange a word between comers? A look? Forgive me, Kit. Another chapter for the fire.

That night, after closing the store, I blew out the porch lantern and drew my chair up to the rail. There was half a moon, enough to distinguish your father from the other men. When his time was up, Swift had to yell to roust him. A discussion followed, Frank shorter by far but standing close, Swift swearing so it carried over the bay. He took Frank by the shoulder and turned him roughly, escorting him to the stern. Frank stepped down into his skiff and rowed—not for the dock but for the end of the bobbing line.

He kept at it all night. I was not foolish enough to stay up watching past the second round, but I heard all about it the next day in the store. *Had her half a dozen times, I'd say. The little one? Yessir. Musta found a good fit.* Laughter. Eventually the talk came round to me.

Guess you got all week to row out there, Viken. You know the smile I wear at such times. I could be any man.

It was a slower Saturday than most, many of the men preferring to line up on the water in their boats. Your father did not come through the door. Toward the end of the day the joke was edging into legend. Starratt wasn't sleeping, wasn't eating. *Found a good fit.* That was the line that came back to me. The one that made my heart grow cold.

11

Knox made sure he was first to share the news. I was in the stockroom, but I knew well enough who had come in—you must have noticed how the bell yelps when it is his hand yanking the door. I walked up front. He had a story about needing some copper nails, though I have never seen him with a hammer in his hand.

"You heard about Frank?"

"What about him?"

"He's taken her. You know, the one with the dark hair."

"—What do you mean, 'taken her'?"

"Taken her. She's gone and so is he." He shook his head. "I knew he'd be trouble."

I turned to the casks. The nails lay at all angles, thousands deep.

"Suppose that's the last we'll see of him."

I said nothing. Then, "He will be back."

"You think so? That Swift fella is pissed."

"He will be back," I said again. "A pound?"

"Eh?"

"The nails."

"Oh, no, a handful will do."

As ever, the store was quieter during the week. I made a virtue of sweeping the porch, one eye on the tug down on the bay. What did I expect to see—Swift running a knife over a whetstone? Foolish. He was big enough to finish Frank with his bare hands.

From time to time a man rowed out to the tug. Nelson more often than not—he was net boss in those days. Never Remy the engineer—he had brought his wife up with him, and anyway, he was a sober sort. Three Chinese went out in a company rowboat, but Swift turned them back. Knox made the trip more than once—that was before he was married. Still, he always waited until after dark. He was younger than me—forty years old at most—but his hair was already two-thirds gone. I remember the moonlight flashing off his scalp.

When the sun was out, Jasmine and Swift spent the slow hours on deck—her with a catalogue open on her lap, him asleep sitting up, or so it seemed. Now and then his hand came to rest on her shoulder, her thigh. Once, he felt me watching and tilted his gaze. I stepped back quickly from the rail.

Jasmine came in on her own in the middle of the week. Skygge must have been out on his rounds. Somehow she didn't sound the shop bell. Soft-footed on the floorboards, she made her way back to the stockroom. I jumped when the curtain moved.

"Sorry," she said. "Didn't mean to spook you."

I waited for her to turn back to the store, but she only stood to one side in the doorway. I squeezed past. "How can I help you?"

"Oh, you know." She followed me up to the counter. "Just getting in the supplies." Her gaze rested on me, then slipped to the row of jugs behind my head. "That stuff'll rot your socks."

I drew the key from my pocket, bent to the cupboard, straightened and set a bottle in front of her.

"That it?"

I stooped again. Two bottles on the counter, three.

She nodded. "That'll do."

A shaft of light cut through the whiskey, and I felt the day's first whimper of thirst.

"This fella Frank," she said. "Eddie says he's a friend of yours."

Eddie? It took me a moment—Knox.

"Yes, he is my friend."

"He won't hurt her?"

A picture came to me, Frank gripping his father's arm just before Frank Sr. kicked him to his knees. "No," I said. "He will not."

It was the only smile of hers I saw that had no target. She turned to survey the store. "Don't suppose you got any gingersnaps. Stanley's got a mean sweet tooth."

◗

In the warming light, the cabin rocks gently, Kit's blood still out in the boat. She shifts beneath the blanket, holding her eyes closed.

Fleet's in tomorrow.

A figure takes shape beside the chesterfield, small of stature, a flood of dark-brown hair. Memory in the guise of a dream.

"We're lucky, you and me." Bobbie sat down. "Your daddy works hard."

Kit reached a hand out from under the covers and touched her mother's leg. "Tell me."

"Tell you what?"

"When you met."

"Oh." A look on Bobbie's face Kit couldn't quite fathom. "Well, you know I was working at the cannery."

Kit nodded. "Packing fish."

"That's right. Kath had heard there was work going, so we came up from the city in this old tug."

"You had a tugboat?"

"Huh? Oh, no, we borrowed it from a fella she knew. Anyhow, we used to bunk out there—better than a shed, we figured—and your daddy used to row out to visit us on weekends. Well, me. I was the one he liked. And that was something, believe me. Kath was the one men noticed."

Kit could picture it: the two friends on deck, Daddy climbing aboard. Of course Bobbie was the one he liked. It was impossible to imagine him with anyone else.

"Lucky thing, too," her mother added. "When we slipped off to get married, Kath kept—well, she kept the manager sweet."

"Mr. Knox?"

"That's right, yeah. We left in the middle of the season, see. We were gone for a week, I think—it took us a few days to catch up with the minister on his rounds. You should've seen us, Kit, me in my best yellow dress and your daddy in his good black coat. He held my hand the whole time the minister was reading the vows, and when it came time for him to answer, he gave my fingers a squeeze. 'I do,' he says, and so do I, and that's it. I'm not Bobbie Holt anymore, I'm Bobbie Starratt."

She lifted Kit's hand and tucked it beneath the covers, then stood and smoothed the blanket up under her chin. "Night, Kitty-cat."

Kit knew not to be greedy. She closed her eyes. "Night."

◗

The day after Jasmine came to the store, word reached Far Cry that Frank and Bobbie had wed. As always, Skygge knew the *Camosun* was coming—he was on the dock with the other dogs long before her whistle blew. I went down to take delivery of the week's order along with the mail.

It was news, all right, your father and his pretty little bride. "That hair," I heard one of the deckhands say. "A man could get himself proper tangled up." The look on Knox's face. At the time I took it to be plain sourness at another man's gain.

It was the first time I was sensible of the line that stretched between your father and myself. She did not cut it, your mother—as far as I know, she did not even try. It was more as though she sat on it, as a girl settles herself on a swing. Slight though she was, I felt the drag.

The following day, I leaned on the porch rail, watching the *Dogfish* motor into the bay. Frank at the tiller, Bobbie in the bow. Swift stood on the tug's deck with his arms crossed, Jasmine beside him in a dark-red dress. She waved to her friend, and Bobbie lifted her hand in return.

Frank tied up and helped his bride out of the boat. He kept hold of her hand and together they ran down the dock and up the stairs, fairly flying along the boardwalk to his shed. Not once did he raise his eyes. The thought of me standing there did not enter his mind.

It was the usual Saturday onslaught in the store, men queued up along the boardwalk and down the stairs. I watched for Frank to appear as the line shuffled forward. He never did. I suppose he had tobacco and a bottle or two left from their trip—or perhaps they were too busy to roll a smoke, too busy even to pour a drink. *She must be wearing him to a nub in there, the lucky sonofabitch.* Frank had been seen hurrying down the cookhouse stairs, carrying food back to her like a fox bringing mice to the den.

I was grateful to be worn out that night, asleep in the armchair with the bottle beside me on the floor. Skygge woke me when it was getting light, up and growling before I heard the heavy tread. Swift was not a man to knock before entering. He filled the doorway, and Skygge drew back barking, crowding the cottage with sound.

"Down, Skygge." I rose and caught hold of his scruff. "Hush."

Swift stepped inside. The door stood open behind him, a frame of grey light and the early quiet of the bay. Then Jasmine appeared. Slipping round her keeper, she dropped to her knees in front of Skygge, who gave a little whine. She went straight for the softness behind his ears. I felt him weaken beneath my grip.

"Your friend's back," Swift said.

"I heard."

"He heard."

"Well, sure." Jasmine had both ears in her fists now. Skygge's eyelids fluttered closed. "Big news around here."

Swift nodded. "Me and him got business to discuss."

"All right," I said. "So why are you here?"

He looked at me, and to my shame I felt a twist of fear in my bowels.

"He's not opening his door," Swift said. "Figured I'd save my boots and let you talk to him."

Jasmine tipped back on her heels and stood. This time Skygge's sound was closer to a yelp. "Aw." She messed the fur at his brow.

"They are married," I said.

"And good luck to them," she said. "Bobbie's our friend, isn't she, Stan. We want her to be happy."

Swift made a low sound.

"It's just, Stanley's only the prince, see. His mama, Vi, it's her place back in the city. That's where me and Bobbie live."

There was something in the way she watched me. Have you ever looked into a creature's eyes, Kit, and seen the question there? The plea?

"Frank does not have money," I said.

Swift held still, but Jasmine made a small adjustment, shifting her hips. "Bet you do."

What could I say? "I will speak to him."

Swift nodded, reaching to draw out a chair. I moved past him to the doorway.

"You got any coffee in?" Jasmine said behind me.

"Help yourself."

Skygge took his time following. He came alongside me at the boardwalk's bend. "So you are coming," I said as he trotted up ahead. "Sure you will not stay with your girlfriend?"

He seemed to know my mind. We might have been on an errand to the cannery or the docks, but he carried on along the boardwalk to the bachelor sheds. Frank had nailed a blanket up over the window— or else she had, I thought, making herself at home.

There were men sitting in front of their sheds, just as I had done in my city years—drinking coffee with rum in it, or just plain rum. The lucky ones with letters in hand, others with a page of the *Colonist* or the *World*. They looked my way like a line of crows—if crows could grin. I nodded and faced Frank's door.

I doubt they heard me the first time I knocked, though I could hear them well enough. I would spare you such details, Kit, but you know better than anyone how they could forget themselves.

I turned my fist side-on and pounded.

"Bugger off!" Frank shouted, and for the first time ever, I heard the father's voice in the son's.

"Frank, it is Anders. Open up."

Quiet. Then the sting of laughter, hers and his.

His face was shining when he showed it in the crack of the door, his beard and moustaches damp. "Congratulate me, Andy. I'm a married man."

"Congratulations," I said. "Get dressed."

So yes, I acted the part of the broker—a strange word for the one who makes the mend. It was true what I had told Swift. There was a fair run that year, but your father was never one to save what he could spend. He had less than a quarter of the price Bobbie's keeper demanded. And yes, as her friend had divined, I had the rest.

Months later, I would learn how Jasmine had helped your mother escape, calling Swift into the cabin for a treat while Frank, last customer of the night, smuggled Bobbie in under the canvas at his bow. He rowed her over to the *Dogfish*, and the pair of them were away. At Duncanby Landing they learned the minister was on the baptism round in Kingcome Inlet, so down they went. I suppose Frank must have thought it all through.

Swift and Jasmine moved on not long afterwards. The girls held each other on the dock while Frank and Stanley stood stony-faced. High above at the porch rail, I watched as Jasmine bent her head, bringing her mouth close to your mother's ear. I wonder now if leaving was her idea. How could people begin to forget where Bobbie came from with that tug still anchored in the bay?

Men learned soon enough not to pass comment in Frank's hearing. His height made some think they could try their luck, but you know how strong he was, Kit, how quick. You might have made a fighter yourself if you had been born a boy. In truth, your mother was far from the first to leave the trade for a proposal. Still, the other wives kept their distance. It did not help when Bobbie carried her bucket down to the community tap and stood laughing with the Oweekeeno women as she waited her turn.

Counting back, I think that first hideaway weekend must have been when you began. I remember the day Frank came into the store to tell me. It was coming on to closing time, only a handful waiting to be served. Still, there were noises of protest when he walked past them to the head of the line.

"Shut your gobs," he said, grinning. "I'm not here to buy." He looked up into my face. "What do you reckon, Andy?"

"I do not know, Frank. What do I reckon?"

He slapped the counter. "She's expecting, that's what."

"Well," I said. "That is . . . excellent news."

He laughed, turning to the room. "You hear that? Frank Starratt's gonna be a daddy!"

I suppose the men in line had the good grace to congratulate him, though I cannot be sure. I was not entirely present, not for several breaths. I forced a smile as Frank turned back.

"Well?" he said. "You gonna shake my hand?"

Yes, of course. I took your father's hand.

Kit moves about the cabin quietly, as though there's somebody there to wake. Feed the stove, cook the porridge, boil the tea. She's planned to spend the day getting her gear sorted for the coming week, but the thought of Uncle Anders on his own with the Saturday crowd makes her miserable. Not long after breakfast she finds herself trudging along the headland path.

By the look of her uncle, she was right to come: shadows under his eyes, a crust of stubble about his mouth. A whiff of liquor off him as she steps in behind the counter. He must be sitting up late on his own.

Two hours into her shift, he sends her to the stockroom to cut a length of canvas. The bolt leans with the other fabric against the back wall. She's measuring a yard against the cut marks when there's a sound behind her, somehow separate from the general din. Looking round, she finds Ida Paul standing in the doorway, the curtain draped down her side.

"Kit."

"Mrs. Paul." Kit pinches the measurement. "Can I get you something?"

Ida shakes her head. She holds Kit's gaze. "That's hard, losing your dad."

"Yeah."

"Bobbie too."

"—Her choice."

Ida's quiet for a long moment. Then, "She's still your mother."

A taste like medicine in Kit's mouth. "Yeah, well, any bitch can whelp."

The look Ida gives her is searing. Kit drops her gaze.

"Kit," Uncle Anders calls from the front. "Hurry up now."

"She wanted you," Ida says before turning. "You were her girl."

Kit passes the rest of the day fetching and carrying—light work compared with fishing, but dull. If only Lys could be trained to climb a stepladder, cut and wrap a pound of lard.

Coming on to the supper hour, the lineup has dwindled to ten or so. Uncle Anders beckons her to the counter. "Go home. Get yourself something to eat."

"What about you?"

"I can manage from here." And when she hesitates, "Go."

She heads for the side door, hangs her apron on its hook. If Lys hears her from the old corner bed in the stockroom, she doesn't rise.

Outside, Kit takes in a lungful—cedar-fresh and cannery-foul. She stares along the headland path, light faltering among the boughs. The thought of the empty cabin at its far end.

She turns left instead, stepping up onto the boardwalk where it joins the storefront porch. Hands braced at the rail, she feels the burden of her shoulders, flesh and bone. The bay is swamp-coloured, crimson where the waves wash back from beneath the cannery floor. At the foot of the long dock, fishermen pass a bottle hand to hand. Standing at a little distance, the young man she spotted yesterday on his way out of the bay.

Kit watches him push a hand through his hair before approaching the group. She can't hear what is said, only the blast of laughter that ends the exchange. The newcomer moves on. Halfway down the dock, he slows where Willie Paul bends over one of the oarlocks in his skiff. The young man speaks, and Willie pauses in his work. There's an unnerving stillness in the newcomer's bearing, the way he leans forward, listening to Willie's reply. A hand raised stiffly in thanks, and he carries on down the boards.

There's something familiar about him, this man she doesn't know. Drawing up to the end of the dock, he stands looking out— rowing in his head, maybe, long, certain strokes. Kit's arms are aching. She lets go of the railing and makes up her mind.

12

I kept my distance from your mother that whole first winter—
quite a trick when three people and a dog live alone together
in a place like Far Cry. I did nothing anyone could put a finger on.
Looked past her when she spoke. Made a point of calling her Roberta
when I saw how it made her flinch.

Frank assumed she was welcome at the cottage. She took no interest in cribbage, as you know, happy to sit in my armchair and turn the
pages of a catalogue, putting in comments and laughing whenever
Frank made a joke. He played badly, lost and seemed not to care.

I might not have minded, but she was with us during the workday too. Your father would not let her lift any kind of weight, but
there was always light work to be done, painting or sanding, gutting
the catch. He took her out in the *Dogfish*, often letting Skygge ride
along. There was room to join them, even as your mother's belly
grew, but I found reasons to stay ashore.

One evening when the two of us sat at the table, my peg ahead of
his, Frank looked across at Bobbie asleep in the armchair. Skygge lay
at her feet. You were there too, in the rise beneath her folded hands.

Frank's cards had tilted so I could see them. I flicked at them with the back of my hand.

He looked at me. "What am I gonna do, Andy? We can't have a baby in that shed."

"Knox will give you one of the cottages."

"Those shitboxes. They're all right for the season, but over winter?" He shook his head. "I don't know if this place is right for a family."

His eyes returned to your mother, and for once I was glad—the fear would have shown on my face. My mind went quiet. Then, "I was over by the stream this morning."

"Christ, you're still swimming? There must be a foot of snow."

I smiled, leaving a pause. "Quite a view from the headland there."

He looked unseeing at his cards. *Quiet, Anders, let it come to him. Let it come.*

There was a natural spot to build, level ground and only a handful of firs to come down. After the felling came the trimming, the stripping. We carried over the cannery saw, cut and fitted the joints.

Your mother was walking with a duck's gait by the time we had finished the outer walls. Skygge stuck close whenever she went to relieve herself in the brush. Then she would be back, tending the campfire, sitting down to take up whatever curtain or cloth she had set aside. The fuss your father made over her jagged hems.

At least he had the sense to leave her behind when we motored back to Shotbolt Bay for roof slates and boards. This time we had to cut away brush and climb in deep. Frank let out a whoop when we found the stove—we were tearing away the floor of a collapsed loft and there it was, hunkered like a bear in its hole. It had a hairline crack along the top, but the body and firebox were sound. Getting it settled in the boat was a chore. I took the tiller on the way home.

Your father had been around boats all his life, but he could get distracted, and the waves were starting to come up.

Bobbie made a project of that stove, covering it with oilskins when it rained, working on it whenever the weather allowed. On the day I am thinking of, the wind was still sharp, but in the clearing you could feel the sun. Your mother had all the brightwork off the stove's body. She was perched on her chair, going at the rust with a wire brush, when she gave a cry. Frank dropped his end of the plank we were carrying and ran to her. She stood up with his help, and I saw where her skirts were wet.

Skygge got there before me, nosing in close.

"Get out of it," Frank shouted. "Get!"

"Oh!" Bobbie's expression twisted. *"Ohhhhh!"*

It was not as though they had no plan. Dr. Pollock had promised to stop by on his way down the coast, but that was not for another week.

I looked at Frank. "We will take her to the cottage."

"No!" Bobbie cried.

"Do not be foolish, Roberta."

She burst into tears. "You don't want me there."

Frank looked from her to me.

"You will be more comfortable." Still she shook her head. It came to me what I must say. "Bobbie. Bobbie, please."

Frank wanted to carry her, but she insisted she could walk. Skygge followed at her heels while I ran ahead to wake the fire in the stove. Bobbie refused to lie down, instead standing behind the armchair, gripping its back with both hands. I stepped out onto the porch, drawing Frank after me and closing the door.

"You must get help."

He stared at me, a look I had not seen since the day we tipped his father's body overboard.

"I will be more use here," I said. We both knew it was true. He had heard the stories—my father up to his shoulder inside a cow, the red mare dropping her foal. Even the cat who chose my quilt as the place to squeeze out her kittens, my boyhood self asleep for the first two births, awake and watching for the third.

"Go up-inlet to the village," I told him. "Bring one of the women."

"Ida!" Bobbie shouted from inside. Somehow she had heard us. "Bring Ida Paul!"

Frank went back in and kissed her. Then he was gone, his boots hammering down the boardwalk, setting off the ravens in the boughs.

I went inside and helped your mother to my bed. She sat quiet as though listening, then fell back with a wail. My hands shook as I unlaced her boots. I remember, I dragged one of her wool stockings halfway off by accident—the shocking softness of her calf as I pulled it back up.

She clawed at her skirt buttons. "Off! Get it off me!"

So, yes, I undressed her, at least from the belly down. Easing her drawers off, I turned my face aside. She gave a mad sort of laugh. "Christ, Andy, you think you're getting through this without sneaking a peek?"

When she was settled under the blanket, I pulled a chair up to the bedside and let her crush my hand. Skygge paced a frantic horseshoe around the bed. Between two pains I jumped up to push another log into the stove. Bobbie's face was red, her hair twisted and damp, but I worried you would feel the cold after months in your mother's insides.

Remembering my own mother at my bedside when I was small, I filled a basin with water from the jug. No rag seemed soft enough—in the end I tore a sleeve from an old winter shirt. Bobbie's eyes closed when I wiped her brow.

My God, the sounds she made. Skygge lay down at my feet, his ears flat. It was as though there was a wolf in the bed, a bellowing stag. As though a storm had come indoors.

When the time came, I went where I was needed. My first and only dealings with a woman's parts—setting aside my own passage into this world. It was impossible that she should open like that, your little mother, but she did. I caught a glimpse—the crown, they call it, the dark slick of hair. I thought she would lift the roof. And then the head, Kit. Your head.

Your shoulder seemed to catch, so I took hold and tugged, then twisted. I had never had cause to be so afraid. Somehow it nudged free. On the following pain, you slid out into my hands. Your mother was up on her elbows. "Is it there? Is it all there?"

"It is," I said, laughing. "She is."

As if to prove it, you gave a cry. Bobbie collapsed on her pillow. The first sob was one in a chain—she lay there shaking while I set you down between her legs. The pair of you were still attached, the cord leading back inside. I rose to fetch a knife.

It wasn't long before we heard the Easthope echoing in the bay. By then Bobbie was propped up on the pillow, holding you against her chest.

"There's your daddy," she said. It would have been the two of you alone in that moment, but she lifted her eyes to mine.

Stepping out onto the porch, I found evening coming on. I understood only then the heat and animal smell I had left. Below, the *Dogfish* was drawing close. There was your father's dark cap and the red triangle of Ida's scarf.

"It is all right," I called down, and both faces turned up my way. One hand gripping the rail, I lifted the other to wave.

Ida leapt out of the boat with a fair gap to go between the gunwale and the dock. You know that measured way she has of walking—she had it back then too, though not on that day. She did not run, but she held her skirts in both hands as if she might.

"It is all right," I called again when she appeared at the top of the stairs. And when she brushed past me, "They are all right."

She nodded, already opening the door. Frank was pounding up the stairs now, the boardwalk shuddering.

"They are all right." It might have been the chorus of a song. He stared at me and then at the door. "Go on," I said, and I followed him inside.

Ida was standing at the foot of the bed, her hand resting on Skygge's back. Bobbie's voice was quiet. "Frank," she said. "It's all right, love." And then he was on his knees at the bedside, his face buried in her lap.

We stood still, Ida and I, even Skygge. You did not make a sound. Not until your father looked up—and then it was only the smallest squeak. He seemed to see you for the first time.

"Jesus."

"Nope," said Bobbie. "It's a girl."

Ida grinned over at me. Then she got to work, washing her hands in the basin, filling the kettle from the jug. I opened the stove door to feed the coals, and when I straightened up, Ida said, "The rest come out yet?" I shook my head. Setting the kettle on the stove, she crossed again to the bed. "You men leave us be."

And so we went, Frank turning back halfway to the door and me holding it open and Ida saying over her shoulder, "Go on, you're letting in the cold."

Next door, I carried chairs out from the stockroom while Frank loaded and lit the stove. I had not thought to bring the cribbage board, but there were packs of cards on the shelf, so I marked

out a board on paper and gave us each a penny for a peg. We opened
a bottle but drank with care. The time would come when the
women would let us back in. When we would be needed again.

◗

Sunday morning, and the clearing is busy with birds. Kit sets a piece
of fir on the stump. Her arms are still sore, but they do as they're
told—hoist the axe and bring it down. The wood splits in two.

She slept in patches last night, her mind waking her to go over
what she'd done. It had been simple enough once she'd decided:
follow the stairs to the dock, the dock to the young man at its end.
He hadn't taken much convincing, her new boatpuller. A surprise,
given the look on his face when she told him her name.

"Starratt," he repeated. And when she nodded, "I'm Jimmy Lo."

It took her a moment, but then she saw it. His father was handsome too.

It was something to think about, the cook's son come up from the
city to look for him. If Bobbie and Lo Yim hadn't gone to Vancouver,
then where? Across the strait to Victoria? As far south as San Francisco's
Chinatown? It was hard to imagine them making a go of it someplace
smaller. Best not to imagine them at all.

Kit centres a fresh piece and lifts the axe—the head weightless
above her before the drop. The blade bites into a knot. She works it
free and tries again, this time finding the grain.

It's unlikely that she hears boots on the path at that distance—
still, the breeze prickles at the back of her neck. She turns, some part
of her expecting Jimmy Lo. In his place, the manager emerges from
the trees.

"Hello there!"

That walk of his—half boss, half shifty little boy. Kit lifts a hand.

"You're handy with that axe," he says, drawing near. "I doubt Mrs. Knox could've lifted one when she was your age. And nowadays, well."

Kit nods and sets a new piece on the stump. Hits it clean along the grain, the halves flying apart.

"You've got your work cut out." Knox stoops for one of the split pieces, setting it on the pile. He brushes the dirt from his hands. "Such a thing as a cup of tea going?"

You bet, her mother would say. *I could use one myself.*

Kit lodges the axe in the stump. "Sure."

He follows her inside. As she stokes the stove, he moves to the table and drags out her father's chair. She fills the kettle and sets it over the heat, scoops tea into the dented pot. What else? Sugar. Reach down a can of milk and push in the opener's tooth.

"Pretty spot, this," Knox says behind her.

She takes up the empty water jug and steps to the door. On her way round to the tap, she catches sight of him through the window, the knuckle between his lips. The kettle's boiling by the time she's back. Pour and carry. Nothing left but to sit and pass the time of day.

"Well," Knox says, "isn't this nice."

She twists the lid off the sugar jar and pushes it toward him, followed by the milk. Rises to fetch a spoon.

"Regular jack-in-the-box, you are."

She sits, waits a little and pours out the tea.

"So," he says, "how are things?"

"All right."

He nods, adding milk to his mug, jerking the can so it blurts. "And how was your first week out on the grounds? You manage all right?"

Manage? You seen my catch. So her father would say. She takes a breath. "Good."

He touches the knuckle to his nostril. "Can't be easy here on your own."

She looks out the window at the smeary movement of trees. "It's all right."

"I'm rattling around myself these days, what with Mrs. Knox laid up in the city." He leaves a pause. "You wouldn't know her, Kit. Skin and kindling. Bald as an egg."

Kit lowers her eyes. She takes a swallow of tea.

"Did you never—" Knox says. "Would you ever think of growing your hair?"

She looks up sharply.

"Kit, I—" He stands abruptly. For a moment she fears he will lunge at her. "I can look after you."

She stares at him.

"She can't last forever. Hell, I'd be amazed if she lasted to the end of the season. We'd have to wait, of course. Not as long as in the city—"

"Mr. Knox—"

"It's all right," he says, crossing quickly to the door. "You think it over."

"There's nothing to think about."

He stands with his back to her. In the stillness, he speaks. "You think anybody gets along in this place without my say-so?"

What is there to say to that? Kit nods her understanding, but he's already out the door.

◗

I fell asleep at the table last night, Kit. Woke at dawn with pencil smudged across my cheek. Even so, I managed a swim before putting the bread dough to rise. Like a good father, I picked the bones from Lys's breakfast of leftover fish.

They say a child changes things. It was not as though people forgot where Bobbie came from after you were born, but by the time the salmon were running again, she was part of the place. I heard the odd low joke about her in the store, but the laughter never travelled far. Only the roughest of men make a point of a girl's past once she has a baby in her arms.

The week was long with Frank out on the fishing grounds. Your mother had chores to do—she kept the cabin clean, and started a garden, and of course there was you. Even a quiet baby gives her mother work. All the same, when the laundry was boiled and wrung out and pegged to the line, she had hours to go until dark.

To begin with, she would come into the store for a can of syrup, a spool of thread. She would set you on the counter in your basket and stay until the shop bell sounded and one of the wives came through the door. Most of them would nod to her, even smile down at you, but they still stopped short of a chat.

There came a day when your mother started shaking out a pile of heavy woollen shirts, refolding them one by one. You had hold of my finger, so I did not notice at first. When I did, I said nothing. Bobbie moved on to the trousers, and from there to a stack of long johns.

"There," she said. Then, looking about, "Those pans could use a dust."

I reached beneath the counter and handed her a cloth.

I suppose there must have been talk. Never mind that I was a "steady" man more than twice her age, or that Frank was known to be my friend. Whatever gossip went around, it died every Friday when the fleet returned. Plenty of women went down to meet the men coming back, but only one of them rushed to the end of the dock, set her baby down and waved with both hands. When your father cast off from the tow line and started rowing hard, she could not help calling out to him, "Frank! Hey, Frank!"

I watched it all from above. Frank throwing Bobbie the painter line, jumping out and grabbing hold of her for all to see. The pair of them hand in hand up the stairs. If it had not been for you in your basket, I believe they still would have run.

By midday Sunday they would have worn each other out. I would finish at the store and go home. If Skygge was asleep on the rug, he would wake. If he was out, he would return to scratch at the door. Not long afterwards, the three of you would arrive, Frank carrying a fish for the pan or a kettle of stew, Bobbie with you in the basket and one of her lopsided loaves. After eating, we would clear away, bring out the board and deal. Bobbie moved to the armchair to drowse, drawing her shawl down over her chest when you needed to feed. Of course, a cribbage board never looked right without a bottle beside it. Frank would have a few, but he knew he'd be back in the skiff and hitching onto the towboat soon.

Mondays, your mother was quiet, missing him all over again.

"You don't mind me working here?" she said one afternoon.

I had a copy of the *World* open on the counter, folded so I could lay it beside you where you slept. I looked up from the page. "Mind? No."

"But?"

"Well, Saturdays are when I really need the help."

I did not think she would come. Leave the cabin and Frank? Leave you in his care? I think that was what made it all right in the end. He would carry you down to show you the boats and show you off. Walk the boardwalk past his old shed where Hanevold had moved in. If the men laughed at him for playing nursemaid, they did not do it to his face. In truth, you were easy to admire, with your mother's flush in your cheeks and your father's dark lashes, your eyes still newborn-blue.

Meantime, your mother was a gift to me in the store. Always ready with a smile or a joke. Women learn how to manage men, or so it seems to me, and I suppose women in the trade learn better than most. There was never a fight in the lineup while she was there.

———

Skygge seemed to know when you were awake. One Monday while I was adding up the weekend sales, he came trotting from the stock-room to sit in front of the counter looking up. Sure enough, you were gazing into the rafters without a sound.

"Kit," I said.

Your mother was kneeling nearby, stocking tins of tea. "Suits her, doesn't it."

"It does."

"Funny that. I meant to call her Kath." She looked round. "You remember Jasmine?"

"Of course."

"—That's her real name. Kath." She held my gaze. "You won't say anything."

I shook my head.

Bobbie sat back on her heels. "She looked out for me, you know? I never had any brothers or sisters. My dad, he went away to work when I was a baby." She paused. "You know the Number One Coal Mine?"

I looked at her. *Nanaimo Mine Disaster 150 Dead.* It was not a headline to forget.

"Yeah." She nodded. "So."

"I too," I said after a moment. "No brothers or sisters."

"Yeah? How come?"

I shrugged.

"You never asked?"

More than that, Kit, I had never even wondered.

"Maybe you were all your mother wanted," Bobbie said.

"Yes, maybe."

She turned back to the shelf. "There's things you can do. Kath knew all about it."

I watched the back of her head, her hair hanging down from beneath a bright scarf, the way Ida wore hers.

She placed a tin and straightened it. "You don't have to worry so much if you have a baby that's still feeding, but after that . . ."

I said nothing.

She was still now, her hands at her sides. "You think it's wicked."

"No."

She turned. "It's just, it feels right, me and Frank and Kit."

I nodded. I cannot say what showed on my face.

"You never thought of it yourself?" she said. "A wife and kids?"

"My mother did. She even had the girl picked out."

"Yeah? What was she like?"

"My mother?"

"The girl, silly."

"Oh." I tried to think, but the only picture that came was Marta Laarsen's yellow braid in the pew before me. Beside it, her brother's shoulders pressed into that jacket, the clean scent of his hair oil when he bowed his head. "She was pretty," I said finally. "Kind, too, I think."

"But you didn't want her."

"—No."

"There must've been someone. All these years."

"Must there?"

Bless you, Kit, you chose that moment to make a noise. You have heard your mother say it often enough, but it is true—you used to mew like a kitten.

"Lord," Bobbie said. "She can't be hungry again." She reached into the crate beside her. "Hang on, Kitty-cat, I'm nearly done." But that sound of yours made Skygge anxious. He went to your mother and pushed his nose into her armpit.

"Jesus." Bobbie laughed. "All right, all right." Then she was on her feet, carrying you next door to feed you in my armchair. It was where you settled best.

Long after Knox has gone, Kit sits at the table, trying to think. His proposal caught her off guard, but it wasn't exactly a shock. Not if she's telling herself the truth.

Things shifted when her mother left. Bobbie had been gone for a week when Mrs. Knox sent her skinny house help, Jessie Potts, to the store. *She says you're to come.* Two rungs up on the stepladder, Kit sighed. Uncle Anders glanced up from the order book and gave her a nod.

The plants on the Knoxes' porch needed watering. Jessie opened the front door quietly, giving Kit a sympathetic look before slipping away down the hall.

Mrs. Knox was in the armchair, her back to the curtains' amber light. "There you are." She waved toward the settee.

The smell was worse than Kit remembered; she moved into the stillness and sat.

"Well, Kit," said the manager's wife. "How are you keeping?"

"All right." Kit felt the ghost of her mother's elbow in her side. "Thank you."

"And your father?"

"He's all right too, thank you."

Mrs. Knox watched her. "The selfishness of the woman." She shook her head. "Never a thought for anyone but herself."

Kit's eyes moved to the window. Her mind pulled the curtain aside.

"Of course, it shouldn't come as a surprise."

The house made sounds. The croak of a floorboard, a clattering from the kitchen that caused Mrs. Knox to wince. From the cluster of portraits, a woman with an iron gaze glared down. Mrs. Knox's mother? Was it possible for a body so solid to give birth to one so frail?

Frail? her own mother would say. *You watch, Orpha Knox will outlive us all.*

"Well?" the manager's wife demanded. "Nothing to say?"

Kit's jaw was a rusted hinge. Mrs. Knox had knotholes for eyes—how had she never seen it before?

"Next time I'll have Mr. Knox bring me one of his filthy fish to talk to." The knotholes deepened. "Well, go on, get out. Get out!"

Kit stood and walked from the room.

"At least your slut of a mother was friendly!"

A few more steps and Kit had the front door open. *Pretty loud for a woman who can't catch her breath.* She pulled the door shut behind her. As she turned, the manager stood up out of a porch chair, making her jump. He was looking thin himself, bluish smudges under his eyes. He might have been his wife's flesh and blood.

"Don't mind her," he said. "She's missing your mother."

Kit nodded. He was standing in her way.

"Did she tell you?" he said.

Confused, Kit glanced behind her.

"Not her, your mother. Did she say anything to you about leaving?"

Kit stood motionless, willing him to step aside.

"It's just," he said, "I can't help thinking, what if he took her? You know, against her will."

Kit wasn't a child. His expression was unmistakable: better to imagine the lovely Bobbie kidnapped than to admit she'd left of her own accord. Kit looked away. Far Cry lay in a jumble along the rocks. High tide grasped at the tree roots down the end of the bay.

She met Knox's gaze. "She liked him."

"Liked him."

"I think so. But no, she never said."

Still he stood between her and the boardwalk back to the store. She edged along the porch railing. Goodbye didn't seem right, but neither did nothing at all.

"Thanks," she said over her shoulder, putting the yards between them.

"Any time," he said behind her. "Anything you need."

13

Midday finds Kit hurrying empty-handed to Sunday lunch. Worry tightens her stride: Should she tell her uncle about the manager's advances or would that only make matters worse? Maybe it will all blow over. Maybe Knox will come to his senses now that he's spoken his madness out loud.

Uncle Anders is frying salmon steaks when she arrives. He's made bread, too—there's even a second loaf for her to take out on the grounds. While she cuts and butters, he carries the pan to the table and slides a bright steak onto each plate. Kit feels the hole where her breakfast should have gone. She takes up her fork.

She can hear it now, how little she's had to say for herself these eighteen years. Bobbie and Frank were the talkers.

Agneta Jensen comes into the store this morning, looks through me like I'm a window.

Not far wrong, is she?

Come again?

That light in his eye. *Hell of a view.*

Across the table, her uncle lifts a curl of salmon skin to his mouth. The cribbage board and cards lie between them, beside the tin of salt. Maybe she should learn how to play.

Her lunch is gone. Uncle Anders has cleaned his plate as well, leaving nothing but bones. The week's newspapers lie untouched on the window-side chair. In the silence, she longs for him to take one from the stack and fold it open. *Listen, now, what do you think of this?*

When she reaches for his plate, he stops her hand, patting it. "I will wash up."

"You cooked."

He rises, turning to the kitchen workbench. "And you have a long week ahead." Setting down the dishes, he moves to wrap the second loaf.

Kit plays with the salt tin, a tiny grinding sound. "Better get some hardtack too. I've got a boatpuller now."

"Oh yes?"

She takes a breath. "That new fella, Chinese. Came up on the boat this week."

Uncle Anders stands still. After a moment he turns around. "You know who he is?"

Kit nods, eyes on her hands. She looks at her uncle. "It's not his doing."

"No."

"I need a boatpuller."

"—Yes."

She stands up, unsure. He hands her the loaf in its square of oilskin, then gropes, like a much older man, for his chair. He sits heavily, enough to cause Lys to shift in her sleep. Kit holds the bread to her chest.

Her uncle nods toward the door. "There is a new crate of hardtack in the back."

◖

Of all the young men to share your skiff with. You are right, of course, he is blameless. What is it, then, that worries me? It cannot be the thought of you and him out there together—I am not by nature a possessive man.

That was your father's trouble—he was always snapping at shadows where your mother was concerned. She received letters, you know. Only from her friend, your namesake, but it was understood that Frank would not like it, just as it was understood that he would not come to know.

Boat day meant it was too busy to keep you on the counter—any baby would have slowed the lineup, but that gaze of yours stopped it entirely, casting a kind of spell. So Bobbie set you on a crate in the stockroom with Skygge lying at its base. I suppose the place was your refuge as far back as then.

The letter was one of the first out of the sack. Print rather than script, the hand unsure, *Mrs Bobbie Starat Far Cry Cannery*. I turned it over to find a Harris Street address on the flap—Shore Street, it was sometimes called in the city, or The Restricted Area. Your mother didn't see me slip the letter under the register—she was busy lining up a load of new gumboots by size. She would enjoy opening her friend's message more after the place had cleared out, I reasoned. She might even read portions of it aloud.

We were kept busy after the initial rush, unpacking and setting out the stock. It was late afternoon when your mother took you next door for a feeding. When she returned, I had laid the letter on the counter. She saw it and let out a cry.

She set you down on the floor in your basket. As though he had been called, Skygge came padding up from the back and nudged at you with his nose.

Bobbie tore open the envelope and drew out a single page with writing on one side. She read silently, her lips shaping the words. She turned it over, hoping for a postscript, before raising her eyes.

"Not bad news?" I said.

"No. Well, a couple more girls have left, but that's good news, right? Even if Vi doesn't think so." A smile, quick as a cut. "Always more where they came from."

You were watching her, your mother. Skygge too, sitting on his haunches looking up. She rested a hand on his head, then bent for the basket's handle. "Better get this one home."

Was it the following day? I remember it that way, so perhaps that is how it was.

"Morning, Andy." Bobbie set you on the counter and turned to the window, one hand in the pocket of her skirt. "Rain again."

"Mm-hm." I looked down at you. Your eyes were open, your bare feet raised to feel the air.

Your mother brought her fist out of her pocket as though to pay. A moment's hesitation, and she set the comb down without a sound.

"What is this?" I said.

"Have a look."

It was heavy in my hand. I had never seen scrimshaw so fine, each sail the very image of the wind. The comb itself was neatly made, a pleasing arc the colour of heavy cream. As always with whale tooth, there was that echo of the deeps.

"Kath gave it to me."

A note of confession in her tone, or was it conspiracy? Perhaps she was only showing me we were friends.

"She got it off some sailor," she added. "She was always getting gifts."

I nodded, placing the comb on the counter between us.

Taking it up, she examined the little schooner in its scene of waves. "Never been on a sailboat. That tug was the first time I went anywhere, and look at me, still here." She shook her head. "'You keep it, Bobcat,' she says to me. 'You're the one with the hair.' Which is funny, you know, because it's not really a comb you need, it's a brush."

"Is that so?"

"Hundred strokes, you never heard that? Hundred strokes a night." She looked up at me. "I used to think about cutting it all off. Can you imagine? Frank would die."

"I suppose he would."

"He didn't used to like it. The comb, I mean. 'Don't ever bring that thing on the boat. Scrimshaw's bad luck.'" She ran the teeth over her palm. "He likes it now, though."

I was quiet. Then, "Oh?"

"I comb his hair when he lets me, but mostly I do his beard."

I cannot say why it shocked me. Another lie—of course I can. It was something between them, or it ought to have been. I could not blame her, though, coming from where she did. How was she to know a private matter from one to share?

"You should see him," she added. "His eyes closed, laying back in his chair . . ."

It was difficult to picture Frank like that, but I did. I closed my own eyes and saw him surrender. I saw it more often than I care to admit.

Your mother wrote back to her friend, but it was at least two years before another letter came in return. You were walking, even running, by then. You were safe enough in the store—you liked to touch things, but you did not grab. Still, we could not have you underfoot in a crowd. Your mother pushed crates together in the stockroom to make a pen. We would look in on you from time to

time. You would be sitting talking softly on your blanket, or standing with your belly pressed to one of your wooden walls, reaching
up to pull on Skygge's ear or feel the soft flesh of his lip. Most often
he was content to lie along the top of the crates. Sometimes, though,
we found him down in the pen, the pair of you curled in sleep.

Bobbie had just locked up. She was about to go fetch you from the
back when I handed her the envelope. She sat down on the stool to
open it, as though she was suddenly tired. I busied myself with the
mops, straightening them heads-up in their barrel, one eye on your
mother as she read.

"Huh," she said. "She's in the rose room now."

"Is that good?"

"Best room in the house after Vi's." She read on, shaking her
head. "Still with Stanley."

Just what did that mean, I wanted to ask, being with someone
under such circumstances? The closest wolf made sheepdog?
Natural enough if you were born into the life, as Kath may have
been. Stanley, the madam's son, certainly was. Your mother, too,
though I learned that later. Everything Bobbie told me, she told me
in her own time.

I should ask you one day, Kit, where does your own memory begin? I
suppose you do not recall the first bad season—you were only four.
The year 1908 saw a decent run on the inlet, but the rain drove the
fish deep so they slipped beneath the nets. It drove spirits down too,
even before Knox dropped the price per salmon and cut hours on the
cannery floor.

A wiser boss would have kept his distance while times were bad.
Your father had always been too familiar with Knox—little jokes
with a bite in them, even a quick suck on his own knuckle now and
then—but I had never before seen him lose control. What was it

Knox said that night over the cribbage board? Something about fishermen having to work hard for a change.

Frank stood up fast. "You little cunt."

A second, no more, but I could see the future unfold—Knox stupid enough to stand and answer, Frank knocking him down. Surprise, that was how I managed to get an arm around your father's neck and steer him to the door. Skygge pushed in against our legs. He let out a yelp when I shoved him back with my boot and wrestled Frank out onto the porch.

"Andy, what the hell—"

"Shut up!"

Rain was slanting in under the overhang. Pushing him before me down the boardwalk, I welcomed the wet on my forearm, my cheek. When he tried to twist free, I drove him face-first into the wall.

"Goddammit—"

"I said *shut up.*"

From the cottage there came the sound of Skygge barking and scrabbling at the door. I prayed Knox would have the sense to stay put.

"You want to lose your place?" I said.

"My *place?*"

"Listen to me. Half the year Knox holds the reins, the other half we're free."

"Fuck that. A man eats shit in this life—"

"No." I brought my mouth to his ear. "Frank Sr. is long gone. Think of Bobbie. Think of Kit."

And was that not what I was doing? Or was I thinking of Anders Viken, on his own once more? Either way, the words had their effect. I felt the fight go out of him. A moment more, and I let him turn.

"That sonofabitch," he said. "What does he know about work?"

"I know." My arm around his shoulder, I led him out into the downpour. "Go on," I said. "Go home."

I made sure Knox stayed on to win that game and the next. Come daylight, I swam, then served the Sunday crowd. No sign of Frank, morning or afternoon. When the towboat made ready to head out, I breathed a sigh of relief at the porch rail to see him row out and tie onto the line.

Not long afterwards, your mother tidied her hair, put you in your best little dress and went calling on the manager's new wife. Who knows what went through Orpha Knox's mind when she opened her door to find the pair of you standing there, you with an armful of the daisies your mother had managed to bring on, even in that sodden year.

◗

Kit should be down on the dock by now, showing Jimmy Lo the ropes. She only came back to the cabin after lunch to pick up her gear, but the sight of the chesterfield flooded her with fatigue. Ten minutes, she told herself. She's been lying here for half an hour.

Eyes closed, she runs a finger over the rose pattern, slippery and distinct. She picked up the habit as a child, when the chesterfield still belonged to the manager's wife. Not that Kit always sat there when they visited; sometimes she watched from the armchair opposite while her mother and Mrs. Knox sat with their heads together, a catalogue laid open across their skirts.

There was nothing good to look at in the Knoxes' parlour: Stiff embroidered pillows, an empty cut-glass candy dish, a spray of dead grasses in an urn. Two dark paintings hung on the wall, a house and a field. The other frames held photographs, family paired up or in lines, unsmiling in their Sunday best. These were Mrs. Knox's people, the Woodleys—the same name as on the catalogue, and on the store Kit's mother had wandered as a girl. *Four whole floors, Kitty-cat. Everything from ribbons to rib steaks.*

"Oh, look," Bobbie said, "this one's velvet. Forest green."

Mrs. Knox nodded in that way she had, as though she were afraid her head might come loose. All the hair she possessed made a bun the size of a walnut. Her part showed a strip of scalp.

"My friend Kath, she can wear any colour, you know? Any cut. Put her in an old bathrobe and she looks like that Lily Elsie."

The manager's wife gave no reply.

Bobbie turned the page. "Oh, now, you'd look a treat in that."

Mrs. Knox looked at her sharply.

"You would," Bobbie said. "Those fine bones of yours. I'd order it if I was you. Geez, all you have to do is write to your daddy—"

"Brother," Mrs. Knox said. "My father passed away."

"Sorry, yeah, your brother." Bobbie paused. "Here, Kit, come and have a look."

Kit went to her mother's side. The dress looked hard to breathe in. Lace dripped from the sleeves, as though designed to get caught in your work.

"Nice, huh?" her mother said. "Look, it comes in rose or cream. Rose, I'd say. Yep, definitely."

Mrs. Knox glanced at them, Kit and Bobbie both. She looked almost pretty, giving in.

Bobbie was excited when the order arrived, almost as if she'd got a new dress herself. Uncle Anders looked up when she tucked the parcel under her arm. "We won't be long. Come on, Kitty-cat."

The Knoxes always had one of the fishermen's daughters for help; this time it was the oldest Memryk girl who let Kit and Bobbie in. She pointed them to the parlour, rag in hand.

The curtains were closed like always, Mrs. Knox in the armchair, wearing some kind of frilled cap. "Oh, Bobbie." She looked past them. "Anna," she called in her breathless way. *Anna.*

The girl came to stand alongside Kit. "Yes, ma'am?"

"Have you done upstairs?"

"Yes, ma'am."

"Skirting boards?"

"—Oh."

The manager's wife closed her eyes.

"I'll do them now," Anna said.

Somehow Kit knew not to watch the older girl go. She could hear Anna behind her, crossing the front hall, climbing the glossy stairs. Mrs. Knox opened her eyes.

"You see? I have to check every little thing."

"Never mind," Bobbie said, stepping through. "Guess what I've got?"

Mrs. Knox seemed unwilling to touch the parcel, almost scared. It was Bobbie who tore the paper, took the dress by the shoulders and shook it out.

"Oh, *look*. And it's as light as anything." She stepped forward, and when Mrs. Knox only stared at her, Bobbie laid the dress over her where she sat. Kit couldn't be certain in that dim light, but the colour looked nothing like the roses she knew.

There came the sound of the front door. *"Coo-ee?"* The manager's voice but higher, as though he was calling a cat. Her mother would make the sound later for Uncle Anders in the shop, then again when the fleet came in and Frank was home.

Mrs. Knox attempted to raise her voice. "We have company, dear."

"Only us, Mr. Knox," Bobbie called out. "Bobbie and Kit."

The manager showed his face at the parlour door. "What's all this?"

"Special delivery." Bobbie nodded toward his wife.

"Well, now. Isn't that a picture."

"You see?" Bobbie said, and Mrs. Knox smiled as though she might cry.

Was the air in there worse than usual? Kit could taste it, like the first soft hairs of mould.

"Well," her mother said. "Andy will be wanting to get the order sorted away."

"Indeed." Mr. Knox stood aside to let them pass.

"Bobbie," his wife said behind them, "I've run out of my salve."

A moment then, so slight it was likely only Kit felt it, a child attuned to her mother's mood. Bobbie nodded. "I'll order some more."

Mr. Knox followed them out to the entranceway. The light there came green through the painted glass. He reached past her mother to open the door. "Shame about the dress."

Bobbie looked at him. "You don't like it?"

"Oh, no, I do. I like it very much." He paused. "Washes her out, though, don't you think? Needs a woman with some colour in her cheeks."

Her mother stood still in the open doorway. Above them Kit could hear movement—Anna Memryk creeping round on her knees. Bobbie reached for Kit's hand and pulled her out onto the porch. "Best be getting back."

◗

You were always one to notice things, Kit, even when you were small. In the cottage, you did regular inspections, your hand pausing to make contact like the nose of a cat. Of course, you found your way to Neville's dictionary on the crate beside my bed.

Somewhere along the way I had taken to using Lo Yim's knot as a marker, laying it down where I had last encountered a word. While your mother stood at the washing-up basin and your father dealt a fresh hand, you slipped the silken knot from between the pages. You carried it to the table, as though it was a feather you had found.

I snatched it from you. You did not cry out, even though the motion was sharp enough to turn your mother's head our way.

"Hey now," Frank said.

I saw myself then—a grown man clutching a child's pretty find. I made myself hand it back.

"Gentle, Kitty-cat," Bobbie said. "That's a treasure."

Was that what did it? Your mother seeing, if not exactly what it meant, then at least how much? I had been drinking, yes, but that had never loosened my tongue before.

"What is it, anyhow?" Frank said.

Nothing, I might have said. "A gift."

"Oh-ho. Who from?"

"Frank," Bobbie said.

"What? We're all friends here."

I closed my eyes and opened them. "There was . . . someone." I thought I would stop there. "A young person who worked in a restaurant. In Chinatown."

"Oh, yeah." Frank grinned. "The old man used to talk about those places."

"It was nothing like that."

"All right, all right. I just—"

"Frank," I said, "I am telling you something."

Bobbie had come to kneel beside you, show you it was all right to stroke the knot's tail. Skygge too had inched in close.

"Go on, then," Frank said. "This girl, she was a Chink?"

I took a breath. "I should not have spoken."

"Aw, no," he said. "Come on, Andy, I'll shut up."

I met your mother's gaze, then yours. When I held my hand out for the knot, you laid it like a payment across my palm. I rose then, or saw myself rise, and crossed to the far corner, to my bed. I remember, Neville's dictionary opened at "witness." As good a word as any, I suppose.

———

It was a relief of a kind, your parents knowing a corner of the truth. I thought Bobbie might bring it up again, but neither of them said a word. Not until the following year.

That season the Hagensborg Norwegians were some of the first to arrive. Once they had signed on with Knox and settled into their sheds, a group of them came calling at the store. Hanevold, as to be expected, and Lund. The Nilsen brothers. Two or three others I had not seen before. They joined the men already drinking around the counter, and I set out a new line of cups.

"What's this?" your father said. "Thought you Bella Coola boys didn't drink."

Hanevold lifted his rum and downed it. "We don't."

Laughter then, the two groups easing into one. Talk of the coming run carried us through the next couple of rounds, then it was on to the manager's wife.

"Pretty, is she?" one of the newcomers asked.

"Pretty rich," said Frank. "She's a Woodley."

The talk turned ugly for a time, women and their worth. I poured myself another and let my attention float.

"What about you, Viken?" Hanevold said, raising his voice for the crowd. "My Tante Nora never married. Maybe she would do for you."

His second big laugh of the night. I gave him a close-mouthed smile.

"Forget your old aunt," said Lund. "Viken wants a young one if he is going to have sons."

"A little late for babies." That was Jakob Nilsen. "He will need someone to wipe his ass in a year or two."

They were roaring now. Hanevold had a light in his eye. "Wipe it?" he said. *"Eller fyll den?"*

The thin, deep-reaching blades of the old language. I felt my smile harden.

"What?" said Frank. "What's he saying?"

I shook my head. *Fyll* is just what it sounds like. You know how men are built, Kit, and women. Do you understand? I believe your father did.

He turned to Hanevold. "You don't know a damn thing about it."

"Oh no?"

"Not every man wants to marry his own cousin."

"Frank," I said.

"Some men want a woman they can't have."

"Frank."

He looked at me. "What, I'm saying nothing. It's none of his god-damn business."

A quiet had come over the room. I could have shut up shop— *Drink up, boys, the storekeeper is tired.* Instead, I reached for the jug. "Who wants another?"

Frank was the first to put his cup on the counter. While I poured, Hanevold looked around at his friends. "Yes," he said finally. "Why not."

Your mother may have understood a little more. There was a story she told me one rainy mid-week day. Were you playing in the stock-room? You cannot have been close by.

She was talking about her mother, and herself when she was a child. "She had this friend called Ernie. Oh, not like that. He wasn't that way inclined."

I could have spoken up then. *She was a he, my Chinese. His name was Lo Yim.*

"He had the milk round," Bobbie went on. "Not on the flats, the cart never made it that far, but he covered Strathcona. Jeannie used to go out walking early sometimes, she liked it better when the housewives were still in their beds. She'd come home and tell me about a new stretch of boardwalk out front of the bakery, or a climbing rose come into bloom around somebody's front door. It was different in the daytime. Even when she had me with her, the women out watering their tomatoes would look right through us. Some even scooted their kids inside."

"Worried the boys would get ideas," I said.

"Or the girls. Some of the older ones would pass by on their way to a shift at the sugar refinery, and here's the women at Vi's and the other houses out smoking and laughing, their feet up on the porch rails. Might look more promising than sweating over the molasses tank, or marrying some fat old bully like their dad." She paused. "Anyhow, that's when she got to know Ernie, on those morning rambles. She used to keep a twist of sugar in her pocket. The milk cart nag would spot her down the end of the street and let out a neigh.

"Sooner or later he started coming by. They'd sit at the table drinking tea, and I'd be lying in our bed, drifting in and out to the sound of them talking. Our room was just off the kitchen—that was a condition of Jeannie's, a room away from the business, with a door that locked, you know, for when she was working and I was on my own.

"Sometimes I would come out in my nightgown and climb into her lap. She'd be wearing some old housedress, her face bare, hair pulled back. Pouring tea for the two of them—hers heavy on the brandy, his with 'just a thimble.' *Miles to go, Jeannie.* He could always get her laughing, even about things that must have made her sad. 'Had a real bungler last night,' I heard her tell him once. 'Couldn't even find his way in.'

"'I'd show him,' Ernie says. 'Back door in my case.'"

What kind of expression did I wear then, Kit? She looked at me, your mother. A long, careful look. My God, the pressure, as though the blood had doubled in my veins. I opened my mouth, and the shop bell rang—like laughter, like a joke. Knox of all people, bringing the rain in to darken the floor.

14

It was early, still dark, but who needs a lantern with a dog in the lead? We passed the sleeping storefront on the way to swim. As I stepped down onto the headland path, Skygge froze. I could just make out the line of his nose lifting, and then he was gone.

I found him by his whine, the sound of his claws at the store's side door. "Mice, is it, boy? All right, we will put down traps after our swim. Come, Skygge." I turned to go, but still he scratched at the base of the door. And so I imagined something larger—rats or even a raccoon.

I got hold of Skygge by the scruff and let us in. "Sit. Skygge, stay." I reached the lantern down from its hook, slipped a match from the box your mother had nailed to the wall. Light, and the two of us listening. Sure enough, a rustle in the stockroom's back corner. I bent to bring my mouth to Skygge's ear. *"Seek!"*

As expected, he made a line to the sound. But then he surprised me. Sitting down on his haunches, he looked back and gave the softest of barks. I came to him. And yes, Kit, you might have been an animal, eyes gleaming, tucked in tight against the wall.

"Hello there." Lowering the lantern, I sat on the floorboards. "Down, Skygge. Lie down." It seemed best to wait for you to speak.

"I took a blanket." Such misery.

"Not to worry."

"I'll put it back."

"Of course. You are good at folding." A pause. "Have you been here all night?"

The smallest motion of your head.

"Have you done this before?"

Silence. I searched for something an uncle might say.

"Do you know, I once spent a whole year on my own. I lived in a little shack on Smith Inlet all by myself."

"Why?"

"Well, I was living down in the city before that—"

"Like Mama."

"Right, like your mama. I suppose . . . I suppose I thought I would be better on my own."

By then Skygge had crept in close. You reached a hand out from under the blanket to take hold of his ear.

"But then I met your daddy, and Skygge also—he was just a puppy then—and the three of us came to Far Cry."

"Mama too."

"Yes, she came a little while later. And then you came along."

You looked at me.

"Kit, what is it?"

I thought you would not answer. I was about to stand up when you said softly, "They were shouting."

"Ah. Well, now—"

"And there were noises."

"Noises."

"Mama and Daddy, in their room."

"Ah." I thought for a moment. "That is only . . . forest sounds."

"No," you said, suddenly older than your years. "It was them."

"Yes, but I mean to say, sometimes when people— Sometimes when mothers and fathers are on their own, it is like a forest."

Did I imagine that would comfort you, a child who had made her way here along a treed and lightless path?

"Come," I said, rising. "Skygge and I will walk you home."

◗

Afternoon light slants along the headland path. Kit can only move so fast with the duffle slung over her shoulder, the grub box jostling at her hip. Passing the old cedar snag, she flashes on Knox stepping out from the trees. She should have known then. He'd never come calling at the cabin before.

Any time, he'd said to her after Bobbie left. *Anything you need.* How long before she'd been forced to take him up on his offer, a week? She'd woken that morning to find her father propped up at the table, avoiding her eye. Not a word when she set his coffee down in front of him. She drank her own standing by the window. She would get something to eat at the store.

When she let herself in by the side door, Uncle Anders looked round, broom in hand.

"Oh, Kit, good. Can you finish tidying up?"

Tidying? The flour barrel was on its side, spilling a pale slope. Splinters of glass glistened, cans lay where they'd rolled to a stop. She glared at her uncle. He knew the shape her father was in; if he had any sense, he'd shut up shop weekend nights, instead of opening the bar.

He stepped in behind the counter, rousing Lys where she lay. "Hanevold made one too many jokes," he said, opening the register. "I had to drag your father off him." He glanced up. "Knox saw the whole thing."

Kit felt the dog's nose at her hand. Watching her uncle count and fold the bills, she understood: it wasn't the first time he'd needed to "pay for the doctor" when someone had rubbed her father the wrong way.

Tucking the money into his shirt pocket, Uncle Anders made for the door with Lys at his heels. Kit was alone then. Three-quarters of an hour spent setting the place to rights, the lineup already forming outside the door. The news was good when her uncle returned: Hanevold had taken the bribe. Still, the trouble showed on Uncle Anders' face. It didn't take a genius to figure it out. It was Bobbie's job to manage Knox, and Bobbie was gone.

On a break to make coffee in the cottage, Kit detoured down to the cannery. The place was going full steam, fairly shuddering with heat and noise. She kept her eyes to the floor. It was easy to lose your footing in all that glittering sludge—besides, she could do without the grins and pitying looks.

The stairs to the office were steep. "Hello?" she called out, nearing the top. "Mr. Knox?"

"Kit." The manager rose as she ducked into the little room. He moved as if to step out from behind the desk, then halted, leaning on the papers scattered there. "I can guess what this is about."

"Sir—"

"I'm a reasonable man."

"Yes, sir."

"It's hard on him, I can see that. But he's making a habit of it now."

"I know."

He raised his eyebrows at her. "It's a big job, you know, running a place like this. I've got enough problems without mad Frank Starratt trying to kill off my fishermen."

"Mr. Hanevold's all right. Uncle Anders talked to him—"

"That's hardly the point."

"Mr. Knox—"

"I don't know what you think you're going to tell me that I haven't already heard."

She made herself hold his gaze. "He's heartbroken. My mother, she broke his heart."

He stared at her. She said nothing until he looked down into the mess on his desk.

"Sir, I was born here."

He shook his head.

"We'll keep an eye on him, I promise. We'll keep him in line."

The manager looked at her. For a second she saw herself through his eyes: hair in need of a wash, trousers shabby with dust. Her mother made young—if her mother had given no thought to her looks.

Knox blinked. "All right, I'll overlook it this time."

"Thank you." Kit's throat was hurting. She turned to go.

"Kit."

She looked out over the cannery floor.

"I'm glad you felt you could come to me."

It was rude to show someone your back when they were talking to you. She glanced back and nodded. Catching hold of the railing, she made her way down.

◗

You have always been good on your own. You watched the other children down on the dock, but when Bobbie told you to *go on, go play*, you were more likely to follow Skygge into the trees. She made sure you knew the dangers, bending to take hold of you by the shoulders and look you in the eye. *You'll die if you eat the white ones, understand? Careful near the edge—you fall in, you drown.*

"I will teach her to swim," I said one day. And when she let go of you to look at me, "Both of you, if you like."

I was wading in the following morning when she surprised me, calling down from above the rocks. "Hey, Andy! Wait for us!"

It was as good a spot as any to start a swimmer off—sand all round the stream mouth, a beach big enough to haul the *Coot* up and still have room to lie drying off in the sun. I had made it my own from that first season, when the bay filled up with cannery slop, the shithouse drift tainting the inlet for miles. Such a blessing there in the lee of the headland, the stream keeping the water clean.

Your mother had grown up on Burrard Inlet, wading along the Tar Flats' swampy shore. Not once had she dunked her head. You watched from the shallows while I taught her to float. When your turn came, I felt the necessary surrender in your skinny back. Have you ever really needed teaching? I remember the first time you took hold of a pair of oars, your strokes shorter than a grown woman's but just as sure. You were dog-paddling before your mother got the knack, Skygge pacing the rocks above you and finally plunging in, putting himself between you and the deep.

You and Bobbie were back the next morning to practise. After a time I felt easy enough to swim my lengths along the shore. That afternoon, the towboat brought the fleet back in. I was in the water before sun-up on Saturday to be back in time for the crush—too early even for Skygge to join me. In any case, I did not expect company with Frank home, and company did not come.

If your father heard about the swimming lessons, he said nothing when he came by the store. Nothing on Sunday either—not until lunch was done. Your mother was curled in the armchair for her customary nap. You and Skygge had gone down to nose around the dock, leaving Frank and me to our game. I remember, our pegs were in close contest, halfway round the board.

"Heard you had the girls out in the water," he said.

"I did."

"Good swimmers, are they?"

"They are."

He was quiet, staring at his cards, his expression dark. Surely he knew how things stood between your mother and myself? I thought of how I might put it. *Frank, she is a daughter to me . . .*

He met my look. "Reckon you could teach me?"

And so it was arranged. Early the following Sunday, I came stroking back from my final length to find him sitting on the sand, leaned back against the transom of the *Coot*. When I reached the shallows, he threw his smoke away and stood.

"Well?" I said. "What are you waiting for?"

He grinned and unbuckled his belt. We had lived in close quarters that first winter, so it was nothing new to see him standing in his smalls. He walked in slowly. Cold showed on his face when the water reached his thighs.

"Take a breath," I said before he could change his mind. "Now shut your mouth and eyes."

I knew he was solid—his tread on the boardwalk that of a much larger man—but I had never dreamt a body could be so dense. I wore my arms out holding him up. He simply would not float.

Skygge had long since waded back to watch from shore. The hundredth time I lowered my hands to feel Frank sink, he swore and buckled at the waist, floundering for a moment before finding his feet.

The sea dripped from his beard. He pushed his hair back. "Fucking hopeless."

I saw it then. It was a matter of belief.

"You know that big fir," I said to him. "The first one we took down?"

"I've had it, Andy. I'm getting out."

"We could not carry it."

"Carry it? Of course not. What are you on about?"

"The sea can carry a log ten times that size."

He looked at me. We stood together in the soft green swell. And no, it was not the next try, or even the one after that, but soon enough I was only holding one hand under his back—and then I was dropping that hand away.

◗

Jimmy Lo is waiting for Kit on the dock when she arrives—that crease in his brow, his long-fingered hands at his sides. Once they get the gear stowed, he sculls them out to the towboat's line. Seven skiffs have already tied on. Hard to be sure who the stares are for, the girl in her daddy's shoes or her new boatpuller. Word will have got round.

Kit has never been the boss. Even with Lys, and Skygge before her, Uncle Anders held a higher, quieter command. She's never been the teacher either, but she knows how she likes to learn. She shows Jimmy how to tie onto a branch of the tow line, then sits with her back to him on the forward thwart. It would only be natural to glance round as they leave the bay, see the open inlet written on his face. She trains her gaze dead ahead.

Most of the others have dropped off the tow by the time Kit demonstrates the trick of slipping the painter line free. With only a few skiffs left, there's no fear of knocking into one as they whirl away over the wake. The wind is with them to begin. She works the sail for a while, then lets her pupil have a turn. Later, he takes up the oars. The sun sinks before them, turning Jimmy to shadow, a shape in the boat.

They make their set at the mouth of Darby Channel, within hailing distance of Willie Paul and Willie Jr. Together she and Jimmy let the net out over the stern. He makes a sound of wonder when it's all played out, the jacklight winking at a distance of three hundred yards. Before she can ask him to, he turns and hauls out the stove.

There are things he already knows. How to move your body in the body of the boat. How to talk when the fish are listening—not all the way under your breath, but almost. How not to talk at all. How to sleep when it's your turn, lie down and turn the light out in your mind.

"Jimmy," she says, an hour before sunrise, and he rolls over in the bow and sits up.

No denying the net comes in easier with two. In the morning twilight, she shows him how to let the fish hang from a finger through the gill, hook the web with the pick's crook and unsnag it, one side at a time. The odd sockeye flops free coming over the roller, saving them the work. In time the fish pile up.

"Some haul," Jimmy says.

Kit nods, hands on her hips, knees adjusting for the swell.

"Should we go again?" he asks.

She gauges the light. "No point, they'll see the net."

When he reaches for the bailing can, she holds out a hand. "I'll do that. You row." She gestures past him as he takes his seat. "See that point?"

Oars in hand, he glances round. "Looks like a rabbit?"

Bunny, she wants to say, Bunny Point. Frank had let her see it for herself—the hunched body of the rock, two firs standing up listening, the bushy ball of salal. *What do you reckon, Kit?*

"Yep." She dips the can. "That's the one."

◖

Only one other letter came for your mother from her friend. This one arrived in winter, your father with us on the dock when the boat came in. The mailbag was light. All three of you were in the store when I dumped the contents on the counter and began to sort. I remember spotting that childish print, *Starat* with its missing *r* and *t*. I slipped the envelope from the pile.

A day or two passed before I could give it to Bobbie. Frank was taking you out to drift for rockfish. I stood on the porch and watched the two of you cross the bay—you rowing a strong, straight line. Early light, the cloud cover low and cold. In time, you rounded Morden Point out of view.

The letter was where I had left it, beneath the register drawer. Skygge came up from the stockroom, not too old to hear purpose in his master's step. The path across the headland was mucky, the branches clotted with snow. I found your mother splitting wood by the cabin door.

"Morning." She laid down the axe and buried a hand in Skygge's ruff. "Hello, boy."

I held up the letter.

"You better come in."

Half a dozen years had passed since Bobbie had last opened a letter from Kath. This time she laid the envelope unopened on the table and boiled coffee for us both. I sat down and watched her pierce a new can of milk, drip a little into her palm and hold it down for Skygge's tongue. He lay down at her feet as she added milk to my mug, then her own. Coffee. Sugar from the jar. Finally she took up the letter and pushed a finger in at the seal.

Again, a single page, a single side. She read it over to herself. Then she read it to me.

I do not know what she did with it, Kit. Whether she burned it and the other two, or tucked all three away. I remember how it started—*Dear Bobcat*—and I remember your mother's face as she read. The house on Shore Street had been shut down, Vi Swift having been given a suspended sentence on the condition that she move on. I was not surprised. There had been stories of the raids in the newspaper for some months—stories I had skipped over when reading to the three of you after Sunday lunch.

The "cleanup" was welcome, or so Kath claimed. She was sick of living under Stanley's thumb, turning over most of what she earned to Vi. She had found a little houseboat not far from Rat Portage

Mill. Plenty of custom, and every penny her own, minus the local constable's tithe.

It was hard to say how much of the strain in your mother's voice was there on the page. "She oughtn't to do it," she said finally. "It's not safe on your own."

What could I say? Setting the letter to one side, Bobbie turned her hands up as if to examine them. I reached across the table to cover them with my own.

15

While Jimmy dozes in the sun beside the pile of net, Kit works a lazy sail. She can make out a dozen skiffs up-inlet, none closer than a quarter mile. Away to portside, shearwaters drop from the sky, diving to fly after the fish. A glance back at her boatpuller. His face shows the pinch of his thinking, even in dreams. She looks away. Unfair to watch someone while they sleep.

A waft of guano reaches her as she draws even with a treeless island. Seals rest among the crags, a handful of females and their pups. Their dark eyes find hers. It's a peaceful scene—or it would be, if only her mind wouldn't go chasing what's lost.

Go on, Kitty-cat. Get.

It was always the same when Bobbie washed the cabin floor: chairs on the table, everybody out. Kit didn't mind—if she had to get through the lesson Uncle Anders had set her, she could at least be sitting outside. Two stories she had to find in the newspaper, one from close by and one from what her uncle called "the wider world." Pick out something they had in common and something different and write it all down.

The ground was just about dry where she was sitting, her back resting against a spruce. Sticky pitch in her shirt again—Bobbie would lay it over the washtub and pour the boiling water through. Kit looked out over the newspaper propped on her knees. The inlet a deep blue-grey, the shushing of Bobbie's scrub brush on the boards.

Even with the season starting up again, their side of the headland had a far-off feel. A ten-minute walk through the trees delivered you from the store to the cabin in its clearing; still, it was rare for anyone but Uncle Anders to call. Even the little beach stayed mostly their own.

It was only natural, then, for Kit to think "deer" when the scrub at the cliff's edge moved. Moments later, Ida Paul stepped out into the clearing, a basket held against her apron. Kit stood up and caught a glimpse of salmonberries, red and gold.

"Mama," she called, her voice like a younger child's.

Bobbie was excited too—Kit could see it when she came to the door. "Ida," she said. "You'll stay for some tea."

With the floorboards still wet, Bobbie had Kit carry the chairs out into the sun. The fourth one served as a little table, crowded with teapot and mugs, milk can and sugar jar, a stack of hastily buttered bread. Ida took her tea the way Bobbie did, sweet and strong. Bobbie couldn't seem to stop talking. Didn't a good crop of salmonberries mean a good run coming, wasn't that what Ida's people said? And what do you do with them, are they good in a pie? Well, the kids would make short work of them anyway, wouldn't they.

Ida had a way of listening, attentive and not, as though a human voice was only one of a dozen significant sounds. Watching her, Kit realized she was a beauty, the only woman she had seen with hair to rival her mother's. Her children never seemed to fight. They were among the few whose company Kit deliberately sought, following the long boardwalk past the cottages and the bachelor sheds, down to the shacks at the far end. The Pauls' true house was in the village at the head of the inlet. Kit had never seen it, but Willie Jr. and Archie talked about it sometimes. They dried their salmon there, then smoked it. In the old days it was all done that way.

"What about in a bad year?" Kit asked once. She and the two brothers were lying on their bellies at the end of the long dock, handlines down in hopes of a rockfish.

"Always a good year someplace," Willie Jr. said. "Some other village gets a good run, they let us fish their inlet. We get one, they come to us."

Ida took a piece of bread when Bobbie offered the plate again. She ate and drank and set down her empty mug. The salmonberries glowed in their basket by her feet. She leaned down for them. "Better get back."

"Oh, yeah. Well." Bobbie stood up after her. "Come again sometime. Any time."

Ida looked from Bobbie to Kit. A small nod, a smile. She left the way she had come.

Kit could make no sense of the expression on her mother's face. Bobbie had Frank and Kit and Uncle Anders; she even had Mrs. Knox to talk to during the season, plus any number of customers who passed through the store. How could she be lonely? She was, though. Clearly, she was.

◗

It was like two lives, Far Cry a ghost town when the season died, a proper one when the salmon ran. Those summer morning swims had a cramped feel—stray too far out and the water turned brown and foul. It helped, having someone besides Skygge to swim back to. Not every morning, but often enough, I would return from my third or thirteenth length to find you and your mother in the water.

In time, she let you come down on your own. You could have done lengths yourself—you had a strong breaststroke by then, and a simple crawl—but you preferred to swim close to the headland, circling out to lie for a time on the surface, then rolling to make for the shallows again.

One morning I came stroking back to find you treading water, your eyes on a spot just off the rocks. Skygge, too, was watching from the sand. A seal, I thought—a decent drop-off there for trapping fish—and sure enough, a dappled head popped up. Another child might have cried out in delight. Fanning your arms, you watched the whiskered face—flaring nostrils, depthless gaze. Eventually, it dove. Only then did you twist to catch my eye.

There were those who hung around to handline at season's end, but Knox was not one to provide free lodging for long. By late September we had the place to ourselves. With the coming of the cooler weather, your father and I ranged over the place again, searching out rust and rot. Hiking the waterline to its head, we checked every join. I carried my .32 on those walks, the trail favoured by bears as well as men.

You and your mother made yourselves useful. I remember looking down from the loft, watching the pair of you move through the deserted cannery, oil cans in hand. Frank was overhead hammering while I felt over the piles of empty cans for any the rain had found. There is little in this world that water cannot break down, given time.

"Anything metal that can move," I heard Bobbie tell you, so while she worked a slow circle around the cutting machine, you passed from hinge to hinge—trap door, window, door. When the hammering left off as your father fitted a new shingle into place, there came the soft *tuck-tock* of the oil can, call and answer, woman and girl. Skygge nosed from one to the other and back, and I thought of my stint as a mill-oiler, the strays I'd kept at bay. You were using proper machine oil, though, not dogfish grease. It was the company Skygge was after, the pack.

———

You know how it happened, Kit. It was early in the season when Skygge jumped off the end of the long dock and swam out of the bay. I was in the stockroom when you came running. The two of us made it across the headland in time to watch him paddle out of sight. It was rare for you to cry, even as a small child, and you would have been eight years old by then. Your wailing brought Bobbie out of the cabin to find us standing together on the cliff. She pulled you close, pressing your face to her chest.

"Hush, Kitty-cat. He'll come back, won't he, Andy?"

I met her look, unsure. "Of course he will."

And of course he did. Not swimming but lying in the bottom of a company skiff, a Wardell's Cannery flag shivering on its mast.

Dan Pike looked too thin to row the three miles up-inlet from Wardell's. Delivering Skygge was a kindness, but Pike also had a tale to tell. That was a late night in the store, the fleet back in and the counter turned bar, empty bottles lined up on the floor.

Pike waited for a good crowd before he began. His bitch, Harebell—half malamute, he had us know, a blue-eyed beauty with a wolf's winter coat—this Harebell had paced the dock at Wardell's all morning, her muzzle lifted to the wind.

"That's right, Viken, your boy there's not the only one with a nose." He had blue eyes himself, Pike. They stood out in his freckled face. "I thought maybe a seal carcass had washed up someplace until I seen him come paddling. Oh, the word went round then. The dock was never so crowded, except when the boat was in. They cleared a path for Harebell, though. She ran to meet your boy where he come scrambling up the rocks. What'd you say you call him?"

"Skygge."

"Right. Well, fair play to old Shaggy, he shakes out his coat and he's on her then and there."

Those gathered gave a cheer, your father among them. Even Knox held up his glass. He had smelled a gathering and followed the boardwalk from his house on the point. Was that where your mother was, Kit, sitting with Orpha Knox? I know she was in the store to begin with—I remember your father standing close beside her and, later, walking her to the door. Perhaps you and she were next door with Skygge, the three of you reunited and relieved.

It was a slow Sunday just past the season's close when Pike came rowing back. This time he had a crate in the skiff. The children seemed to know—you were waiting on the long dock with half a dozen others whose families hadn't yet moved on. Bobbie heard the excitement and stepped out onto the porch. She stuck her head back inside the cottage with a grin. "Come on, you two, never mind your game." Skygge lifted an ear. "You too, Skygge, you lazy bugger. Come see."

We found Pike on the dock, kneeling by his crate in the crowd of kids. He rose and stepped toward us. "Andy. Frank." Your father stood at a little distance while I shook Pike's hand.

"Hello, Dan," Bobbie said.

"Missus." He cleared his throat. "Harebell's had her pups. Got a couple left."

She moved past him for a look. "Oh, aren't they beauties!"

I saw them then—one on its hind legs in the crate, front paws braced at the rim, the other in one of the Jensen boys' arms. And I saw you, Kit. Standing at the edge of the group, a look on your face as though you were holding your breath.

"Black-and-white one's a dog," Pike said. "Little grey's a bitch."

The cries they made. Skygge pushed into the group to smell them—the grey stretching up to lick his muzzle, the other wriggling in the boy's arms. Did they know him for their father? Surely he, at least, understood. The nose that had caught wind of their mother from three miles off must have recognized them for his own.

"Thought you might like one, Andy," Pike added. "What with your boy there getting long in the tooth."

Something inside me went cold. Long swim or no, Skygge was spending more and more time on the rug. A decade had passed since he had been a puppy himself, a long life for a dog his size. A spawning salmon gives up eating at the river's mouth—might not a dog take a new life in the house as a signal to let go of his own?

"Thanks," I said. "But we are fine as we are."

"Lars! Lucas!" That was Agneta Jensen, calling her boys. When the one with the pup in his arms turned and saw her standing at the head of the dock, he placed it back in the crate and ran after his brother to follow her up the stairs. A blessing for Ida's three. They got the black-and-white in the end.

Pike pushed his cap back, rubbing at the line it left. "How 'bout you, Missus? Wouldn't your girl here like one?"

Was that what did it, him showing he'd taken notice of you both? Or was it the smile your mother flashed, unguarded, even warm?

"What do you think, Frank?"

Your father looked past her to Pike. "Dog's a lot of trouble."

"Honey, for Kit—"

"Kit's fine."

Your mother fell quiet.

"Come on, *Missus*," Frank said. He took hold of her hand as he had in their early days and led her away. At the stairs, he gestured that she should go first. She mounted them with him close behind, neither one of them looking back.

"I will take her," I heard myself say. "I will take the grey."

But grey was not quite right, was it? Silver, you have said, and so she is.

We returned to the cottage to find the cribbage board abandoned, your parents gone home. So it was the three of us—you, Skygge and I—left to watch the silver pup explore.

"What will we call her?" I said.

You thought for a moment. "What does *skygge* mean?"

You knew the answer, Kit. I told you again. "Shadow."

You nodded, watching the puppy follow her father, light after dark.

"Ah," I said, understanding. *"Lys."*

It was selfish of me, I know, keeping Skygge's passing for myself. Perhaps if I had found him by daylight. If Lys hadn't woken me in the dark.

"Hush," I said. And then, as sometimes happens when I am half-asleep, the old language drifted up. *"Stille."*

But she would not be quiet. When I reached a hand down to push her from the bedside, she took it gently in her teeth. That way they have of using their mouths as hands. I was awake then. I knew.

He had become lighter with age. Leaving Lys crying in the cottage, I carried him with ease along the back headland path. It troubled me, laying him down on the pebbles while I dragged the *Coot* down the short slope of the beach. I feared I might lose him in the dark.

I rowed out farther than need be—it was March, the water as clean as it ever gets. Out past Squid Island, to where I could feel the falling tide keenly against the hull. No sense lingering. I touched the fur at his brow, the dry sponge of his nose. I heaved him overboard.

Rowing back, I saw the headland lighten and take shape with every glance round. How long were you standing there, I wonder, before I made you out?

◗

With the wind tearing up the inlet and the sail no longer any use, Kit sees what her boatpuller's made of. Steady, the best rowers are, a fluid, seemingly endless strength. His face untroubled, Jimmy sculls through the whistling sound at the top of a wave, the thud as they drop into a trough. Kit relaxes into the ride.

In time he brings them round into the Carmen Island channel. It's quieter here, only one other skiff down the far end. Hanevold, it might be, that green cap of his—hard to be sure in the failing light. Either way, she'll take care to stagger the set so there can be no talk of cutting a fellow fisherman off.

Jimmy works wordlessly beside her, letting out the net. Later, when the coffee's coming to a boil, she's almost surprised to hear him speak.

"I can't get over the smell."

She breathes in through her nose: coffee, yes, and woodsmoke, but mostly ocean, the cold, ongoing clean.

He shakes his head. "In the city it's always smoke and horseshit. False Creek has the swamp and the slaughterhouses, the mills. You ever been?"

"Once."

"You know the Main Street Bridge?"

"Yeah."

"Okay, so on the south side, down on your left, there's a dairy ranch."

Kit pictures it—the boxy brown bodies, the startling grass. "Yeah," she says, "that's right."

"Far edge of the paddock, there's a creek there, Brewery Creek."

And so there is: beyond the grazing beasts, a cut of water, sparkling, dark.

"This old guy," Jimmy says, "one of the regulars at the restaurant, he used to let me and a couple of the other kids borrow his boat. We'd row across to the creek for eels."

"Eels?"

"You never had them? They're good." He pushes a stick of wood into the flames. "I always loved it in the boat. Your head feels better."

Kit nods. "And your chest."

He looks at her. The stove's heat plays on her face; she must be lit up like he is, flickering. She wraps her hand in her sleeve and lifts the pot off the fire. Jimmy holds out his cup.

◗

Knox was here earlier. All these years and still the man has not learned how to drink. I keep a special bottle for his visits—did you know? The good stuff, he thinks, and so it was before I watered it down. Even so, he gets loose-tongued after one, and clumsy after three. More than once he has stumbled out to be sick over the porch rail into the salal bushes below.

I suppose it is not such a high price to pay, the occasional cribbage game. Even your father managed it most of the time. In the early years he would sometimes catch my look and let the boss win. It was something between the two of us, a game within the game.

Things were better once Knox had his bride to keep him home— weeks would pass without his footfall on the boardwalk, his face at the door. Nights when he did show up, he was always crowing or moaning, or both—full of having won himself a Woodley girl, even if she was the runt. That is his word, Kit. All the same, it seems hard-hearted copying it down here.

"You don't know your luck, Starratt," I remember him saying one night when he and Orpha had been married a few years.

"Luck?" Frank said, skipping his peg down the track. "Try skill."

"No, not—" Knox gestured to the board. "Your wife. And your girl, just as bonny as her mother."

Frank winked at me. "If it's kids you want, there's not much of a trick to it."

Knox looked up. "My Orpha, she—she's not strong."

You might feel sorry for the man, reading that. I almost do, writing it. And then I recall the look on his face. Even then, drunk as he was, there was that twinned intent he was never without. Never a word, never a thought without its shadow riding along.

Take tonight. He took his time working round to it. We were well into a second game before he mentioned your father's name.

"Won't be the same without him." A pause to pick up his hand. "Too quiet by half."

I nodded, throwing two low cards to the crib.

"Out of his misery, though," Knox added.

I looked at him.

"Well, he was never quite right after the war, was he? And then, when his missus up and left . . ."

What could I say to that? He laid his discards over mine. I waited for him to cut for the starter card.

"I still can't believe it," he said. "A woman like that going off with a—"

"Married, you mean." I cut the deck myself. "A married woman."

"Sure, but you know what I mean. She could've had her pick."

"Frank," I said. "Frank was her pick."

"I know, that's what makes it so hard to believe." He kissed his knuckle before sniffing it, then laid the first card of the play. "You never know, though. Maybe things weren't so rosy in the old log cabin after he got back."

Did he notice my stillness? Just how many drinks had he had?

"You had to feel for her," he added. "The girl, too."

That set my teeth on edge. He had known you all your life—why not call you by name?

"How's she doing, anyway?"

"Kit?" I said. "Fine." I played a card for fifteen—enough to turn his expression sour.

"Can't be easy, her mother running off like that. Then, what, not even a year later, she loses the old man."

He poured out the last of the watered whiskey. I rose for a fresh bottle. So what if he ended up sick.

"You know she's got this boatpuller now." He gave a snort. "Didn't know the buggers could row."

"Yes," I said. "I know."

We played to the go and gathered back our hands. He sucked his knuckle as though it was the knob on a chicken leg.

"You're not worried?" he said. "The pair of them out there day and night?"

I met his look. "Kit is a sensible girl."

"Sure." A pause. "I just wonder if she should be out on the grounds at all."

"She has been fishing all her life."

Setting down his cards, he took up his pipe and lit it, the coal fizzing. "I could always train her up in the office."

He could feel me watching him, I know he could.

"How is Mrs. Knox?" I said finally.

"Orpha? Not so good."

"She will be missing you, down in the city on her own."

"Yeah, well, this place doesn't run itself."

At long last, he counted his hand. I counted mine along with the crib, pegging my share of points. I wonder, Kit, will you learn to play when the season closes down? It will be just the two of us then, and Lys if she lasts.

16

Kit was ten years old when the world came to blows. When it began, the war moved like a deep-sea current, distant and unseen. By season start-up, it was coming into shore.

"Heard about Memryk?" her father said one evening over the cribbage board. Kit was curled up on the rug, her head resting on Lys's back.

Bobbie looked round from the basin. "Fedor?"

"You know some other Memryk?" When she said nothing, Frank added, "Bugger's gone. The whole family, sent to one of those camps in the interior."

"I wondered," said Uncle Anders.

"What camps?" said Bobbie.

"Internment." Uncle Anders looked across at her. "They are all going, Galicians, Hungarians, Austrians. Germans too."

"Best place for 'em," said Frank.

"Frank."

"There's a war on, Bobbie. Enemy's the enemy."

"I know, but . . ."

"I suppose I should count myself lucky," said Uncle Anders.

"How's that?"

"Norway is neutral."

Her father made a noise. "No such thing."

"Frank," Bobbie said again.

"This is my country," Uncle Anders said. "I left Norway over thirty years ago."

"Yeah, okay. I'm just saying, a man has to stand up for something. Fight for what's his."

Bobbie dried her hands and came to lay them on Frank's shoulders. "Don't you go getting any ideas. Married men need the wife's say-so, remember?"

Kit saw her father's face harden.

Her mother must've sensed it. She swung round and dropped into his lap. "How would we get on here without you?" She looped a hank of her hair around his wrist. "Hm? How would I get on?"

Frank's mouth softened, a release Kit felt in her chest. As she worked a hand into Lys's ruff, Uncle Anders pushed his chair back and stood. She thought he would speak, but it was only a fresh bottle he was after. High in the open cupboard, it sent back the light of the lamp.

◗

I told myself it was a surprise, but looking back, I can see the steps your father took—one after the other, like stones laid out across a stream.

I remember when they began printing the casualty lists, all those names framed in black. Your father asked me to read them out.

"Frank." Bobbie shot a glance your way.

"You don't think they deserve our respect?"

I see now how I played a part—bringer of bad tidings, teller of chilling tales. The news reached us late, but it still reached us, copies of the *World* piled on the table to be read in order, day by day. There are those who skim the week's headlines, eager to bring time back in line. I prefer to make my way through each edition, building on the stories that came before.

Your parents trusted me to read anything of interest aloud. Names and the numbers of lives lost. Mons into Marne, Ypres as 1914 wound down, then again with the coming of spring—this time under clouds of killing gas. Weeks later, a U-boat's torpedo sent the *Lusitania* to the sea floor. Do you remember, Kit? *Many children and little babies still lie in the morgues like so many dolls.*

Your mother stood up from the table when I read that line. "Come on, Kit, planting to do."

Lys followed you out—to lope ahead to the cabin, I suppose. Nose out voles while the two of you worked on Bobbie's tub garden in the sun.

Frank watched the door for a moment after you were gone. He shifted his gaze to meet mine. "Go on."

I finished the article, then turned the page to read about the trouble down in Victoria, Germans beaten, their shops destroyed.

"Serves them right," he said. "Sons of bitches."

"You think so?"

"Don't you?"

How did I answer, Kit, a conciliatory nod? Or did I just read on?

Bobbie was the one to speak up when I read the latest about Minister Hughes. He was still refusing to replace the Canadian-made Ross rifles—never mind that our soldiers were snatching up the sturdier Lee–Enfields from the British dead.

"God," she said, "he really is a mad bastard."

Frank flinched. "It takes a hard man to lead."

"Yes, but—"

"Yes-but, yes-but, that's all I hear out of you these days."

You will not have forgotten that moment, Kit—I remember you glancing up from the page of equations I had set. Your mother looked as though she had been slapped. Your father's face did not move. Inside, though, he was in motion. Landing on one stone, gathering himself for the leap to the next.

It was Knox who got him the rest of the way there. Late July, was it? One of those disappointing Saturdays when he showed up for a game.

"I was saying to Laramie," he said, looking over his hand, "you have to admire these young fellows, going over to do their part. Envy them even." He poured himself two fingers from the watered bottle, plucked a card and laid it down. Lifted his glass in Frank's direction. "Course, it's different for old married men the likes of us. Mrs. Knox would have something to say on the subject." A laugh. A little shake of his head. "Doubt they'd have us anyhow, me with my back and you being, well, on the smaller side."

Your father sat still as a portrait. I knew then, Kit. Why else, in the days to come, did I fail to read aloud the notice that married men no longer required permission from their wives to enlist? Frank must have heard talk of it among the men. Perhaps even Knox himself, come down from behind his desk to make a show of inspecting the catch.

However he got wind of it, your father took the news to heart. Not long after the season closed, he let himself out into the moonlight, careful to wake neither his daughter nor his wife. He picked a path down to our little beach, pushed off in the *Coot* and rode the falling tide to the inlet's mouth. At Duncanby Landing he paid young Travis Mead to tow my little *reska* back to Far Cry, while he caught the *Camosun* on her southbound stop.

To think he might have come back to us on her next northbound pass. If only the recruiting officer had been a man of fewer words. Half an inch under regulation height. Frank tried out his charm, but there was no bending the rules. He was almost out the tent door when the officer added, "You might try the Medical Corps."

Imagine, Kit, the height requirement an inch shorter for those men who would carry the injured, the dead. I suppose Frank saw himself pounding across a muddy wasteland, one end of a stretcher on his shoulders, a soldier's blood running down his back. At least he would be part of things. Anything was better than boarding the steamer for home with his tail between his legs.

◗

Full moon, the net glinting as they bring it in. Kit's hands begin to burn after the first couple of yards. She looks to her boatpuller, whose alarm is beginning to register on his face. She was small the first time she felt the stingers' fire. She tells Jimmy what her father told her then: "Jellyfish. It'll pass."

He shakes his head, digging with his pick to twist a salmon loose. With the next length of net, a fat, translucent jelly drops over the rollers to wobble on the boards. The net still wound in her fist, Kit hooks her pick on her belt and stoops for the bailing can. Scooping up the jellyfish, she slops it back overboard. It's the first of several. Those that land out of her reach, Jimmy shovels her way with his boot.

With the catch aboard, Kit shifts to hang her swollen hands over the side. Jimmy shuffles the other way on the forward thwart, sweeping his hands in the sea. When the cold gets too much, they sit facing each other, hands in their laps. Moon-eyed salmon crowd around their boots, some still clenching, others reduced to a flutter about the gills.

"There's time to make another set," she says. "Reckon you can row?"

Jimmy flexes his fingers and nods.

As he hauls on the oars, Kit looks past him to the moon's white road. Nothing so cold as that light, so clear. The night her father left for the war, it lay in a drift across her bed. She woke to hear him go. Out to the privy? Strange to need more than the pot at that hour.

Maybe he just couldn't sleep. Run out of drink, gone walking the night path to let himself into the store.

It had the feel of a lie even as she thought it. She lay listening for him until her breath betrayed her, deepening into sleep. The next sound was Bobbie crying. Kit should have known—the hour, yes, but also his step. It had been wrong somehow. Too soft for a man doing anything but slipping away.

◗

It made sense for the three of us to take supper together once Far Cry emptied out. I would have been happy to eat at the cabin, but your mother preferred to come to me. To begin with, she made every day Sunday, carrying over her stew kettle and a loaf of bread. By mid-winter she was cooking at my stove.

With Frank gone, the two of you helped more than ever with the off-season upkeep. Bobbie and I were replacing a stretch of the cook-house stairs when she caught her thumb with the hammer and cried out. White-faced and wincing, she brought her hand to her mouth.

"Are you all right?" I asked.

Lowering her hand, she held it to her chest. "I used to see him, you know, the first month or so after he left. But it would be a branch moving. One time it was the water bucket, just hanging there on its hook." She examined her thumb. "That's over now. My head knows, but the rest of me . . ." She looked at me, dry-eyed. "The other night I went into Kit's room and sat there. You know, just to hear somebody breathe."

I nodded. You will remember Skygge's way of sighing in his sleep. Lys is quieter, but I can still reach down beside the bed and find her moving flank.

And what of me? Did Anders Viken, storekeeper, miss his friend? I did not realize how much until late May, when Far Cry began to come to life. The Knoxes were back, along with a few early-bird fishermen and the cannery's set-up crew. The first time I heard the manager's hard-heeled boots outside the cottage, I felt a gladness that caught me off guard.

Clearing the smile from my face, I opened to his knock. The winter had aged him—less flesh on his bones, more scalp showing through his hair. He had an armful of the cannery books, carrying them home. I used to wonder, did he leave all the tallying to Orpha, or did she only check over his work?

I had not thought to water down a bottle. Before long the whiskey loosened his tongue. He had had enough of Orpha's brother lording over him at the family store. "Manager? Sonofabitch couldn't manage his own asshole. Get him up here, see what running a real operation looks like."

I cut the deck and pushed it toward him. "Your deal."

"Got half a mind to move up here year-round."

I looked up sharply.

"See how the little shit gets along then." He worked a clumsy shuffle and tossed down two hands.

I took mine up and discarded. Knox peered at his hand until I tapped my two cards in the crib.

"Hold your horses, hold your horses." His first card hovered partway to the crib. He snatched it back and chose another, along with the one beside it. Laid them face down on mine.

"And Mrs. Knox?" I said.

"What about her?"

I cut the deck again. "How would she fare up here in winter?"

"Yes, well." He turned up the starter. "Who knows how long the poor girl will be with us."

Sober, he never would have said it out loud. Still, he arranged his expression well enough—long-suffering, resigned. He played a card, then I did. Then he.

"I suppose none of us knows," he added.

My card, his.

He grinned. "Thirty-one."

Thirty-two, in fact. I let him have his point.

"You take Frank," he said, gathering his cards back for the count. "What are the chances he'll come through it all?"

He held his thin lips straight, but he could not quite dim the light in his eye. Of course, I had noticed him watching your mother—men did. Until that moment, though, I had failed to see how deep his interest ran.

The following day, I waited until the trickle of morning trade had subsided and you had taken Lys out for a row. Bobbie was passing a sieve through the flour barrel, looking for bugs. I let my broom bring me close.

I could not repeat what the manager had said. We had an understanding, your mother and I—we would never speak of Frank not coming home.

"You know Knox has his eye on you," I said finally.

She looked round, the sieve in her hand, flour dusting the floor. "You think I can't handle a mouse like him?"

"Are you certain that is all he is?"

"Mouse, rat, either way." There was a hardness in her gaze, a glitter I had marked years before in the eye of her friend.

"All right," I said, and I believe I thought it would be.

17

Kit's war was made of stories. Tales overheard on the docks and in the store, articles her uncle would read aloud and those he wouldn't. Sometimes Kit picked up a newspaper on her own. She was twelve, then she was thirteen, old enough to understand. "Casualties" meant both injured and dead. The dark-bordered lists broke down: *Killed in Action. Presumed to Have Died.* Her father wasn't "in action," so far as they knew. Still, she moved a finger down each column of names.

Died of Wounds. Wounded and Missing. Wounded and Gassed.

An army marched on its stomach—she'd read that in the *World*. All right, she couldn't go out with the fleet, but fish-pitchers played their part, and a cannery couldn't run without its store. She was helping. What more could she do?

The answer came through her mother, a message from the manager's wife. Kit and Bobbie both—all good women and girls, in fact. They could knit.

Bobbie had long since given up dragging her along when she went to sit with Mrs. Knox. The parlour was as Kit remembered—close and dim. There was a fire in the grate, as though it was January and not June. Windows all round, casements fastened, curtains drawn. What was the point of living on the point?

Mrs. Knox took her role as teacher seriously. She sat on the chesterfield between them, a big-eyed bundle of twigs in a heavy shawl. On her lap, she held three sets of needles, three balls of dark-grey yarn. *In, up, around and off*—the veins stood up in her hands, as though the yarn were spooling through her too. Bobbie got the hang of it right off, but Kit struggled. Funny, given how good she was at mending nets.

Once they were under way, the manager's wife gathered herself and walked carefully to her chair. The effort set her coughing, a raw, upsetting sound. Bobbie rose and went to stand behind her, rubbing her back. Catching Kit's eye, she raised an eyebrow. *The fuss.*

In time, Mrs. Knox settled and returned to the balaclava she was knitting; a pile of them sat on the small table beside her, dark, flattened heads with holes where the men's faces would go. Meantime, Bobbie worked on the tube of a sock. That left cholera belts for Kit. Apparently, if the men wrapped up their middles, their organs would remain sound. Each belt was to be six inches wide and as long as a soldier lying down. Kit couldn't imagine finishing one, let alone the dozens Mrs. Knox had in mind.

The manager's wife talked in breathy bursts. What if Mr. Knox should take it in his mind to enlist? Worse, what if conscription came and all the able-bodied men were called up? Kit felt her mother smile inside. *Able-bodied? Knuckles Knox?* Out loud, Bobbie offered assurances. He would never. He knew he was needed here.

Kit sank beneath their talk, like dunking your head with the gulls still crying above. Her father's name called her back.

"And Mr. Starratt?" Mrs. Knox was saying. "Have you had any word?"

Bobbie kept her head down, needles ticking. "Still working at the hospital in Taplow so far as we know."

"You'll be glad of his pay."

"Gladder to have him home."

The manager's wife left a pause. "We'll have the Prohibition soon. That's one good will come of all this."

"You think so?" Bobbie said.

"Oh, yes, certainly."

"I can't see how it would last."

"Why ever not?"

Bobbie glanced up. "People need a way out of themselves."

Mrs. Knox pursed her lips. There came a stretch of no talk, only the negotiating needles, the rhythmic rat-squeak of their hostess's breathing.

No matter what Kit did, her stitches tightened down. Bobbie showed her how to hold the yarn loosely, shake the tension out of her hands. Still, each row lay shrunken atop the last. Kit's eyes began to smart. She was jamming her needle's point into a constricted loop when she felt her mother's gaze.

"Why don't you go round to the woodshed, Kitty-cat. Split some wood for Mrs. Knox."

"Oh, no," said the manager's wife. "Mr. Knox can send up one of the cannery lads."

But Kit was already standing, dropping the sad inches of knitted belt.

"It's all right," Bobbie said. "She doesn't mind."

Kit took her leave before Mrs. Knox could speak again. Round back of the house, she stood for a moment, letting her eyes reach out to sea.

When she'd split and gathered a healthy stack, she filled the wood-box and let herself in through the kitchen door. Here too the fire was stoked up high—heat and the smell of something yeasty, though there was no sign of any rising dough.

Mrs. Knox's voice reached her from across the hall. "He won't touch me."

Kit stood frozen, the box dragging at her arms.

"Oh, now," Bobbie said.

"It's true, not so much as a kiss."

"He's careful of your health, that's all."

"He thinks I'll break."

"Oh, Orpha—"

"He said so. He said it would snap me in two."

Quiet then. Kit imagined her mother laying her needles aside.

"I'll put the kettle on. You'll feel better after a cup of tea."

Kit was still standing there when Bobbie came in. She opened her mouth, but her mother shook her head, gesturing for Kit to set the woodbox down. "Go on," Bobbie whispered, nodding toward the door.

◗

You will remember the day your father's first letter arrived. No word of apology for leaving the way he had, or if there was, your mother did not read that part aloud. *They had us like fish in a hold on that damn train. By the time we got into Halifax every other bugger was burning up with the measles. Lucky boy Starratt already had it. Just about killed me when I was a sprog.*

The shortness of the letter should have come as no surprise—when had you ever seen him write more than a handful of words? An item or two on the list for catalogue orders, notes on a sketch for a new shed. Rooster scratch, Bobbie called it, though she was never much of a writer herself. If you recall, I was the one who made sure we sent a letter out on every boat.

Two months passed before we heard from Frank again. By then he was overseas, posted to the Canadian Red Cross Hospital in Taplow, England. *Tell Kit they got a cat in the kitchens here called Kit. A real mouser. Tell Andy I cleaned up at cribbage last night.* A little about his days, his duties, his bunkmate—a fellow orderly who farted in his sleep. It seemed they spent most of the workday cleaning and carrying. *No weight like a dead weight. At least those poor buggers are quiet.*

Eventually, he wrote with the happy news of his posting to a hospital ship. *About time too. I been telling them since I signed up the likes of Frank Starratt is wasted on land.*

◊

Mrs. Knox's chest was bad. "She can hardly catch her breath, poor cow," Kit's mother reported one day in the store.

Uncle Anders made no reply, but it was as though Kit heard him nod. She was down the back, tidying after the weekend crowd.

"That new tonic they've got her on smells like tar," Bobbie added.

Kit drew a toppled stack of overalls toward her; behind it on the shelf, the telltale rise of a mouse nest. She bent closer. No pups in this one, thankfully. Last time had been like finding four pinky fingers cut off and come to life. Unable to make herself step on them the way her father did, Kit had carried the nest out the side door and set it in the crook of a branch. Not a kindness—she didn't kid herself. A meal for a raven or whatever got wind of them first.

"I told Knox I'd help with the books," her mother was saying now.

Was there a shift in her uncle's quiet?

"You needn't look like that," Bobbie said. "It's only an hour or two in the mornings. Not on boat days, and I told him I couldn't do weekends."

Finally Uncle Anders spoke. "He is paying you?"

"Of course he's paying me. What kind of a goose do you think I am?"

Kit sat back on her heels.

"Well then," Uncle Anders said.

"Well then. All right then." Bobbie gave a short laugh.

After a moment, Kit reached to close her cloth over the nest. Sweeping the pale jumble into the dustpan, she recognized threads of blue. Somewhere in a stack of work shirts, she would find the one the mouse had made its own.

The store had been busy for a mid-week morning. When noon came around with no sign of her mother, Kit went next door to the cottage to cut sandwiches for lunch. She made enough for three, but only Uncle Anders came to join her, Lys at his heels. When they were done, he rose and wrapped the last sandwich in a clean dishtowel.

"Take that down to her. He cannot keep her working with nothing to eat."

The whole of Far Cry reeked during the season; even so, as Kit stepped into the cannery's high gloom, she fought the urge to plug her nose. A few strides in, she felt herself break a sweat. Down the far end, light from the fish-ladder door streamed across the gut shed. It broke into colours where water splashed down from the overhead pipes. Ida Paul looked round from the washing table, and Kit found herself holding up the sandwich, part explanation, part wave. Ida nodded, or seemed to in the scattered light.

The din of the place. The clank and whine, the ongoing roll of running water and drumming knives. No need to tread carefully on the climb to the manager's office—no one would hear the groan of a stair. The thought came to her, though, didn't it? Step after narrow step, her hand grasping the rail.

Her mother's voice reached her as she drew near the top.

"Now, Ed, get a hold of yourself."

"That's not what you said on the tug."

"Ancient history, boss."

Kit stepped up into the office doorway. Bobbie was sitting at the desk, ledger book open, pen in hand. Mr. Knox was standing over her. No part of them touching, so far as Kit could see.

She stood stiffly as her mother's face formed a smile.

"Hi, Kitty-cat."

The manager straightened up. "Well, now, to what do we owe the honour?"

Kit held out the sandwich.

"That my lunch?" Bobbie said. "Well, bring it here."

She moved into the little room and handed it over. Her mother set it on the desk.

"Is that the time?" Mr. Knox said. "Mrs. Knox will be waiting."

"You go on," Bobbie said. "I can finish up here."

"Right."

Kit drew back to let the manager pass. He descended quickly, both hands on the rails.

She looked at her mother. Bobbie unfolded the towel and took up the sandwich. "Is this the tomato relish?"

"Was he bothering you?"

"Knuckles? I'd like to see him try." Bobbie took a neat little bite, chewed and swallowed. She met Kit's eyes. "Every man's got a tiller on him, Kit. You know what you're doing, you don't have to touch it to steer."

Kit knew she should look away. Her mother's gaze hardened.

"You think it's different anyplace else? You've got no idea, you know that? No blessed idea." She grabbed hold of Kit's wrist. "This is our home. You and me and your dad when he comes back. Uncle Anders, too. This is where we belong."

Kit nodded. A moment more, and her mother let go. Bobbie looked down at the sandwich on its cloth. When she looked up again, her face was quiet.

"Off you go," she said. "I won't be long."

◖

War or no war, off-season was a peaceful time at Far Cry. No Knoxes, no crowds. You and your mother and myself and Lys, plus the odd trapper or handliner in for supplies.

I could do nothing about the war tax on coffee and tobacco, but the rising cost of spirits was another matter. Remember, Kit, the sour fug seeping from the padlocked shed? I had only a rough recipe to begin, much of it gleaned from those single-pint trips to the tavern with my father. Moonshine is a pretty word, but somehow it is always *hjemmebrent*—home-burned—that comes to mind. My occasional customers offered tips. *Gotta pour off the early drop, Viken. That last batch was foul.* By the time Prohibition came in, I was known for bottling a clean brew.

The *World* still reached us, the *Camosun* on a fortnightly schedule through the stormy months. On the day I am thinking of, you and Lys were out fishing, so it was just your mother and me in the cottage, along with the latest bundle of news. A parcel of yarn had come in too. Bobbie had made progress on the first sock by the time I worked my way down to the copy from December 6.

Of course, it could happen. How many times had I stood on a Vancouver wharf watching the ships ease round each other like dogs? In Halifax Harbour two of them had touched hulls.

Your mother looked up. "What?"

"'Large section of Halifax destroyed,'" I read aloud. "'Several hundred lives lost in explosion. Collision of munition ship with another liner cause of tremendous disaster. North end of city is in flames.'"

Bobbie's hands were still—the wool and the needles, the dark sheath of the partly formed sock. "Go on."

Waterfront buildings had been blown to pieces, fires were raging for miles. I read down through the conflicting reports from Montreal, Truro, New York. Then on to the December 7 edition, where the number of dead doubled, survivors cut and blinded by flying glass. I paused to meet your mother's eye. She nodded and I read on. "'The busy and thriving North End, from the sugar refinery to Creighton's Corner, is just a mass of broken, splintered timbers, of powdered brick and stone, and human bodies crushed to pulp or charred and blackened by fire.'"

Canada is vast, Kit, thousands of miles from its eastern to western shores. Still, we felt it. We felt the war find us at home.

◗

Kit wakes with a start, no inkling of her dream beyond a sense of something wrong. She sits up in the bow. Jimmy's perched on the aft thwart, watching something away off the starboard beam. In the dawn light, only the rim of his face is visible—jawline, cheekbone, the edge of an eye. She directs her gaze after his in time to see the eagle drag its talons across the sea.

Brown wingbeats now, the focus of the snowy head. It climbs, a sockeye kicking in its grip.

Jimmy looks round. "Did you see that?"

"You should've woken me."

"It's still early."

"It's already light." Rocking up onto her feet, she makes her way aft. "Come on."

Together they haul in the net. Salmon come flashing over the roller, but only for the first hundred feet. Then trouble: the twisting, clay-coloured shapes of dogfish.

"Careful," she says sharply as Jimmy moves to grab one.

He looks up. "I'm not stupid."

"Not the teeth, the back. There's a couple of spines."

"Oh." He peers at the dogfish. "Right."

"Grab the back of the head," she adds, but he's already got hold of it, working the mesh out of its gills.

Yard after yard comes up loaded with them, the net well and truly fouled. Kit grabs another, cursing under her breath. Ugly things. Sharks in miniature, thin through the body, not one of them longer than her arm.

There's a snaky strength in the ones that haven't been snagged long. She's feeling the strain when a big one comes writhing over the roller's turn. It arches and flips loose. She stops herself from reeling back as it lands across her boots, and then Jimmy's there with the club, one motion, one blow. She's seen him smile before, but close-mouthed and fleeting, almost a flinch. This is the first full grin. She returns it without thinking, and he bends down before her, hooking the dogfish by the tail and dropping it over the side.

Fifty, sixty more follow by the time they're done.

"Fatten up the others," he says, watching the last of them sink.

She nods and moves past him, toeing the meagre catch aside. She'll pull the stove out in a minute. Just now, she needs to sit down.

"Bad luck," Jimmy says, skimming the can along the boards.

"Could be worse. Sometimes you get sea lions after the catch, or a pod of blackfish. Sharks too, proper ones."

"Yeah?"

"Sure. Tore the net to pieces one time when I was out with my dad."

Jimmy nods. He sits down on the opposite thwart. "I heard what happened to him."

She looks at her hands. Blood on the right thumb, not much. She wipes it on her trouser leg.

"Your mother and him," Jimmy says. "Were they, you know, happy?"

The midline puddle sways between her boots. "What kind of question is that?"

"It's just, my dad never said why he was leaving. Work, right, that's why people head north. But he had work, he had the restaurant. That's all he ever did."

Kit closes her eyes. Yes, Jimmy's father had come north. She sees him on that first day, parting the onlookers, dropping to his knees where Uncle Anders lay howling on the dock. Kit crouched with her mother close by. She hadn't known a shoulder could leave its socket, had never seen her uncle in such pain. It was all right, though, the newcomer knew what to do. In moments he was standing, having put the trouble right.

"I just wondered," Jimmy says, "if maybe they knew each other before."

And there it is—sharp, like a sliver in the memory's palm. Her mother smiling up at the stranger, reaching to pat his calf.

Kit raises her gaze. At the head of the channel, a twist of steam, the distant white wedge of a bow. "Collector," she says, pointing with her chin.

"—Right."

"Well?" She looks at him. "You gonna bail?"

18

F rank had been away for two and a half years when Dan Pike motored up-inlet with the news. Out splitting wood in her slicker, Kit spotted him in the distance, his boat bucking over the chop. Her stomach dropped: manning the telegraph was part of the winter watchman's duties at Wardell's.

She ducked inside to tell Bobbie, and the two of them hurried over the headland, not a word passing between them through the rain. Uncle Anders was already down on the dock, Lys wet-furred beside him, her nose to the wind. Dan Pike eased his speed entering the bay. "It ain't him!" he shouted over the engine's stutter. "It ain't Frank!"

Kit looked to her mother for a shaky smile. As the boat drew closer, she saw Dan Pike had grown a beard, rust-coloured and thin. Harebell lay in the bow. She sat up when they came alongside the dock, white hairs showing about her muzzle and eyes.

Uncle Anders caught the line and tied it. "All right, girl," he said, and Lys jumped down into the boat to smell her mother's tail end.

Dan Pike held up the telegram. "It's for you, Missus." And again, for good measure, "It ain't him."

Bobbie reached for it. Kit opened her slicker to keep off the rain, though the paper couldn't get any more wet. Dan Pike's printing was careful, the pencil pressed hard. He stepped up among them, Lys following to sniff at his pant leg, his boots. He messed a hand in her sopping ruff.

"It's Kath." Bobbie looked up. "They're burying her tomorrow."

Uncle Anders nodded. The *Dogfish* would never get them down to Vancouver in time.

"Thank you, Dan," Bobbie added. "You'll stay for some breakfast."

Dan Pike grinned. Kit couldn't blame him—winter watchman was a lonely job. But Uncle Anders was already striding for the stairs. Shoving the telegraph into the pocket of her slicker, Bobbie shrugged an apology, whirled and hurried after him. Dan Pike couldn't hide his disappointment. "Thanks," Kit called over her shoulder as she ran.

In the store's overhang, her uncle stopped to explain. They would motor down to Duncanby Landing and try to catch a ride.

"We can't," said Bobbie. "Can we?"

Already the sound of Dan Pike's boat was dwindling. Lys pushed her nose at Kit's hip. "What about Lys?"

"We will leave her with Jess Mead at Duncanby," Uncle Anders said. "Hurry up now, both of you. Get what you need."

Back at the cabin, Kit laid her rucksack on her bed. She had only ever packed for days out on the water. She would need knickers, a sweater—what else?

"Bring a dress," Bobbie called from the far side of the wall.

Kit looked at her grey housedress hanging on its nail. There was the brown poplin rolled up at the bottom of her trunk, but the last time she'd worn it, it had made her ribs hurt.

"Here." Bobbie stood in the doorway with the yellow dress folded over her arm. No denying it was a pretty shade.

"Come on," her mother said. "Get a move on."

As luck would have it, they reached Duncanby in time to signal the *Fulmar*, a shrimp boat en route from the Kodiak to Vancouver with a laden hold. They left Lys howling after them on the dock, Mrs. Mead leaning on her cane beside her, a red-and-black men's work shirt buttoned over her dress. Her grandson Travis wore one too, rowing them out to the ship.

The *Fulmar*'s captain was a hard-faced Scot, but when Uncle Anders shouted up the nature of their errand, he had the ladder put over the side and handed them aboard. Kit had been to the inlet's mouth before; she knew well enough the rush of the open sound. To carry on southward, though, that was new. She hung at the rail while daylight lasted. Darkness fell as they entered Queen Charlotte Strait.

They only spent one night aboard, but it was a long one—no porthole in the crew's closet, Kit and Bobbie pressed together in the lower berth with Uncle Anders snoring above. Her mother's back was hot. When Kit finally drifted off, she dreamt of the shrimp crawling over each other in the hold below.

Come daybreak she was back at the rail. The mountains were there as always, a reminder of the true valley beneath them, the ocean floor. Islands and shoals, clear-cuts and burns, trees from the time before time. Nothing she didn't already know of the world, yet everything was somehow changed. When a gull banked down to rest on the transom, it wore a black ring about its bill in place of the familiar red spot.

They docked at Vancouver around midday. The wharf was heaving, men in uniform threaded throughout the crowd. Of course, Kit's father was not among them. Still, her eye caught on one man, short and powerfully built, black hair showing beneath his cap.

"Kit."

Uncle Anders was at her shoulder. They might just make it, but not if she stood dreaming on the gangplank, blocking the way.

◖

I wonder, how does the city strike a girl of fourteen who has grown up at the green edge of the world? You had known docks all your life, but nothing to prepare you for the smoky sprawl of Vancouver's wharves. You stuck close to your mother and me to begin, but by the time we reached Main Street, you were venturing a little way ahead. I was accustomed to seeing you in trousers or plain skirts. Strange, then, to watch a girl in a yellow dress move through the crowd, turning the soldiers' heads.

Down the end of the block, the tram rounded the corner into view. Bobbie looked at me, and when I nodded, she cried out, "Kit, that's it!"

It was a pretty sight, mother and daughter breaking into a run. I caught up just in time to swing aboard.

Mountain View Cemetery, away out on North Arm Road. The size of the place brought home just how much the city had grown. I do not suppose your mother expected to meet a crowd, though she may have hoped for more than three. You remember, Kit—Vi Swift in that black platter of a hat, enough feathers to build an ostrich of her own. Her hulk of a son at her side, and, standing at a little distance, the grey-haired houseboy, Wing. No sign of the gravedigger. Certainly no minister to speak a blessing over the hole.

Your mother suddenly seemed very young. Crouching at the graveside, she scraped up a handful of earth. She let it fall, then rose, wiped her palm on her skirt and shook hands all around.

"Where's your manners, Bobbie?" Vi Swift said, smiling past her.

When I stepped forward, your mother said, "This is Mr. Viken. And you needn't look like that, Vi, my Frank is serving on a hospital ship. Anders is a family friend."

Vi Swift looked me over. "Never dreamt otherwise."

Stanley seemed to see me then, or to remember. We exchanged a nod.

"And this is my girl," Bobbie added. I suppose you might have shaken hands also, if your mother had not kept hold of yours.

"She got a name?"

"Kit." Bobbie took a breath. "Katherine."

The son closed his eyes. Vi Swift nodded, something like sorrow, or at least softness, passing across her face. "You'll come back to the house with us," she said. "Have a drink."

"We won't, thanks, Vi."

All sign of feeling left the woman's face. Her hand came out quickly. You cannot have forgotten, Kit, the long, single stroke she delivered to your hair. You wore it in a ribbon that day, instead of the customary braid—another concession to your mother, I suppose, along with the dress.

"She's got your gift, Bobbie," Vi Swift said. "Remember, Stan? Jeannie had it too."

Your mother pulled you close. "You tired, Kit?"

"A little."

She gestured to a stone bench tucked under a dark-limbed spruce. "Go sit down for a few minutes."

"I'm all right."

Her hand at your back, a gentle push. "Go on."

She watched you cross the grass, winding a path between the stones. Then she turned to Vi Swift. "What happened?"

I thought Stanley would speak, but a glance from his mother shut his mouth. She took her time, nudging the loose earth with her well-made boot. "Jail."

Your mother blanched.

"Infecting a soldier," Vi Swift added. "That's a crime now, if you didn't know. I don't suppose the prison doctors were the best." She nodded, and for a moment I imagined that great shelf of feathers slipping free. "I warned her not to go out on her own," she said, looking straight at your mother. "Stubborn little bitch."

From the shaded bench, you saw your mother stiffen. You stood up as I caught hold of her arm.

"Come, Bobbie." I said it firmly, as though I was speaking to Lys. "Time to go."

❦

Kit's mother was quiet on the tram back from the cemetery. When the three of them stepped off into the jangle of downtown, Uncle Anders led them to a greengrocer's, where he bought apples and stubby bottles of lemonade. From there it was on to a butcher's for three steak pies. Kit had never seen so much meat. There was a cool smell of pennies about the place, crossed by the odd waft of rot. A picnic, her uncle announced, turning from the counter. Something to cheer them all up.

They caught the Chilco tram to its terminus, alighting where an enormous fir stood at the park's entrance, just as Bobbie had said. Together they crossed the bridge. Geese glowed white on the hemmed-in lagoon; the road, when they reached it, though, was plain grey gravel. Bobbie didn't seem to notice. A sign read: *No Autos 2–5 pm Saturdays & Sundays. To Right, Buffaloes. To Left, Big Trees.* Kit went right, assuming.

"Kit," Uncle Anders called after her, and she turned to see her mother walking the other way.

Bobbie didn't look back, nor did she look toward the birds on the lagoon. Soon they departed the gravel drive for a path that cut inland, leading on to a grove. Kit was no stranger to mammoth trees; all the same, these were a wonder. Seven towering firs—no, that one was a cedar. The forest floor lay bare about their roots, reddish. Light fell in trembling shafts.

"The Seven Sisters," her uncle said.

Bobbie stepped in close to one of the great boles, pressing her palms to the bark. "You know those Sutherland Sisters?"

Uncle Anders nodded. Kit too had seen the advertisements: Seven Sutherland Sisters Hair Grower—*Permit us to remind you that it's the hair, not the hat, that makes a woman attractive.* The photograph showed seven grim-faced women, their dark hair down to the ground.

"We saw them one time," her mother said, "me and Kath. They were sitting in a drugstore window—McDowell's, you know, over at Granville and Hastings. All seven of them crammed in there, brushing their hair. They'd pulled a good few gawkers, too. That didn't stop Kath, though. She could part any crowd.

"'Hey, girls,' she says when we get in close. If they can hear, they don't make any sign. 'Not much to look at, are they?' Kath says, loud as anything. 'Bunch of dogs next to you, Bobcat.' She gets a laugh for that, and a few dirty looks too.

"'You call that hair?' she shouts through the glass. The sisters hear that all right, you can see them brushing harder, keeping their eyes to themselves. Kath has her arm around me now. Before I know it, she's got my hat off. 'Quit it,' I tell her. 'Kath, let me go.' But she won't. She's pulling at my hairpins. 'See that? Now that's a head of hair!'

"The crowd's roaring now—the men are, anyhow—and my cheeks are burning, but I can see she's happy, she's wild with it. Next thing you know, she grabs my hand and we're off, belting out of there like we're ten years old."

Uncle Anders said nothing. Her mother stood as though she was listening, her hands pressed to the tree. Finally she turned. "Let's go."

Kit imagined they would walk back the way they'd come, maybe have their picnic overlooking the lagoon. Instead, Bobbie headed off down a broad path into the forested heart of the park.

She set a punishing pace, scarcely looking up when the occasional walking party passed. Kit took her cue from Uncle Anders, nodding politely, *afternoon, afternoon.*

When they came out at Prospect Point, Kit spotted a gazebo and hoped again that they might stop. Her mother stood with her hands on her hips, staring out across Burrard Inlet's mouth. A minute, no more, and she was off again, following the grey sweep of the drive southeast.

The road passed through copses, hiding and showing the sea. The weight of Kit's rucksack was beginning to tell; still Bobbie marched on, as though she was expected and badly behind time. Uncle Anders caught Kit's eye once or twice, but for the most part he strode wordlessly beside her, keeping her mother in sight.

At length they came to a great clearing marked by a high wooden arch. A number of parties had spread their blankets about the grounds—families small and sprawling, soldiers and their girls. Again Bobbie halted.

"The beach, I think," Uncle Anders said, coming alongside and taking her arm. He led them to a quiet spot. To Kit's relief, Bobbie sat down on the sand with her back against a log. Uncle Anders settled beside her and opened his pack. Kit gathered up the nuisance of the good yellow dress and knelt. When her uncle folded back the brown paper, she reached for her pie. The crust broke buttery against her tongue; the meat made her eyelids flutter closed. While she ate, Uncle Anders pried the caps off two lemonades and set them on the sand. Then he drew the flask from his jacket pocket and drank.

Bobbie held out a hand, tipped the flask to her lips and grimaced. Kit caught a poisonous waft of her uncle's *hjemmebrent* as her mother reached for a chaser of lemonade. Kit took a gulp from her own bottle to match, then chose an apple, cut the skin with her teeth and worked a steady circle to its core. She felt her mother's gaze.

"You were hungry, Kitty-cat."

Kit nodded, tossing the core into the saltgrass.

"You get enough?"

She nodded again. Bobbie watched her for a moment longer before patting her thighs. Kit felt her mind go soft. Crawling close, she laid her head in her mother's lap.

Waves and the high talk of gulls, the sounds of others picnicking on the green.

"Funny," Bobbie said, "I'd swear that road used to be white."

"It was," Uncle Anders said. "I believe the shells could not stand up to the mud."

"Huh." Another swallow, another whiff of the flask. "They dug them up, you know. Those shells."

"A midden."

"What?"

"Midden," Uncle Anders repeated. "That is the word."

"Geez." Bobbie laid her hand on Kit's hip. "You oughta be a schoolteacher."

"Ah, well." There was a smile in his voice. "Schoolteacher, store-keeper . . ."

"Butcher, baker—"

"Candlestick maker," Kit murmured.

"That's right, Kitty-cat, dead right." The slightest stumble in her mother's voice. Why didn't she eat something? Kit closed her eyes.

"What happened, anyhow?" Bobbie said.

"Hm?"

"The Indians, where'd they go?"

"Oh. They were moved on." Uncle Anders paused. "Those who did not die of the smallpox. The village was burned."

"Jesus," Bobbie said. "Why does everything have to go to shit?"

"Kit," Uncle Anders said, "take a walk now, see what you can find."

Kit stared at the water beyond her mother's boots. Then she rose and did as she was told.

◖

You were too old to be sent off in search of treasures, I know. For a time I thought your mother would not speak. She waited until you were a good way down the beach.

"Vi bought the place on Shore Street in 1901," she said. "Jeannie wasn't right for months before the move. Her monthlies stopped. She might've worried about a little brother or sister for me if it wasn't for the pain.

"Our room in the new place was the size of a pantry—you had to climb in over the trunk. She went down fast after that. You wouldn't think a body could get that thin. Normally Vi wouldn't have opium in the house, but she bent the rules.

"I was sixteen when she died. Vi got into the whiskey at the wake—she put her arm around me, and I guess I was lonely enough to let her. The next morning, she comes up behind me when I'm stirring the porridge and starts plaiting my hair. I remember, I held really still. She gave the braid a little tug. 'Time to start earning, my girl.' That same day, she had Stanley take the lock off my door.

"Vi taught me the basics. It was Kath, though, who really took me in hand. She was only a couple of years older, but she knew everything there was to know. 'Most of them, you just grin and bear it, but there's some can give you a real grin.' She told me how that worked too.

"It was her idea, the night we came here to the park. There was Wing's bicycle with the basket—I rode that one—and Kath had one of her own, a present off one of her regulars. 'I coulda had his pocket watch off him before he shot off,' she says to me. 'Coulda had the hand he wound it with.' I know, I know, she was hard. But not with me."

Bobbie reached again for the flask. I recall a shameful wave of drinker's fear. There would be bottles tucked away throughout the city, dry province or no, but where? Would I find one before the steamer cast off the following day?

"You have to remember," she went on, "not one in twenty was any way sober. Most of them were just clumsy, but some were cruel. 'You don't have to take that,' Kath told me. 'You just yell for Stan.' Sometimes, though, the guy would get a few licks in before Stanley could get there. There was one sonofabitch pushed a dresser up against the door and just about choked poor Bess to death. It was rare, though, that one of us got properly roughed up. There were things they could do, mind you, things Vi considered part of the service." She was quiet for a moment. "Sometimes it was just too many of them, you know. Payday."

I closed my eyes and saw the lineup of fishing skiffs, the tugboat's long, wagging tail.

"That night, the night we rode out here, we were coming off a round-the-clock stretch. CPR men, I think it was. Kath found me in my bed. I wasn't asleep exactly—I used to get these staring spells. She took my feet in her hands and rubbed them until I came back. 'Come on,' she says to me, 'I know what you need.'

"I remember, she had on this dark-green housedress. Mine was one of Jeannie's, red with little flowers. Kath showed me how to tie the skirt up in a knot to keep it from getting snagged. I guess she saw me wince when I got across Wing's bike. 'Hang on,' she says, and she takes off her cardigan and ties it over the seat. I told her no, she'd be cold. 'The hell I will.'

"I had my work cut out keeping up. Sometimes all I could see of her was the gaslight in her hair. She never said where we were headed—all I knew was it was farther than I'd ever been. And she was right, you know. It was what I needed. I remember pedalling home with the sun coming up down the end of Hastings, like we were riding toward a fire."

She looked at me then, your mother. Beyond her shoulder, movement caught my eye—you returning from your search of the sand.

Bobbie saw my gaze shift. She twisted round. "What you got, Kitty-cat?"

You know this part. You balancing your way toward us along the silvery log, standing in front of your mother with one hand behind your back. It was the largest abalone shell I had ever seen. The bowl held all the colours of sea light, private and smooth. Ah, Kit, the way your face fell when she began to cry.

I wonder, did you find your way to sleep in that clapboard hotel, sharing a bed with your mother down the corridor from my own? I know I lay awake. Being back in the city had turned over the stone in my chest and set things crawling. How many blocks to the spot where I had seen him standing beside his plain little woman? How many years since I had watched him hold up his prize of a child?

I would not have known the Union Wharf the next morning, had we not found it at the foot of Carrall Street where it belonged. There were train tracks down to the dockside, and the sheds had tripled in number and in size. Even the smell had changed, with the fleet gone over from coal to oil. I feared I would lose you both in the crowd. As we made our way to the *Camosun*'s berth, Bobbie gripped your arm with one hand and the back of my jacket with the other. Behind us the city rumbled. I was never so glad to leave a thing behind.

19

H alfway through the week and Jimmy's just about got the hang of the sail. With both water cans empty, he guides them toward shore, one eye on the silver scribble of Trapper's Creek. Kit says nothing, letting him learn. He's a quick study on the whole.

The wind lifts her hair, messing it about her face. For a second Knox is before her—*Would you ever think of growing your hair?* Some chance. There are times when she feels the ghost of her braid, but that's not the same as wanting it back.

There was no actual moment of deciding: the kitchen shears were hanging on their nail, then they were in her hand. She was alone in the cabin, her mother at the store, helping with the pre-season over-haul. Kit found herself standing before the washstand mirror. Her hair was out of its braid, not down to the ground like the sisters in the shop window, but easily down to her waist. Some three or four weeks had passed since the lady in the black feather hat had petted her. *She's got your gift.*

The shears closed by her ear with some trouble—her father was the one who kept things sharp. A hank came away. She let it drop.

That side of her head felt better. Another handful, the shears gnawing, getting through. Dark on the floor at her feet, but she wouldn't look. Another and another. In no time the thing was done. Kit shook her head carefully, then with abandon. The relief nearly made her wail.

A glance in the mirror now, a genuine jolt. She let herself look down. Was there really so much of it? She thought to open the stove door and shove it in by the fistful, but that would stink the place out. Besides, she had a creeping feeling that somehow it wasn't hers to burn.

A thrill of shame then—she must clean it up, clear away every last strand. Her eye travelled the kitchen workbench to catch on the large saucepan. All right, yes. Anything with a lid.

She was sweeping up the remnants when the door opened, letting in the day.

"Kit!" Her mother stood staring.

Kit leaned the broom against the washstand. Bobbie came at her, half a dozen swift strides. Catching her by the shoulders, she gave her a shake.

"Mama—"

"Mama nothing. Shut your mouth." Bobbie let her hands drop. She closed her eyes for what felt like forever, then opened them and looked about. "Where is it?"

"What?"

"*What.* Your hair!"

Kit looked to the saucepan and her mother whirled, snatching off the lid. "Shit." Her eyes filled up. "Shit, shit, *shit.*"

"Sorry," Kit said. "I'm sorry."

Bobbie set the lid down and took hold of her again, this time by the arm. She turned Kit to the mirror and stood behind her, bringing her face in close. Two heads on Kit's shoulders now. Together they took in the change.

"I'll be damned," her mother said finally. "It suits you."

Kit took a breath. It was true: her face looked right in its boxy new frame.

Bobbie clucked her tongue. "God knows what your father will say."

Their eyes met in the glass. What they wouldn't give to hear him shout.

◊

What use was I, the day we got the news? It was a big delivery, I remember—I did not get to the newspapers for hours. What did that matter when the thing had happened a week before? Five days for the story to reach Vancouver, another two for the steamer to carry the headline north.

Huns Deliberately Send Hospital Ship to Bottom of Sea.

"Herregud," I said. My God.

You looked up from the crates you were unpacking, you and your mother both.

"What?" Bobbie straightened and came to the counter, but you stayed where you were.

By then my eye had found the ship's name, the *Llandovery Castle.* The numbers were there also—twenty-four rescued out of 258 on board.

"Andy, what is it?"

I skimmed the front page. Torpedoed with all her lights burning, including her red hospital cross. The lifeboats shelled. I could hear your mother breathing as I turned to where the story carried on. *Survivors Accounted For.* Navy came first—the captain and other officers, purser, lamp trimmer, able-bodied seamen. A list of Medical Corps, the orderlies left to last. Four names in a row, not one of them Private Frank Starratt. I looked up into Bobbie's face. She grabbed at the counter, already going down.

The shop bell rang as we crouched beside her where she lay. Agneta Jensen stood open-mouthed on the threshold. "Frank's ship," I said, and even that much felt like a betrayal. "The store is closed."

You know what happened next—I carried your mother back to the cabin. It shames me now to find you missing from that part of the memory. I remember Lys loping ahead of me down the path. You must have been following behind.

I know you were beside me when I tried to lay her down, and she woke with a frightened cry. We sat her at the table like a doll. I boiled the tea she would not drink, cut the sandwiches she would not eat. All the while you stood at attention alongside her chair. Lys let the scraps I dropped for her lie. You know there is grief in a house when a dog pays no heed to ham.

Cry your eyes out. It is a thing people say, but it seemed as though Bobbie really would. How long before she gave in? The two of us half carried her to bed, you easing her boots off once she was lying down. It felt unnatural to leave you both as night came down, but I knew I must. Even then, on that worst of days with the worst of news, there would have been talk.

At the door, you looked through me. I laid a hand on your shoulder. "I will see you tomorrow." The best an uncle could do.

Lys lit the way, the twilight gathering in her fur. That was when I truly felt it, on the walk back to the cottage where I would never again pour a drink or turn a card for my friend. I halted. I stood with my eyes shut tight. In time I heard Lys pad back to me, felt her muzzle move over my hand.

I opened the store late the next morning, having broken a rule and taken a bottle with me to bed. Not five minutes after I turned the sign, the shop bell began to sound. Word had got round. Every sale came with condolences, a query about the widow and yourself.

The fleet came in that evening, and like their wives before them, the fishermen bowed their heads. Bill McNally was sorry for my trouble, Hiroji Yamashita offered regrets. I feared Hanevold would have something sly to say, but he and the others were decent. *Jeg kondolerer, Anders.* It pained me to be comforted in the old tongue.

That night I managed to hold firm, sitting at the table with Lys at my feet and the lamp unlit. Stumbling to bed in the small hours.

Saturday in the store on my own—a hard prospect made worse by Knox coming in to act the shocked and sorry friend. The way he sidled along the line, his hands landing on the men's shoulders. Their faces closing as he drew alongside. He just about hid his pleasure, stepping in at the counter, making them wait.

"A terrible thing, Andy."

I forced myself to nod. He had come round to the cottage the night before, he wanted me to know, but the place was dark. Bobbie must come to the house just as soon as she felt able. Mrs. Knox would only worry until she did.

Yes, I would pass the message along. I looked past him to the restless line.

"Time and tide, eh, Andy? Time and tide."

I worked until the crowd dwindled and was gone—eight o'clock? Nine? I remember walking the headland path in the dark. Again you met me at the door. She had eaten nothing, had managed a cup of tea. And you, Kit? You were all right. Lamplight at your back, your face in shadow. You were fine.

The day ended. Another one broke. Can a man go swimming when his friend has been lost at sea? By then I had made myself read the article with care. *Canadian Nurses Missing. Fourteen Sisters and 80 Officers of Army Medical Corps Have Disappeared.* Please, God, say he went down quickly. Say he did not fight.

No swim, then, and not the newspaper either. As always, I closed the store at noon. I did not expect you and your mother for lunch, though I lit the stove and tidied the cottage as if I did. I suppose I ate something. And yes, I drank. Sunday evening, the fleet gone out, a new week come around. I walked to the cabin with Lys at my heel. By then she knew we would not be going in.

◖

Kit had heard all manner of sounds issue from her mother's mouth, but never the likes of this. A high, dangerous wail. She lay on top of her covers, listening through the wall. When she could bear it no longer, she sat up, then stood. How long since she'd escaped to her little bed in the corner of the stockroom? The three years her father had been gone, certainly, but somehow it felt longer than that. Had there been fewer fights with the passage of years? Fewer bouts of making up?

Her mother's noise rose behind her. Through the window, the faraway moon. Kit couldn't seem to feel her hand on the sill; her bare feet, too, felt dead to the floor.

She pushed through her bedroom curtain. In the main room the sound was wider, the moonlight shivery, almost blue. Bobbie's net was clotted with shadows. Kit heard it then, a lower frequency than her mother's howling: the scritch and listen of a mouse. In the morning she would find a scattering of droppings, gnawed crusts on the buttered bread her mother wouldn't touch.

Her eye found the lamp. Was there sufficient life in her fingers to strike a match? She made herself. Take up the light. Turn back to your mother's room.

In the flicker of the wick's flame, Bobbie's face was a ruin. She stared at Kit, her eyes streaming, then she held up a corner of the sheet. It was the thing Kit wanted most and least: to crawl in beside her mother. To cry.

◖

Over the coming days, women walked the headland path to leave food at the cabin door. Soft-spoken Gladys Winslow brought her offering to the store.

"I wouldn't want to trouble them," she said, setting a quart jar of stew on the counter. "Venison," she added. "Sam sent a quartered buck back on the collector. He always takes the gun out in the boat."

More words than I had ever heard her speak. I picked up the jar, still warm. "It is good of you."

She shook her head. A sorry smile, and she took her leave.

I carried the stew to you that evening and the story to go with it, reasoning that it could not hurt to hear something of life in the store. At the door, you held your hand up in refusal. Over your shoulder, I caught the glint of other jars unopened, lined up on the kitchen workbench.

Boat day came again, a week gone by. With you and your mother still absent, I enlisted a couple of cannery hands to haul the week's delivery up the stairs and pile it in the stockroom however they saw fit. People would be hungry for their mail. Let them wait. I left the door bolted, the blinds drawn. Lys lay on the floorboards looking up. I bent to the first bundle of newspapers and cut the twine.

I did not see the headline at first, tucked away under the fold. *One More Survivor Found.* My vision blurred. It could not be him. How could it? I forced my eyes to clear.

Bless you, Kit, you had coaxed your mother outside to sit where the sun cut through the trees. Do you remember how we came running, Lys and I? I shook the rolled-up copy of the *World*. "They found him!" I shouted. "He is alive!"

20

Bath day, a November wind crying at the casements. While Kit stoked up the stove, her mother filled the kettle and both saucepans. Kit dragged out the washtub, and together they waited for what Bobbie called a proper boil.

When the water was a foot deep and tempered with cold from the jug, her mother stood pinning her hair up by feel. "You want first go?"

"I don't mind."

Bobbie smiled. "You're a good girl."

She slipped out of her dress and dropped her underskirt, lifted her heavy chemise. Men's long johns and grey woollen socks—everything went over the back of a chair. It was no shock, the sight of her mother's body; these days it was closer to Kit's own than ever before. The hollows above the collarbones, the small, neat breasts below. There was a softness Kit didn't have—the upper arms, the belly, the thighs. More hair down there, and darker, but Kit's was coming in.

Bobbie dipped a toe. "Jesus!"

Kit reached for the jug.

"No, it's good, it's good." Bobbie stepped into the tub, stood for a moment then squatted. Took hold of the rim and sat. "Mmm."

Kit went to fetch a flannel sheet from the trunk. When she returned, the water had coloured her mother in halves: pale above, rosy below.

"Hand me the soap, will you, Kitty-cat?"

Kit obliged, then fed the stove, then sat to wait her turn. Outside, the whipping branches, grey glimpses of sea. She could hear the waves tearing at the beach below.

Her mother held out the washcloth. "Do my back?"

Kit rose to the sound of the door's singing hinge. She felt the cold come in. Her mother spoke: "Frank."

Kit turned. Her father's beard was grizzled. His hair was still black, except at the temples, where it looked to have been rubbed through with ash. He dropped his duffle and shut the door. "Now there's a sight for sore eyes."

Kit heard the falling water as her mother stood. She shrank back out of her father's way.

"Oh, God," Bobbie said as he caught her in his arms. "Frank, *Frank.*"

In time, she held out a dripping hand. Frank too, the pair of them beckoning. Kit stumbled a little, stepping into their embrace. Her mother's warm, wet skin, her father's woollen coat. He smelled of salt air and pomade, of sour clothing in need of a wash. As ever, he smelled of drink. Kit's arms were longer—eleven years old when he'd left, and now she was fourteen. Even so, there was less of him to hold. Only one letter had reached them after the *Llandovery Castle* went down, and the nursing sister had wasted no words. Private Starratt had suffered a shock. It would be some months before he was fit to travel home.

Frank made a noise in his throat. After a moment, he stood back. "Christ, Kit, what's with the hatchet job?"

It took her a second to remember her hair. Feeling for the blunt ends by her jaw, she caught her mother's look.

"Never mind that," Bobbie said, reaching for the sheet. "How'd you even get here?"

"Got a ride as far as Duncanby and Travis Mead brought me from there. Had to pay him double, if you believe that. Lazy bugger didn't want to come out in a gale."

His wife gazed at him. "But you're here."

He nodded. "In the flesh." He took hold of the sheet where she'd draped it round her shoulders, pulling it snug. Without a word, he reached for her piled-up hair. She let him dig for the pins. Piece by piece, the dark of it came sliding down.

"Run and tell Uncle Anders," Bobbie said, talking to Kit but looking into her husband's eyes.

"Didn't he meet you at the dock?" Kit knew it was a stupid question even as it left her lips. Her father nodded but didn't speak.

"You go on anyway," her mother said. "We'll be along in a bit."

But Kit was already turning, leaving them alone.

◖

It was foolish to imagine the same man would come back to us. He could not seem to settle. He would get up in the middle of a game and cross to the window, return to take up his cards, then set them down. Watching his hands crab along the table planks, I thought of my grandfather—a man I knew through story alone. My mother was the last of nine children, the only one still at home when it came time for her father to die. He was devout in the way of a drinking man, prone to fits of prayerful remorse, but when she read to him from the Bible, he clawed at the blanket and tried to rise. In desperation she reached for a book of fishermen's tales. They were not happy stories—I remember one about the *draug*, a demon who rode the sea in a half-boat, grinning at the men he had come to drown. Even so, my grandfather quieted when she read them aloud.

I had no such tales for your father. Instead, I gave him what I believe my grandfather had truly craved. For months after he came back, I let Frank fill the glasses, reasoning that it was only fair to allow a man in his condition to take the lead. Some mornings I was too sick and headsore to swim. I woke up on the floor more than once, Lys whimpering when I opened my eyes.

You will not have forgotten the time he went missing. Your mother sent you over to me in late morning—I remember, I was propped up over the *World*, watching the newsprint twitch. I could not be certain what time your father had left.

"Have you tried the cookhouse?" I asked. "We were going to do the puttying today."

It was a lie and not. Your father and I had spoken about the rattling windows, the damp coming in—one of many jobs piling up in our minds. Oh, but the flash of hope on your face. Lys read it and came to your side.

I followed the pair of you out the door. There was a chilling rain, and the swollen boardwalk dulled our steps. While you led Lys up the cookhouse stairs, I looked down over the railing and counted skiffs. They were all there, bobbing and rubbing on the swell—long past when we should have hauled them out.

At the edge of my eye, you appeared at the cookhouse door. I made myself straighten and wave.

"Try the sheds," I called, and you nodded, already on your way down.

Could he have taken the *Coot*? Head pounding, I hurried along the back headland path. When I broke from the trees, Bobbie was standing twenty yards distant at the top of the rocks.

"Great minds," she called out.

But the *Coot* was dragged up high and dry, and there were no boot prints on the sand. I picked my way toward your mother, pushing through the brush where it grew out over the edge. When I reached her, she turned to look out.

"The skiffs are all there," I said, "and the *Dogfish*."

She nodded. "Where's Kit?"

"Checking the sheds."

"He say anything last night? Anything to make you—?"

"—No." She looked at me. It was not a time for being unsure. "No, Bobbie."

"Then where the hell is he?"

"Asleep somewhere," I said. "Sleeping it off."

Better to imagine that—your father out cold and snoring while I looked in the store and the stockroom, even followed the boardwalk to its end, checking that the manager's house was still locked. Frank had never set foot in the place, but who knows how a man might think with his brain swimming in whiskey and the night.

Better to think he was sleeping while you and your mother went from dwelling to dwelling, as far along as the last of the shacks. The two of you stood in the cannery's echoing cold, Bobbie calling, *Frank, Frank*, and then your voice, *Dad!* I joined you there, my next idea to go back for the rifle and walk the waterline trail. I did not notice Lys sitting by the net loft ladder, looking up. None of us did. We were on our way out when she barked.

Better to believe that was what woke him. That he could not have lain up there with his hand around the neck of an empty bottle, listening to his family call. His eyes were open when I reached the top of the ladder. He looked through me, then he blinked and seemed to see.

◗

Jimmy's dead asleep, head in the bow, boots pointing to the sky. Kit could reach out from where she's sitting and tap his soles. Instead, she leans back, her arms along the thwart.

The first set is holding well, the current drawing it taut. It's a clear night, the moon large and on the wane. Her uncle's lessons hold true above: the bears are there, daddy and baby; no sign of the hunter and his dog. The North Star hangs where it ought to, the Morning Star still tucked away.

In the quiet, a salmon-sized thud against the hull. Kit's stomach complains. Careful as she can, she unwraps the wood, loads and lights the stove. Leaning over the grub box, she pries up the lid and digs for the bacon. Straightens and steals a look. His long, silent form.

Seated on the thwart, she waits for the flames to settle before balancing the pan across the oil can's rim. It's a good bit of bacon Uncle Anders has given her, plenty of meat wound through the fat. Slipping her knife from its sheath, she cuts chunks against her thumb, dropping them into the hissing pan.

Smell that, will you.

Her mother, poking at the spitting rashers in the pan. Kit was setting out the knives and forks, moving around her father where he sat. He'd been home a few months, his face still thin under a winter beard.

"Filthy beasts, pigs," he said.

"Suppose so," Bobbie said.

"Eat anything."

Her mother nodded, not looking round. "Same as crabs."

Laying down her father's fork, Kit pictured herself out in the *Coot*, hauling the clicking crab pot aboard.

"Makes for sweet meat, I guess," Bobbie added.

"You wouldn't say that if you heard what I heard."

"Yeah?"

"This one fella, it was all he could talk about. Him and a couple other privates get sent out on retrieval, and damned if they don't find this big sow standing over one of the bodies, eating her fill."

"Frank!" Her mother whirled to stare at him.

He looked up, startled. "What?"

"Jesus, you can't—" Bobbie shook her head. Her eyes found Kit's. "Take the scraps out, Kitty-cat." She nodded sharply to the pail.

Kit felt her stomach shrink. It couldn't be right, could it, what she thought she'd heard? She looked to her father, but his gaze was flat.

"Kit!" her mother barked. "Now!"

"Hey," somebody says.

Moonlight, and the weight of something in her grip. Not the handle of the scrap pail, Kit realizes, but the hilt of her knife.

Jimmy lifts his head from the pillow he's made of his rucksack. He sits up, pushing back his hair. "Geez," he says, smiling, "that smells good."

◑

After we found your father in the loft, I took over the pouring again. Work helped. We set the cookhouse windows snug in their frames, mended the net loft ladder where Frank had put a boot through a rung coming down. Heavy jobs were best—he was calmer after a morning spent shoring up pilings or splitting wood. Your mother too did her utmost to wear him out. *Remind him he's home,* she liked to say. Something else she ought not to have told me. Nothing you do not already know.

By the time Far Cry was coming back to life for the season, Frank could make a fair show of being the man we had known. Of course, he had never been a man without a temper. Knox knew that better than most.

He came calling on his first night back—late May, the weather soft. We got along all right through the first game, Frank grinning whenever that knuckle slipped between Knox's lips, making the odd sideways remark. He never reminded me so much of his father as when he sat down across from the boss.

By the second game, even watered whiskey was enough to make Knox bold. He wanted to hear all about the sinking. "Is it true they were shooting at men in the water?"

Frank met his every question with a short, dark joke. I thought Knox had taken the hint, until Frank piled up the points and left our pegs behind.

"Still," Knox said, "good to see a little action after all."

Frank's face went quiet. He spread his hands over the table. "What would you know about it."

"Frank—"

"No, Andy, I want to hear what this stay-at-home fucking pansy thinks he knows about action."

Knox sat up straight. "You watch yourself, Starratt."

"Or what, you gonna shoot me with your pen? Chuck a can of fish at me?"

"We did our part!" Knox's voice came out in a strangle. "Army travels on its stomach, you never heard that?"

"Oh, I heard it. I seen what the army does to stomachs, too. Better stick to your books."

Knox glared at him. Frank turned his hand over in the lamplight. I should have said something, made some kind of joke.

"Speaking of," Knox said, "your missus has been a real help."

Frank looked up. "What?"

"She didn't tell you?" Knox gave a little twisting smile. "She's been filling in for Mrs. Knox these last two seasons. Brightens the place up no end."

I moved to come between them—a decade since the last time, and I was not quite so fast. Frank landed a punch before he was fully standing, a cut to the jaw that sent the boss over backward in his chair. Knox let out a honk like a goose, then came the thud of his skull hitting the rug. Again I wrestled my friend to the door. This time it was Lys growling, crowding close.

"Down!" I shouted. "Down, Lys!" I shoved Frank out and followed him into the night. When he turned, I pressed a hand to his breastbone. *"Enough."*

"You heard him—"

"She does the bookwork. Anything else is Knox getting at you."

He stared at me in the window's weak light.

"Are you going to let him?" I demanded.

A moment more, and he leaned like a dumb beast into my hand. I could feel his heart pounding. A gentle push was all it took—he tilted back and caught himself. Eyes on the boardwalk, he turned. I watched until he stepped down onto the path, then I let myself back inside.

Lys rose from her crouch. I drew her head against my thigh. "Good dog."

Knox had made it up onto all fours. I went to help him stand.

"That's it," he said, feeling for the table's edge. "That is *it*."

"Let me pour you a drink."

"Oh, no. No you don't." He pulled himself up to standing. "He's done it, Andy. That sonofabitch has done it now."

"Come on, Ed, sit down."

But he was walking, one foot after the other. They carried him out the door.

———

I woke in the half-light with Knox's words in my head—*That is* it.

Dressed in a sweater and trunks, I stepped out onto the porch. No signs of life about the docks, no stovepipes smoking—not even the cookhouse. The headland was awake, though, the high-up talk of ravens, the smaller birds calling for dawn. I took the back path. The tide was on its way out. I shucked off my sweater, laying it across the *Coot*'s keel. Three strides in and I dove.

A last long swim before the season dirtied the inlet—before whatever end the day would bring. I kept up a crawl for as long as I could, then fell into a breaststroke, a comparative rest. Around me, the odd flash of a salmon as the sun rose over the trees. The drag was strong when I came around Squid Island—it carried me at speed along the outer shore. All bluffs and beaches until the gouge of Deep Cut Cove. Not far from there to the island's tail end, the hard-a-port turn back to shore.

It was full morning by the time I stood up out of the sea. Bobbie was sitting on the little apron of beach. I stepped past her and took up my sweater.

"It's all right." She stood, brushing the sand from her skirts. "I've been to see him."

I looked at her. "Knox?"

"Who else?"

I did not ask what Frank had told her, or how. Perhaps you were there for the shouting, lying with the covers drawn up about your ears. Or perhaps you had climbed out your window into the dark.

"He was in the office this early?" I said.

"He was." There it was again, that glitter—as though her eyes had been cut to catch the light.

I drew the sweater around my shoulders. "What did you say to him?"

She smiled at me, your little mother. "Wouldn't you like to know."

21

C hanged or not, your father still liked to talk. Sometimes, after a drink or two, he would get started on his time away. He had been glad of the transfer to the hospital boat. He was still an orderly, but at least he was changing sheets and dressings at sea.

"We used to take the walking cases up on deck most afternoons," he told me one night. "A group of us had a running game of Crown and Anchor going—just penny stakes, patients and orderlies, a few of the crew. Denny Coates, he was this private with the Patricias, belly wound. Funny-looking kid, yellow hair standing straight up on his head. Field stubble, he said his mother called it.

"There were some who thought he talked too much. This one day, he really gets going. It's all about the mud, how you're walking along the duckboards with your coat soaked through—he said it's like wearing a dead body, that coat—and suddenly the guy ahead of you stumbles and just kind of tips into the muck. So then you're down on your knees, holding your gun out like a branch, but the poor bastard, Phelps, it's Phelps, he just watches you as he sinks. He doesn't even reach up to grab hold.

"The group's gone quiet now, some of them looking at their shoes and some looking sour at Denny, and Denny's breath is coming fast. I get up to help him out of his chair.

"'Aw, c'mon, Frank,' he says, reaching for the dice. 'I'll play, I'll play.' But I just stand there until he takes my arm. He was slow, shuffling back, but that didn't keep him quiet.

"'You'd think you wouldn't do it,' he says to me. 'You'd look out on that mess of shit and bodies and say no chance. The joke of it is, if all the time there's somebody telling you what to do—get up, brush your teeth, clean your rotten stinking feet, stick your head up so the fucking Boche can shoot it off—you just . . . do as you're told.'

"We were at the ward door by then. I closed my hand on the knob and pushed, and then the nursing sister was with us, asking did Denny get some sun, and was he all right in himself. 'Oh, yes, Sister, A-one. Just a little tired.'

"Next morning, Denny didn't make it out to sick parade. It must've been coming on to noon before I could check on him. I took a pack of cards with me, in case he was up for a game. I thought he was sleeping, but he opened his eyes when I sat down. Big black pupils—I guess the bluebird had been round to give him his shot. Sister Nolan, she was all right. No cards allowed on the ward, but she'd turn a blind eye.

"Old Maid was about all Denny was up for, and even that didn't last long. I was used to him looking pale, but he'd gone a really bad colour. Shiny, you know? I figured I'd let him rest, maybe put a word in the sister's ear, but when I'm clearing up the cards, he grabs hold of my arm.

"'You like swimming, Frank?' No kidding, that's what he says.

"'Sure,' I tell him.

"'We got this swimming hole,' he says. 'Down past the back field, down in the trees.'

"'Yeah?' I say.

"'My dad, he tied a rope around one of the branches. He put a knot in it, you know, so you can keep hold. You get a run at it, see, you swing way out and—'

"'Splash.'

"'Yeah,' he says. *'Splash.'*

"I started working his fingers loose, not rough or anything, just one by one. He watches me do it. Then he looks me in the eye.

"'Hang on, Denny,' I tell him. 'I'll be right back.'

"Sister Nolan was over on the far side of the ward. She was changing this soldier's dressing—I remember thinking what a big bugger he was, must've been twice Denny's size. I stood behind her until she turned round.

"You could tell from across the room. It didn't look a thing like sleep. Sister Nolan felt for Denny's pulse, but that was just for show.

"It was me and her got him ready. He'd bled to death inside— you could see it, like somebody'd put the boots to him. Only so many stitches a man's guts can hold. Anyhow, everybody who can get out on deck does, walking cases and a few of the ones in chairs, orderlies and nursing sisters and MOs, whatever crew can be spared. Even the captain shows his face. He says a few words, and then over Denny goes."

He was quiet then, your father. "Not like the old man," he said finally. "Remember that, Andy, the way the old man went down?"

I nodded, and he nodded back.

"Yeah." He looked away. "Denny had way more of a drop."

❨

Opening day, 1919. Kit rushed through Sunday lunch, left her parents and Uncle Anders still eating and made her way down to the docks. Her first season as boatpuller on her father's skiff. She'd already checked the gear that morning, but she went over it all again.

By the time Frank showed at the top of the stairs, all but a few stragglers had already tied onto the towboat's line. Watching him descend and make his way along the boards, she saw he'd had more to drink than he should. He wasn't staggering, just a familiar deadness to his step.

At last he stooped to loose the painter line from the cleat. Stepping aboard, he set the skiff rocking, like a man unused to the sea. They were the last to tie on, her father leaning out to snatch up a branch of the tow line with a cold whip of spray, fumbling as he fed their painter through the eye. When Kit reached for the line, he gave her a hard look. Did she think he couldn't secure it himself, the man who'd taught her every bowline, every hitch?

She felt lighter once they were under way. Frank sat on the forward thwart, eyes fixed on the doubled column of skiffs before them, the bare bones of fifty swaying masts. They left the bay behind. Kit glanced over her shoulder, catching sight of the cabin between the trees.

Coming round Squid Island, they met the falling tide. Kit looked overboard into the deep, then forward to Dawsons Landing, a smudge on the far shore. They steamed across the current, the mountains watching them go. Her hair lifted away from her face, evening light along the chop, the touch of it still warm.

In time Walbran Island loomed to portside. The towboat came round, her tail of skiffs beginning to curl. Southwest into Schooner's Pass—a chance for Frank to look behind him, maybe even give her a grin. Instead, he felt for the painter line. Wait, she would've told him if he'd asked. Let the others stagger their nets across the narrows; down around Welch Island the fish will be running hard.

But her father braced himself, so she did too. Without a word, he pulled the knot undone. Gripping the painter line, he grabbed for the tow line's branch where it hovered above the surface, stiff with strain. Inch by inch, he let the painter line out through the branch line's eye. The skiff's bow nosed outward on the towboat's wake. He waited, then one-two, he let go. The painter snaked on the water as they bucked and spun away. It was a clean drop. Drink or no drink, he'd managed it well.

Kit moved forward to take up the oars. Shifting to the aft thwart, Frank nodded toward the island's shore.

By the time night was falling, he had them tucked into a cove. "All right. This'll do." And when he saw the look on her face, "You got something to say?"

She shook her head, but he was already standing to let out the net. Pulling on the oars, she watched the jacklight bob away on its float.

The current wasn't nearly sufficient to keep the set taut—that would be her job for as long as her father chose to sit there smoking. Between sessions at the oars, Kit dragged out the stove, lit the kindling over a nest of wood shavings and set the coffee to boil. The coals were sufficient to warm a can of beans, and there was Bobbie's bread. Her father said nothing when she handed him his plate. She rowed a little, pulling the net straight, before taking up her spoon.

When the washing-up was done, she dozed, head on her knees, hands clamped on the oars. Tree boughs whispered from shore. Her father's smoke drifted through the dark. There came the sound of him striking another match, unscrewing the cap of his flask. After a time his weight shifted as he stood to piss, the sound making her want to go herself. She'd hung over the side in his presence a thousand times—he'd held her by the hands when she was small. Tonight, she felt shy of him, as though he were a stranger in the boat. She'd go in the bailing can when he was asleep.

Head down, her own damp breath. He would've woken her, she supposed, but as it was, she roused herself every so often and straightened the slackening net. Two hours, three. In the end they brought in a dozen fish.

"Yeah, all right," her father said, though Kit hadn't uttered a word.

She rowed them back out into the pass. Jacklights dotted the way down-inlet. Catching the tide on the turn, she pulled hard to starboard, stroking away from the pack.

The darkened shore slid by, the mountains like wading giants. Drawing past Dawsons, she made for the skinny scrap of Carmen Island. Her father said nothing. She could almost forget he was there.

Slipping into the narrows along the island's inland shore, Kit saw there was no one there. The passage was often overlooked by both fish and men. Sometimes, though, on a gentle night, the salmon came driving through.

"You go on," Frank said when they'd made the second set. Taking a seat, he nodded toward the bow. She made her way past him and lay down.

No rain and none coming, a crescent moon stamped on the blackness, a nail-hole pattern of stars. Waves tongued the boards. Kit drifted off. From time to time she opened an ear, then an eye. He was still sitting on the aft thwart—the coal of his cigarette, the glint of his flask.

The next time she stirred, the stars had withdrawn into the pre-dawn gloom. She looked down the length of her blanket, over the hills of her boots. Her father hadn't moved. No smell of coffee, the stove unlit. *Morning*, she was about to say, when something bumped against the hull.

She heard her father inhale. On the second bump, he let out a cry.

Kit scrambled to her feet. "What is it?" But she could already see thrashing along the length of the net, the corks jumping. "Dad!"

He was hunched over on the thwart, his eyes shut tight. No time to find her apron, let alone tie it on. Hunkered low, she made her way hand over hand along the gunwale. Beside him now, she saw he was shaking. She pushed past him and bent to the net.

Fins sheared up through the surface, just as suddenly dropping away. Salmon sharks, heavy through the body, as long as, or longer than, a man. Were there ten of them? Twenty? Each strike at the net sent a juddering through her bones.

She hauled the net in over the roller, picking frantically as she went. In her haste, she made a mess of those fish that were still whole. At one point a shark drove in hard, yanking her so she barked both knees on the gunwale, almost going in. "Dad!" she shouted again. A wild over-the-shoulder glance showed him still frozen, his back to the scene. She braced herself and hauled again.

It was sun-up by the time she dragged the jacklight aboard. Her arms threatening to fail her, she bailed. The last of the sharks swirled like mist about the hull, then dropped away. Kit stood trembling, the net beside her, a torn and sodden heap. Only then did her father move. As though shoved from behind, he tipped forward onto his hands and knees. Crawling away from her through the ruined catch, he curled like a dog in the bow.

Her clothes were wet through—she ought to have lit the stove. Instead, she sat staring out over the stern.

She came back to herself when the collector swung into view. Archie Paul had taken over her spot as pitcher; even at that distance she could read the happy length of the inlet in his wave. All that time she'd spent waiting to be out with the fleet; now she longed to travel back to the previous season, climb aboard the collector and pick up the pew.

"You guys okay?" Archie shouted.

Kit stood up, unstable on her feet. "My dad's not right," she called. "We need a tow."

Her mother said not to fret. If Frank wasn't feeling steady in the boat just now, there was plenty of work to be had on shore. Kit tried to imagine her father pitching or gutting, lined up with the women along the washing table.

"Net boss," Bobbie announced, back from the office for the midday meal. "What do you say to that?"

Frank didn't answer.

"Paulson's useless. He's had his card marked since last season." Her mother set down the stew plates, one, two, three. She took a seat. "Knuckles saw sense for a change."

Frank nodded slowly, as though to himself. Bobbie had forgotten the bread, so Kit rose to carry it over on the board.

"Butter," her mother said, and Kit fetched the dish.

Now they were all in their chairs. Kit cut slices and buttered them. Her mother was already eating, her father yet to begin.

"Saw sense," he said.

Bobbie nodded, swallowing. "Doesn't want to lose his winter watchman, does he. No way Andy could hold this place together on his own."

"No," Frank said. "Don't suppose he could."

"There you are, then."

Her mother took another mouthful, and her father took up his spoon. It was all right now. It would be all right.

Of course, if Frank wasn't going out with the fleet, neither was Kit. There was nothing to stop her handlining, though, when she wasn't needed in the cabin or the store.

"You keep close to shore," her father said when he saw her heading out with her line.

She turned, her hand on the doorknob. Behind him, Bobbie's expression: just play along.

"I mean it, Kit," he said. "No more than a stone's throw."

22

The following winter was hard, ice on the boardwalks to welcome the new decade, snow heaped up dripping among the trees. All around them came the crack and whoosh of branches giving in. Then rain. Some days Kit had to bail within minutes of pushing off. Still, she dragged the *Coot* out whenever the swell allowed.

Lys came with her if the downpour wasn't too heavy, Uncle Anders joining them from time to time. No point asking her father along. When she left, he'd be awake but still lying in bed—resting up, Bobbie had taken to saying—or sitting red-eyed and silent with a mug in front of him, or, on better mornings, already bent to some job. Her mother smiling for both of them. *Go on, Kitty-cat. Catch us a big one.*

Spring came around, with catalogue seed packets and the occasional day of sun. The dress her mother had ordered in the dead of winter finally arrived. Kit was starting supper when Bobbie tried it on. A certain blue, it turned her mother's eyes into flowers.

Frank took a moment to speak. "Who'd you buy that for?"

"What do you mean? You, you idiot."

Standing at the kitchen workbench, Kit laid a fillet on the plate of flour.

"Found something to spend my money on," her father said.

"I work in the store."

"And the office."

"Yeah, and the office."

Another fillet: this side, that side, set aside.

"—Cozy."

"Jesus, Frank, we've been over this."

"You've been over it."

"Yeah, all right, forget it. Just forget it."

Kit didn't mean to look round. Her mother was fumbling with the buttons, tearing free of the sleeves. The dress dropped down around her. Suddenly pale in her underskirt and chemise, she stepped out of it and kicked it aside.

◗

It was late, you and your mother gone home, the bottle getting low. I cannot say what brought the story to your father's mind—perhaps it was always there, waiting to be told.

It was his turn to deal, but he pushed the cards aside and began rolling up a smoke. "We were a week out of Halifax," he said. "Summer's night, smoothest crossing yet." He licked the paper, pressing it closed. "That's the thing about a U-boat. You never see the fucker coming."

I nodded, nudging the matchbox his way.

"There was one hell of an explosion. *Boom.* Lights out all over the ship. By the time the order came to lower the boats, she was already sloping to the stern. We'd had the drills, but it's another thing altogether when the bow's sticking up like a mountain under the moon. Still, they managed to lower a couple on the port side, and we got five down on the starboard. Two of them were swamped right off, I guess, so we were five all told.

"The nursing sisters were in one of the boats, fourteen of them, and maybe the same number of men. I was rowing hard away when I caught sight of their boat, lowered all right but caught in the ropes and bashing against the ship's hull. It'd gone dark an hour since, but the moon was getting on to full. You could see the sisters' white veils, and a couple of them were white all over—already in their nightdresses, I guess. I was too far off to tell which one was Sister Nolan, but that's how I picture her, you know, shivering there in her nightdress, the lifebelt round her waist. Lot of good it would've done. They say the men in the boat broke their oars trying to keep off the hull. When they finally got free, they could only drift into the suck of the ship going down."

He was quiet then, taking up the matchbox and setting it down. He laid his unlit smoke on top of it, like a body on a bed.

"It was fast," he said. "Can't have been ten minutes between the torpedo and the last sight of the *Castle*'s bow. We were maybe fifty feet off the hull by then, far enough to keep clear. There were a couple dozen of us in the boat, crew and Medical Corps. Men were yelling in the water all round, swimming or hanging on to whatever scrap they could find. We rowed to man after man, hauled seven, maybe eight fellas aboard.

"It's true, you know, what they said in the paper. Those sons of bitches were running men down in the water, on the lookout for our boats. They caught our bow on one of their passes, flipped us like a coin.

"All right, I'm thinking, I'm done. And then it's like my arms remember—hey, Frank, you can swim, Andy taught you. So I do, I swim until I hit something—a board, a piece of decking maybe—not much to hold on to, but enough. I could hear the U-boat plowing back and forth through the wreckage, and men shouting. An hour or so, maybe longer. I don't know.

"There wasn't too much of a sea, no big drops. I was up on a swell when I caught sight of one of the boats. It had a sail up—to catch the moonlight, I'm thinking when I spot it. I wasn't thinking right.

"Anyhow, there's no way I can get any speed up dragging that board along, so I let it go. Crawl, that what you call it? That's what it felt like too. I crawled up and down, up and down, every rise showing me that sail. That was when they started shelling. Water spraying up all around, and the next swell I manage to climb, that lifeboat is gone.

"Time to go. That's what I'm thinking, roll over, Frank Jr., slip away. Only right about then something bumps against my leg. You know when you're cold, the way you feel something when you can't? *Bump.* Like that. *Bump.* Denny, I say to myself. Little Denny Coates with his field-stubble hair come bobbing back up from the deeps.

"I know—I said I wasn't thinking right. So, yeah, another shell hits a ways off, the sea going up like a fountain and Denny bumping up against my dead legs. That was better than what I thought next, though. Sharks.

"Now I really want to sink. Fuck it, I'm telling my arms, just quit. And that's when I see something rising up on a swell. I thought it was a raft. Then a door. Two doors, actually—a wardrobe, floating high on its back. Cedar, you know, a good one. Officers' quarters.

"Christ, Andy, I don't know how I even caught hold of the thing, let alone climbed on. I guess I would've made some target, laid out there like a starfish. And what if the buggers did shell me? Even with that wardrobe under me, I was more than ready to go.

"I can't say how long it took, but in the end things went quiet. The sharks did come, right about sun-up. Blues, I'd say, long and fast. One fin, then three or four. For a while I counted a dozen—and that was only looking one way, my cheek flattened to the wardrobe door. They were close, I know that. I had an idea that I might touch one if I could make my hand let go. Anyhow, they moved off. Bodies in the water, I guess. I don't know, by then I was dropping in and out."

I watched him take up his smoke and light it. "How long?"

"Well, it was sundown when I caught sight of her, I remember the colour in her sails. The *Snowdrop*, how's that for a name."

"Twenty-four hours," I said.

"Hm? Oh, no."

"Near enough."

"—No. They found the others on the morning of the twenty-ninth. The captain's lifeboat was the only one left. No, it was after that they sent the ships out."

I was not sure I had understood. "Two days you were out there?"

He nodded. Then, after a moment, "And two nights."

It took three months before the doctors judged your father well enough to travel home. I know only scraps.

"Ever hear of soldier's heart, Andy?"

"Something about bravery, is it?"

That made him laugh. "You could say that. You get it on the battlefield mostly, heart starts hammering and won't stop, feels like you're gonna die." He paused, eyes on his cards. "Sometimes you get it later on, when there's fuck all to be scared of. Pounding and pounding, piss yourself, shit the starched sheets. Christ, I'd like to meet the bugger dreamt up shocking a man who's had a shock. That's right, Sister, hook him up—*gggzzzzzzzt!*" He gave me an ugly grin. "If that doesn't work, stick him in a bath, hold him down. Best thing for a man who's been lost at sea."

I looked at him then, my friend. Kit, there are troubles in this life for which there is no comfort. Every word that came to me was wrong.

◗

It wasn't the first time her father had yelled in his sleep. Usually, Kit could hear her mother talking him down—*Wake up, Frank, you're home now, you're home*—but this time Bobbie cried out too. Kit stood up, the air cold through her nightdress. Fumbling for the matches, she lit the lamp.

"Wake up!" her mother shouted. "Jesus, Frank! *Frank!*"

Kit took a breath and dragged her parents' curtain aside. Bobbie was sitting up in bed, holding Frank twisted against her, pressing his face to her chest. "It's all right," she said to him. "You're all right." Meeting Kit's gaze, she gestured with her chin.

Kit turned and hurried to the kitchen shelves. Two inches left in the bottle, no more. Setting the lamp on the kitchen workbench, she tucked the whiskey under her arm and reached for a glass—wait, her mother might want one too. One inside the other. Kit held the glasses to her breastbone and took up the lamp.

By then Frank had curled down to hide his face in his wife's lap.

"Here." Bobbie shoved a catalogue off the bedside crate.

Bringing the light close, Kit saw the mark around her mother's eye.

"It's all right," Bobbie said again. "He didn't mean it, did you, Frank. He did it in his sleep."

Her father said nothing. Bobbie lifted a hand to stroke his head. Kit stood watching, night around them in the corners.

Her mother looked up. "Do me a favour, Kitty-cat."

Kit nodded.

"Fetch another bottle from the store."

23

Thursday morning, the collector come and gone. Passing the net over her knees, Kit checks for tears. Meantime, Jimmy cooks the last of the bacon, soaks hardtack and fries it in the fat. Gulls drift in to ride the scented smoke. Sea lions yelp from the rocks as he divvies up the meal.

He has a careful way with a fork, each bite seemingly full of thought.

"What?" he says, glancing up.

Kit drops her gaze. "Nothing. It's good."

Later, when he fills the kettle to do the washing-up, she takes it from his hand. "You go ahead, get some rest."

"Yeah?" he says.

"Yeah."

When she looks again, he's lying on his side, his back shaped to the starboard hull. One arm folded beneath his head, the other across his chest. The slightest rise of his breath.

The smell of boiling sea water settles her to the task. She fills the basin and adds a mugful of cold, gets soap in the rag and goes at

the mugs and plates, the forks and the blackened pan. Setting everything to drain on the lid of a crate, she tosses the washing water
over the side.

She sits down, resting her eyes on the fins of a far-off pod of
blackfish, the occasional breach. From here she can enjoy their black-
and-white beauty. They're headed down-inlet, away from the nets.

The sun is fierce, tilting off every facet of the sea. Her back aches
as she eases down to lean against the thwart. Pulling her hat down
over her face, she's assailed by the familiar smell of dirty hair.
A private, degenerate odour, it clung to her father more often than
not over the previous year. Whiskey, Kit was used to, rum and fish
and rolled cigarettes, but in the past his hair had always smelled of
beeswax and gingerbread, Kingfisher's Best pomade.

She takes another breath before pushing the hat back and drawing
in the clean sea air. Wash your hair every fortnight, her mother had
insisted, brush the oils through each night before bed. These days Kit
only ever drags her fingers through her dark mop. The whale tooth
comb is broken, and Bobbie took the hairbrush with her when she left.

It still surprises her, the thought of her mother here one day, then
gone. How had Kit missed the signs? Maybe because her parents had
always fought. It was worse, though, admit it. Dark and darker since
her father came home from the war.

Jesus, Frank, I married you, didn't I? I chose you.

Her mother's voice through the bedroom wall. Kit rolled over
in her cot.

"Yeah?" her father said.

"And when you fucked off and left us, I waited for you!"

"Is that right."

"Yeah, go on, have another drink."

A lucky thing about growing up small: at fifteen she could still fit
through the little window above her bed. It was pouring, but that was
all right—she'd taken to keeping her slicker in her room.

Night eyes open wide. Her hands anticipated the soaked, low-hanging branches; her feet recalled where the trip roots lay. The world swayed about her, wailing. *Only forest sounds.*

Finally, the clapboard corner of the store. She felt along the wall, stepped up onto the wooden walk. Was that when Lys heard her? The dog's nose came out damp and seeking the moment Kit cracked the cottage door.

Inside the store, she hung her dripping slicker on a nail. No point feeling for the lantern—they both knew the way. She often slept best on the little pallet, the dog tucked against her belly or pressed along her back. Lys nudged her now as she knelt down, a tongue at her cheek, a waft of meaty breath. "Get off, you. Lie down."

It was an animal sound that woke her—rain, yes, but also an urgent rhythm on the far side of the wall. She sat up in the blackness and felt for Lys, already standing beside her. Something was choking. No, someone was being sick. Her father, his voice inside the sound. Lys gave a low growl, and Kit brought her mouth to the dog's ear. "Hush, Lys. Down."

Outside, her father retched until there was nothing left. A shudder as he slumped against the wall. Kit closed her eyes and pictured him, back to the boards, face buried in his hands. Her mind began to work as if at one of the calculations Uncle Anders set—weights and measures, revenue and cost. How long to see if he came to his senses and staggered back to the cabin? She could hold still and hope, or she could creep out into the downpour, cut through the trees and double back, pretending to have come looking from home.

"Frank?" Uncle Anders' voice. "Is that you?"

"Who else."

"Are you all right?"

"Hell yeah, right as rain." Her father laughed at that, a sound akin to the one that had shaken her from sleep.

"Come on, we will get you home."

"Fuck that." A small commotion. "Fuck off! I mean it, Andy, leave me alone."

Quiet for a stretch. Rain.

"What is the trouble?"

"Trouble. Same trouble as always. You marry a whore—"

"All right, Frank."

"What. You never liked her, not back then."

"That was a long time ago. Bobbie has been a good wife to you."

"What would you know about it?"

"And a good mother to your girl."

"If she is mine."

"Frank, you only have to look at her."

Was that when Uncle Anders realized? Lys not in the cottage when he'd woken, four ears listening from the far side of the stockroom wall. Kit heard a note come into her uncle's voice—brassy, false.

"Come, we will have a game."

"—You got anything to drink?"

"What kind of question is that? I am the storekeeper."

"Ha. Yeah."

A sound like shifting sacks then, as her uncle helped her father to stand.

"Perhaps some bread and butter too. You need something on your stomach."

"Yes, Mother."

When they were gone, Lys sighed beside her. One then the other, they lay back down.

◗

Your mother had never been one for a springtime swim. I thought at first it was you sitting on the little beach—something about the way she had her knees drawn up, her hand resting on Lys's head. As I swam closer, she came clear—not a woman who had woken early, but one who had been awake all night.

I got my feet under me, waves lapping at my chest. "Everything all right?"

"Oh, you know." She took up a stone and held it. "You think he's getting worse?"

"Worse?"

"I don't know, his . . . temper."

I was warm with exertion, but in that moment I felt the ocean's cold. "Has something happened?"

"No. Well, yeah. He broke my comb."

"The one your friend gave you?"

A flicker of alarm. "My mother. My mother gave it to me."

"Of course," I said. "My mistake."

She glanced away. "It's just, when he used to get angry, it would burn off. We burned it off together, you know."

I looked down. My body wavered in the water's bend.

"Nowadays he can't even manage it half the time. I'd say it was the drink, but—" She gave a short laugh. "Oh hell, forget it. It'll pass."

I searched my mind in silence.

Bobbie tossed the stone aside and stood. "How many?" she said.

"—What?"

"Lengths."

"Oh. Six."

She started back up the rocks. "Better get on with it, then."

I watched her climb, then turned and plunged away. Swimming clears the mind, you know that, Kit. Not that time. Your father's voice was with me. The harder I swam, the louder it got.

"Don't look at me like that, Andy. Maybe you can live like a fucking monk—"

"All right, Frank, I am not looking like anything."

"Okay, but you don't know. The smell on those wards—Christ, it was worse than the cannery any day. You're peeling back dressings and draining off pus, or cleaning shitty sheets, or shuttling DIs up to the ward." He shook his head. "*Dangerously Ill.* That's Medical Corps for damn near dead.

"Come nighttime, if you're not on the wards, you're laying there in your cot, listening to some other bugger pull himself off. I'm just saying, by the time you get overnight leave, your balls feel like they been beat with a club. I never went the first time, all the others but not me. The second time, though, I'm saying to myself, why not? If I wear a safe and treat the girl nice, where's the harm?

"It was this row house, you know, curtains in the windows, drinks with the old lady in the parlour, three or four girls upstairs. I took my turn. Not straight after the fella in front of me—the girl, she wanted a minute to clean up. Then she calls out to me, 'All right, pet, in you come.'

"She was a pretty thing, blond out of a bottle but who gives a shit about that. She had on some kind of slippery robe with flowers on it. Never mind how many she's done before me, she gives me this sweet little smile and drops all those flowers to the floor. She's got a dark bush, like I figured, and a stand-up pair of tits, but it's like I'm dead from the neck down. All right, I was pissed, but I was still on my feet, and anyhow, that never troubled me before. She tried her best—oh yeah, she tried out her bag of tricks. Finally, she just lays back and lights a smoke. 'Never mind, love,' she says to me. 'Takes us all different ways, this mess.'"

24

It was the usual mayhem when the boat came in. Your father was helping ready the week's shipment to be loaded after the freight had come off. Bobbie was with me, lining up sacks and barrels for the count. There was a pig that week, do you remember? The children crowding round the beast on its chain while you quieted Lys, making her sit. Crates of chickens, too—all part of the cookhouse order that was piling up.

Knox left the *Camosun*'s master and came to hover at my side. "Where the hell's the cook?"

"Chu Ming," I said.

"What?"

"The cook."

"Yeah, all right, where is he?"

"How would I know?"

He glanced around. "Kit, fetch the cook for me, would you? There's a good girl."

You looked to me, and I gave you a nod. Lys followed you to the foot of the cookhouse stairs, but by then Chu Ming was on his way down. He looked different in his street clothes, no more apron and little white hat. He had a carrying basket in each hand.

"Shit." Knox hurried to meet him. "Chu, what's all this?"

Chu Ming shouldered past him, his eyes on the boat. You know how hard it is to keep a cook up here, Kit—you have seen a dozen come and go. I have told Knox he should hire a kitchen helper, but the best he will do is to get a girl from the shacks for the washing-up. *I'm paid to manage this place, Andy. We're all buggered if I take my eye off the ball.* Or as your father liked to say, old Knuckles would rather shit a dime than share it.

"Good luck," I said to Chu Ming, and he nodded as he passed.

Knox came to stand beside me, hands on his hips. "Lazy bastard. We're better off."

I looked at him. "Without a cook?"

"You need cook?"

Yes, Kit, it happened like that—the voice first, then the man. He must have passed Chu Ming on the gangplank. I turned around— Anders Viken, storekeeper, sixty-one years old. I stood there in my body. He had aged, of course, but he was the same.

"What," Knox said, "you're a cook?"

Lo Yim nodded. "Good cook."

Knox barked a laugh. "You hear that, Andy? Must be my lucky day."

I wonder, Kit, did I manage to speak?

"Right, then," Knox said. "You better come with me."

In the moment before following, Lo Yim met my eye. It was then that I understood. I had been waiting—every steamer, every unknown boat that had come alongside the dock. I had been holding my breath for years.

A man with a divided mind has no place on a busy dock. A cask of nails, I think it was. I tripped and went down without warning, caught myself with a straight arm and heard the shoulder go.

The sound of a grown man screaming is a frightening thing. I saw the shock of it on your face, then your mother's, the pair of you like flowers nodding close. Lys barked back the crowd. Frank got hold of her scruff—I could hear him yelling at her to lie down.

Then another voice. "Okay, okay."

Lo Yim knelt beside me and said something in his own language. When he touched me, I feared I would lose consciousness. He was quicker about it than Mrs. McClintock had been. He held my arm as though listening to the bones. Stillness, then movement—a great key clunking in its lock, and the shame of an unbridled cry.

Is there any peace like the end of pain? While you and your mother helped me sit up, Lo Yim rocked back on his heels and stood. By then Lys had slipped your father's grip. She pushed in close, bringing her nose to mine.

"Okay," Lo Yim said again, and before I could speak, he moved off into the crowd.

"All right, Viken?" Knox now, using his manager's voice. He stood in front of me, looking down.

"Fine," I said. "I am fine." And I was. Mrs. McClintock had sent me to bed with a bottle, but no one had taken a boot to my ribs this time. Besides, it was boat day. I made a sling of your mother's shawl and got on with my work.

We kept busy for the rest of the afternoon, you and Bobbie sorting the delivery while I saw to the special orders and doled out the mail. The shop bell rang and rang. Even so, your mother could tell there was something amiss. Did I speak too little? Too much? Either way, she asked me back to the cabin when I locked up after the last sale. The first bush beans were ready, and you had trapped some fair-sized crabs. Far too much for the three of you to get through.

"Thank you," I told her, "but I am tired."

That night I drank my supper, forgot Lys's scraps until she sat by the icebox and cried. Come full dark, I dragged a chair out onto the

porch with my good arm. No lights in the long body of the cookhouse, not even in the cramped cook's quarters at the end. Lys
would not lie still. She tracked back and forth along the boardwalk
until I rose and went indoors.

The next day was Friday, the fleet due in. I told myself Lo Yim
would be run off his feet. Then came the Saturday lineup, the store
so hectic there were moments when I almost forgot. After closing,
the drinking crowd stood round the counter until all hours. Again the
cookhouse lay dark when I finally stepped out into the air. I stood
facing it, God only knows how long.

Late to bed, early to rise. A stumble along the headland path,
a few sore, half-hearted lengths in tight along the shore. Half day in
the store, then the same family lunch and drawn-out game as
always, the habit kept up even though Frank was no longer going
out on the evening tow. I let myself match him, drink for drink. I do
not know when you and your mother went home, only that I woke
in my clothes, lying face down across the bed. Whether I had
stepped out to watch the sleeping cookhouse, I cannot say.

Monday morning was quiet in the store, your mother gone to
the cannery office, your father mending nets at the racks. I suppose
you were out in the *Coot*, dropping your line. I drew up my stool and
stared unseeing at the week's accounts. *Add up a column, Anders.
Set the figures down.*

How long before the shop bell shivered? I stood up quickly and
felt my head spin. "Good morning."

He closed the door and came to stand before me. "Good morning, Anders Viken."

I had not expected it somehow, the sound of my name on his lips.
I suppose it frightened me. "I trust you are well," I said. "You and
your family."

A flicker of his eyes. Then the click of Lys's claws as she came trotting up from the stockroom. Lo Yim held a hand down for her to

smell. From there she nosed at the leg of his pale trousers, pausing at a bloody smudge.

"Leave it," I said. And when she looked up at me, "Sit." I made myself meet his gaze. "What can I get you?"

"I make soup," he said.

"All right."

"No barley."

"Barley." I tried my legs and found them willing. Walking back to the grain barrels, I felt him follow. Then Lys, judging the sit to be over, click, click, click. I took up the scoop. "How much?"

He looked about. "You have sack?"

"In the stockroom. Twenty pounds all right?"

He nodded, and again he followed me, Lys at his heels. "I carry," he said when I bent to the sack, but I held up a hand. Alone, I would have taken care to bend my knees. As it was, I heaved the sack onto my good shoulder like a young, unthinking man.

My back bore it. I walked to the front and dropped the barley by the door. "Is that everything?"

He watched me for a long moment. Then he spoke. "I am well. My family one son. My son well."

I moved to put the counter between us.

"This son, my brother son," he said. "My brother die in ninety-eight. My brother son, my son."

The surprise must have showed on my face.

"My brother wife, my wife," he added. Then, "One more son."

What did my face do then, Kit?

"This son too small, too soon." Lo Yim glanced away. "My brother work hard before he die. I work hard, my wife work hard. My son also." He left a pause. "Every day I work in kitchen. Sometime I sit down, eat something, smoke, drink tea. Sometime I hear men talk— how make money, go home China or stay. One day one man, he talk about the North. This cannery close now, this cannery China House

burn down, twenty-nine men dead. I listen now—I know this life.
This cannery good, he saying, Far Cry, he take a crew there. China
House okay, manager pay late sometime, but he pay." Lo Yim nodded
to himself. "Then he say about Far Cry store. This good too, same
price for Chinese, even whiskey, same price. Storekeeper Norway
man, name like Viking. This storekeeper, even his dog like Chinese."

I made a sound, a sort of hollow cough.

"My wife dead four year," Lo Yim said. "My son grown." His eyes
rested on me. "I come north."

The shop bell made me jump—Agneta Jensen, leading with her
basket, her skirts noisy with starch.

"Good morning, Mrs. Jensen." I spoke the words loudly, like a
man unused to the stage. Then to Lo Yim, "I will put it on the cookhouse account."

He lowered his gaze. Lys pressed in close as Lo Yim moved to the
barley and dropped into a squat. He closed his arms around the sack,
hoisting it and rising in one. Youth in those thighs, despite the years.
Agneta Jensen stood back out of his way with a tight little smile. He
moved past her and was gone.

◗

Kit was used to her father coming in at all hours. Still, she roused at
the sound of the cabin's front door. As her eyes made sense of the
dark, she heard the bed boards creak on the far side of the wall—her
mother rolling over, sitting up. Then her father's boots, one—a pause
while he struggled with his laces—two. The deeper groan as Bobbie
shifted to the edge of the bed and stood.

"Found your way home, then." Her mother's voice was close by.
She would be leaning in their bedroom doorway, arms crossed.

"This mine?" her father said.

"You're lucky to get anything."

"Is that right."

Cold bully beef and mash left out on the kitchen workbench. Kit had tried to cover it with a bowl, but her mother had said to leave it. Kit had gone to sleep with the thought of mouse tracks across her father's potatoes like sign in the snow.

The sound of the plate dropping onto the table, the chair scraping out. "What's up your ass?"

"Like you give a damn."

"Didn't I just ask?"

Bobbie moved then, her tread light even when she was angry. Kit lay still. Her mother was near the table now. She might even sit down.

"What?" her father said.

"What. Fucking Orpha Knox, that's what."

"What about her?"

There, the second chair.

"How many years have I been listening to that woman whine? When I do get a word in, it's always what can I say to cheer her up."

Frank made a sound, his mouth full.

"She was going on about her brother's wife getting the china with the fucking bells of Ireland pattern. I don't know, I just snapped."

"Yeah?" Frank said. "What'd you say?"

"—*Poor baby.*"

Her father's fork hit his plate.

"I did," Bobbie said. "*Poor baby*, just like that."

Her laugh was quicker, but his was loud and long. Kit listened. She let her eyes fall closed.

"Christ," her mother said finally. "She threw me out, you know that? That wheezy little voice of hers. *I think you should go.*"

"Bitch," Frank said. "I don't know why you bother."

"—I have to."

"You eat shit in this life, it's shit you get served."

Silence. Kit's eyes opened again.

"You're kidding me, right," her mother said. "Who the hell do you think keeps them sweet?"

"Keeps who sweet?"

"*Them!* Fucking Ed and Orpha Knox!"

"Ed? Fucking Knuckles can go fuck himself."

"But that's just it, isn't it? He can't go fuck himself or we'll be out on our asses."

Kit sat up in her cot.

"Bullshit," her father said.

"You think so? You think you'd be net boss if it wasn't for me making nice? You think you'd have any kind of job?"

"Shut up."

Kit pushed her covers aside and stood. The window was partway open; she shoved it wide and climbed up onto the sill. The softest of drops. Moss under her feet, moonlight.

"I've been carrying you, Frank Starratt!" her mother shouted. "I've been carrying your sorry ass for years!"

Kit curled forward, hands over her ears. Then she came back to herself and ran.

25

It was all I could think of—Lo Yim had come north, Lo Yim was in the cookhouse, just up the hill. The *søvngjenger* led me through the following few days. Nights were harder, no matter how late I sat up alone or with your father, how many glasses or games. Come mid-week, I woke in darkness from a dream of the kind I had not suffered in years. Lys shifted at the bedside. I sat up and held my face in my hands.

After a time, I lit the lamp. My pocket watch lay alongside Neville's dictionary—nearly three o'clock. Why not swim in the dark? My shoulder wasn't bad. There would be the cold light of sea fire where the current was slack, and I could leave the lantern burning on shore.

I dressed quickly, stepping out of my smalls and making a rag of them, wiping the dream's mess away. Summer or not, the night air would be cool. Trunks and a work shirt, jacket and boots. I lit the lantern and blew out the lamp.

Lys slipped past me through the door. I stepped out after her onto the boardwalk's wooden drum. "Let's go, girl." No sooner had

I spoken than I froze. Away up the hill, a light was burning—life on the little porch at the cookhouse's far end. I watched as the figure that was Lo Yim set down his lamp and opened the door to the coop. My hand felt for the serrated wheel on my lantern, turning the wick down and out. Beside me, Lys made a huffing noise out her nose.

"Come," I said quietly, stepping back inside.

How do you keep a secret in a town built of echoing stages and stairs? No lantern, for starters, no boots. I bent to undo my laces. Lys whined when I held a hand down to stop her following, but she did not bark.

Still the lamp burned above me, the coop door open, the treed night crowding round. The moon had set. I blinked in the blackness. Eggs—that would be the story. How many people knew I got mine from your mother? Even if they did, hens are not always inclined to lay. All right, then, bootless and begging eggs in the small hours. You see what happens when a man moulds his thinking to his desire.

Gradually my field of vision grew—the smudged line of the boardwalk, the deeper shadow of the stairs. Down a dozen steps, then several soft paces before the turn to the long flight up.

Barefoot, a body feels the spring in the wood. At the top, I fought the urge to look back. I knew what lay below—darkened dwellings, the black hulk of the cannery jutting out over the bay. Stepping close, I fitted a hand to the doorknob and felt it give.

I walked a straight line between the long tables to push through the swinging kitchen door. Passing the stove, I felt the breath of the banked-up coals. Now I was through to his quarters—which is to say, the closet where he slept. A cot and a trunk, a door standing open, letting the lamplight through.

He had heard me coming—the set of his back told me so. With measured movements, he reached for his basket and closed the coop door. In their boxes the chickens murmured. Lo Yim took up his lamp and turned. I wonder, Kit, are you old enough to know how the mind stacks up time? He turned on the cookhouse porch and he turned in the South Arm Cannery and he turned on the moonlit sand. His face was all planes and shadows. It was the face I knew.

Lys was close by the door when I let myself back inside. She gave a woof, and my hand found her head. "All right, girl." It would be light in an hour. I would swim as though it was any other morning, keeping to the stream's cleaner current, length after length. For now, though, I stood breathing in the darkness. I felt into my jacket pockets, each hand closing around an egg.

◗

Kit's got a hunch about Borrower's Bay, so Jimmy's been rowing for a couple of hours, following the northern shore.

"The storekeeper," he says, though neither of them has spoken for miles, "he doesn't like Chinese?"

"What? What makes you say that?"

"He sure didn't want me in his shop."

"That's not—" She shakes her head. "Your dad, I guess Uncle Anders blames him."

"He's your uncle?"

"Not by blood. But yeah."

Jimmy nods, his expression closed.

"I'm telling you, he likes Chinese just fine."

He looks past her, hauling on the oars. "I guess you've never seen a parade."

"Me? No."

"Me neither until I was six." The crease in his forehead deepens. "They came down Pender Street, hundreds of them, I don't know, maybe thousands. The Asiatic Exclusion League. Smashing shop windows, setting fires. We stayed upstairs with the lights out. They were beating up anyone they could catch." A hitch in his rowing. He glides, then brings the oars down.

"What happened?" Kit says.

"They moved on to Powell Street, scare the shit out of the Japanese too. By the time they circled back to Chinatown, the police were there. Took a few hours to clear the crowd. My father went down at first light to board up the restaurant window and sweep up the glass. They came back again later that day, but the streets were roped off and there were constables standing guard. He carried bricks up to the roof anyhow, in case the crowd broke through. Everyone did. My mother was laid up in bed, but I helped."

Kit pictures it: a small boy, a single brick. She thinks of what she might say. "That was a long time ago."

He gives a short laugh. "You think so? They already put up the head tax here—used to be Chinese had to pay fifty dollars to come in, now it's five hundred. There's still plenty pushing for an Exclusion Act like they've got down south."

"What, you think they'll send you back?"

"Back? I was born on Pender Street, Kit."

"—Sorry."

"They want to stop any more of us from coming. Keep us from marrying, having kids." He shakes his head. "My mother, she wanted me to finish high school, but what's the point? I'm lucky I had work in the restaurant. Nobody will hire you outside Chinatown. Doesn't matter if you're Canada-born."

"I'm sorry," she says again. Then, "You like fishing, though."

He makes a sound through his nose. "Yeah," he says finally, "I do."

◖

The boat came in again, Lo Yim and myself working on the dock alongside everybody else. So far as I know, he did not once look my way. Nor did he leave a light burning that night.

The dreams came as they had when I was young, but instead of a shadow, or even poor Marta Laarsen's brother Nils, the visitor was Lo Yim. During the days, my mind made a surface, choppy then smooth. By the time he returned to the store, I had myself just about under control. My heart kicked at the sight of him stepping through the door.

He gave a nod. "Anders Viken."

Your mother stood up suddenly on the far side of the shelves. "Hello."

Lo Yim did not startle.

"Bobbie," I said, "Mrs. Starratt, have you met—"

"Lo Yim," she said. "Not properly." She came forward, dusting her hands off on her apron. He shook the one she held out. "Settling in all right? Cookhouse up to scratch?"

Again, the neat little nod. "Cookhouse fine."

"Good." She glanced at me, smiling.

"What can I get you?" I said.

A pause before he answered. "Molasses, two can."

"I'll get it," your mother said, already turning.

He watched me then, and I him. The blood roared in my skull. Bobbie was back in moments, the cans stacked up against her chest.

Lo Yim took them from her. "Thank you." And to me, "Cookhouse account?"

"Yes." He didn't move. "Is there something else?"

He looked down on the cans and up again. "You know good beach for clam?"

"You bet," your mother said, "Burntwood Bay." Then, before I could think, "We could take the *Dogfish*."

"Oh, I—"

"Low tide's around seven. What say we meet on the dock after supper?" She looked to Lo Yim for a nod, then back to me. "Come on, Andy, Kit'll love it." There was a lightness in her voice I had not heard for some time. "We might even get Frank to come along."

❏

Kit wasn't sure she'd heard her mother right. It was true that the tide would be perfect, but they hadn't taken the *Dogfish* out in over a year.

Bobbie picked up Frank's supper plate, laying a hand on his arm. "What do you say? Dig a few clams, have a few drinks?"

He didn't look up. "You're keen."

"Come on, you love a good chowder." And after a moment, "We'll keep in close to shore."

He stood up quickly, forcing her to take a step back. "Suit your-self. Some of us got work to do."

When the door slammed behind him, Bobbie shot Kit a quick, afflicted smile. There came the sound of Frank splitting wood. Kit looked down at the last rasher on her plate and didn't want it. She rose and carried her things to the basin, took up the kettle to fill it from the jug.

"Leave that," her mother said. She grabbed the empty water bucket in one hand, the scrap pail in the other. "Fetch the shovel, Kitty-cat."

Uncle Anders and the cook were already waiting in the *Dogfish*. True to Bobbie's word, they ran along not far from shore.

Burntwood was more of a dip in the coastline than a proper bay. The beach was vast, ridged and glimmering in the sinking light. A string of logs marked the high-tide line, except where the trunk of a great cedar lay crossways over the flats, its crown point-ing out to sea. Her uncle brought them in as close as the prop allowed. Kit dropped anchor and watched it catch. Lo Yim shucked off his slippers, the rest of them working free of their boots. While Kit and the men rolled up their trouser legs, Bobbie gathered her skirt and tied it in a knot, showing her legs to the knee.

Lys quivered in the bow. "All right, girl," Uncle Anders said, and she leapt overboard.

Lo Yim was nearly as fast, one hand on the gunwale, a spring and a splash. Standing in the shallows, he steadied the hull and offered Bobbie his hand. Kit thought nothing of it, her mother smiling as she gripped the cook's hand, that girlish hop into the sea.

The beach was spurting, crowded with clams. Kit's shovel scraped shells going down. The sand was heavy with mud, but she warmed to the work, turning over cut after cut while Bobbie pushed her fingers into the sludgy piles. Uncle Anders and Lo Yim were somewhere on the far side of the cedar's dividing line, but Lys dug furiously beside her, jumping back whenever a squirt hit her nose.

First came the rosy littlenecks, then the bone-white butter clams, siphons tonguing the air. As ever, mother and daughter made a good team: within an hour, both bucket and pail were full. They would sit the clams in sea water when they got home, leave them to pump out the grit. It was a trick of her father's. *See that? Buggers clean themselves.*

Bobbie held a hand out for the shovel and drove it in to stand beside their haul. She glanced across at Kit and grinned. Without a word, she began walking in place, stamping the sand beneath her from solid to soup. Kit copied her, and together they began to sink. Lys stood rigid, then dropped back on her haunches, tail going like mad. Bobbie gave a yip, and that made it a race—who could tread herself deeper, be the first to be mired to her knees. Eyes on the shuddering slurry around her calves, Kit pictured the clams retreating, tunnelling for their lives. The mud breathed up sulphur laced with an iron tang.

"Geez, Kit," Bobbie said. "You have beans for supper or what?"

Did anything come close to her mother's laugh? It loosened Kit's limbs, made her long to pelt across the sand. But before that, there was the work of dragging her feet out, thrill building to panic before the suction finally gave way.

"Oh-ho," Bobbie cried. "No you don't!"

But Kit was already stumbling free, running toward the water's edge. A line of sandpipers skittered in the shallows, lifting when she thundered close. Lys came romping, and Kit plunged after her, splashing and rearing, the pair of them wild. A glance over her shoulder showed Bobbie watching, waves lapping at her ankles, hands on her hips.

Away down the beach, Uncle Anders had come back into view. The cook too, both men bent over their shovels, hard at work. The tide was on the turn, the sun disappearing down the inlet's curve. Lys woofed and Kit took her meaning: a good stick floated within reach. She scooped it up and sent it arcing through the air.

26

A drinker portions off part of his mind. Where is the nearest bottle and when will it run dry? How many glasses, and when is it safe to let go and lose count? Now a new pocket was taking shape in my thoughts. Where is Lo Yim? When will I catch sight of him next?

Days passed, and the *Camosun* came round again. I knew the yeast belonged with the cookhouse order—the store stocked smaller cans. All the same, I set it down on our side of the dock. Yards away, Lo Yim was overseeing his part of things, calling directions to the men Knox had lent him to carry the cookhouse delivery up the stairs. I bent my head over my order book, following his voice through the din. The thrill of him speaking quickly, at home in his own tongue.

Later, when the mail was sorted and the delivery packed away, Bobbie sent you next door to make coffee. I had set the can of yeast to one side. Now I took it up, study of a man finding something amiss. *Must be part of the cookhouse order.* I said the line over in my head, then spoke it aloud. Next I would sigh and step out from behind the counter—only your mother was already untying her apron.

"I'll run it up there."

I have an image of myself standing there, clutching the can to my chest.

Bobbie looked at me. "Unless you want to."

"No, no. I have had enough of stairs for one day."

She smiled and took hold of the can. I followed her out—not right away, I was not that far gone. She was halfway up the cookhouse stairs by the time I eased out onto the porch with my broom. I did not know your father had come up from the cannery for coffee. How was he so quiet walking up behind me? It was his custom to shake the boardwalk as though he was his own father's size.

"Where's she going?"

If I jumped, he did not seem to notice. His gaze was trained on your mother, now nearing the top of the stairs.

"A mix-up with the delivery," I said. He made a low sound in response.

Above us, the cookhouse door swung open, and Lo Yim stepped into view. He greeted your mother, receiving the yeast with what may well have been a smile. I suppose she smiled too—at such a distance, how can a man be sure?

We stood side by side, your father and I, watching them pass the time of day.

"Chatty fucker," Frank said.

Thankfully, their talk reached an end. Lo Yim carried his yeast inside, and Bobby turned. Catching sight of us, she gave a cheery wave. I lifted a hand in return, but your father wheeled away, striking off down the headland path.

You leaned out the cottage door. "Coffee's ready. Where is everyone?"

◗

The sky darkens an hour before it should. While Jimmy rows, Kit tents the canvas across the bow.

"Here's good," she says when they pass Devil's Club Head. Jimmy ships oars and rises. Together they let out the net, feeding lengths over the roller to follow the jacklight's drift.

The rain comes when it's ready, a dark lake overturned. Kit drops to all fours and crawls in under the shelter. Twisting to rise on one elbow, she can just make out the droplets jumping around Jimmy's boots.

"Come on," she calls.

He crouches, his face in shadow, running with rain. *For chrissakes,* her father would say, *you wanna drown?*

"Come on!" she shouts, and this time he obeys.

Commotion then, close quarters in the dark. Jimmy wriggles over on his back, his legs jutting out beside hers into the rain. Kit digs for the rolled forms of the aprons. Together they curl up to shake the oilskins out over their knees. It's one thing to get wet, another to lie like a dead thing, letting the deluge have its way.

Quiet then, aside from the din of the rain. Jimmy keeps to his side of the keel line, his arm pressed against hers. "Almost as packed as the China House in here."

"Come on, it can't be that bad."

"You ever been inside?"

"Not for a few years."

"And not when it's full."

"—No."

"Put it this way, if it was a boat, it wouldn't float. Actually, scratch that. The ship my father came over on, there were hundreds of them in the hold."

She tries to imagine it: a young Lo Yim crushed in with his countrymen, breathing the airless dark. Jimmy shifts beside her. The skiff lifts and settles, the heavens sluicing down.

"My mother hated rain," he says.

Kit blinks, and her own mother shines in the dark—standing among her plants, hands upturned to a summer shower.

"She was sick a lot," Jimmy adds. "My little brother, he was stillborn. After that she was never very strong."

Kit glances his way. She can't make out his expression. "She didn't have any other kids?"

"No. My dad was good to her, you know, he looked after her, but . . ." He pauses. "What about you, any brothers or sisters?"

"Nope, just me. It's strange. It's not as though my parents didn't—" She catches herself, her face growing warm.

"They were happy," Jimmy says.

"—I don't know about that."

"But they loved each other."

She stares into the darkness. "Yeah."

◖

The counter can be a comfort, you know that, Kit. But it can also be a trap. Knox had come in for a half pound of Orpha's pastilles and stayed on to complain. I was thinking of ways to nudge him off home when the bell sounded. He turned to watch Lo Yim step inside.

"Boss."

"Afternoon."

Lo Yim stood with his hands clasped behind him. "I hear squid by island."

"Squid Island, you mean?" Knox grinned back at me over his shoulder. "Sharp, this one. Doesn't miss a trick."

"Okay I take rowboat tonight?" Lo Yim glanced my way. A moment's quiet, my head going under, the sea in my ears.

"What the hell for?" Knox was saying as I surfaced. "Plenty of bait in the gut shed."

"Not for bait. Chinese like."

"Christ, not fussy, are you?"

Lo Yim left a pause. "Okay I take boat?"

"Long as you're up to get the breakfast."

Lo Yim nodded, then lifted his eyes to mine. "You have jig?"

I would have led him to the spiky bundles, but Knox looked round again, a smirk on his face. "Buggers'll eat anything."

"Back wall," I said, and Lo Yim turned.

Your father came round that night. One game bled into another, me listening past him for the splash of Lo Yim's oars in the bay. It was after midnight before I could get Frank to go home. Lys had taken herself over to the rug by the bed. She got to her feet when I snatched up my trunks.

"Lie down, girl." She sat and watched me change. "Lie down, Lys. Stay."

A crescent moon showed through the trees. I made myself walk along the back headland path—it would have been madness to run. On the beach, I stuffed my shirt under the *Coot* and kept to the pebbles, leaving no sign.

Out past the headland, the water grew foul. I plowed across the shithouse drift in my hardest crawl, praying enough clean current lay ahead to wash the stink away. The inlet was calm, the tide a constant pull. In time I drew even with the island. If he was there at all, he would be around the far side—the jigging said to be best in Deep Cut Cove. I stroked along, not far from the outer shore. At last I rounded the rocky bluff.

The cannery rowboat sat at the heart of the cove. Lo Yim had lashed one jacklight to the bow and another to the stern, laying light over the water to call the squid up from the depths. With its two glowing eyes, the boat might have been the head of a great water snake, its body going on below.

He must have expected me to come in a boat. When I got close enough for him to see I wasn't a seal, he let out a laugh. "You swim all the way?"

"So you see."

Squid swarmed about the boat. I bobbed up to hang off the side, their small, soft bodies glancing off mine. Lo Yim drew up his jig and plucked the last of his ghostly catch from the tines. Ink flowed down his fingers. Like a boy, I tucked and dove, passing beneath the rowboat, parting the slippery school. I surfaced on the far side and gave a tug on his oar. "Come on."

No one would see—the island a blind between us and Far Cry, the inlet open wide. Even so, he turned the wick out on both lanterns before taking his seat.

There was sea fire as we drew close to shore, flashing blue-green off my arms and Lo Yim's rising oars. It is a good distance, as you know, even for a true swimmer such as myself—a man of my age ought to have been tired. I stood up in the shallows with the years running off me. Grabbed the rowboat by its bow and hauled it ashore.

"Careful you shoulder," Lo Yim said, but I was already lifting him, carrying him up the sand.

Later, when the moon had set, I sat beside him. In the darkness, I dared to speak. I began by telling him about the cove on Smith Inlet. "Like this one," I said, "only smaller, not so deep." The trouble was not the place, I told him, though the place was hard. The trouble was that I was alone.

I told myself he was listening. I went on. Come the close of season, he could take the steamer south, but only as far as Port Hardy, say, or Port McNeill. I would fold up my life at Far Cry, and early one morning I would row away. Each night he would look out for me from the government wharf. I would be there within a week.

You might wonder if I spared a thought for your mother and father, for you. I did, of course—you were my family. But Lo Yim was my love.

In the blackness, I laid out the story of our life. We would row until the world felt far enough away. We would find a cove and build a cabin, fish and trap and live. When I fell quiet, Lo Yim made a noise in his throat. Then he kissed me, something I took to mean his assent.

27

There had been sun for a week, not a spit of rain. Bobbie tested a drooping bean plant with her finger, then crossed with her watering can to the tap.

"Damnit, your father said he'd check the line."

Kit saw the silvery trickle. She set down her trowel. "I can take a look."

"That'll take ages." Her mother stood with her eyes closed. "You mind doing some hauling?" But Kit was already reaching the bucket down from its hook.

It was a chore she knew in her bones; they had lived ten years in the cabin before Uncle Anders talked Frank into running a second waterline. The salal bushes had overrun the clifftop walk, so she took the rocky way down, jumping the last few feet to splash in the incoming tide. She followed the stream a little way inland to make sure the water would be sweet.

A full bucket on the way back meant thinking through the familiar climb—no problem if she didn't rush.

"Yeah." Her mother's voice reached down to her from the yard. "I do all right."

"You get rot?"

It took Kit a moment to recognize Lo Yim's voice—known to her after the clamming trip, but out of place.

"Sometimes," Bobbie said. "Not this year, fingers crossed."

"Good sun," Lo Yim said as Kit crested the cliff. He feathered a hand across the onion greens. Bringing his fingers to his nose, he smiled.

The smallest of movements on the path beyond. Kit set down the bucket. Her father was leaned up against the cedar snag.

"Here's Kit with the water," Bobbie said to their visitor. "Would you like some tea?"

Kit watched her father push off the tree. "Sounds good," he said, walking toward them.

"Frank," Bobbie said. "Lo Yim's come for a look at the garden."

"So I see."

For a second no one moved. Then Lo Yim nodded—to Bobbie, to Frank, a quick glance round to Kit. "I go."

"Not on my account, I hope," her father said.

Lo Yim stepped past him. "Work to do."

As he disappeared down the path, Kit took up the bucket and moved into the yard. She poured it out, half over the tub of onions, half over the beans.

"Kit's had to haul water," her mother said.

Her father gave no reply. Kit turned and made for the cliff, the empty bucket in hand. Behind her, Bobbie spoke again.

"You gonna fix that line?"

"That depends," Frank said. "You gonna make me that tea?"

——

Kit cooked supper that night, frying sliced potatoes and rockfish while Frank sat at the table and drank. Bobbie worked in the garden until Kit called her in. Not a word while they ate. Kit cleared away, set the kettle to boil and carried the jug out to the tap. It took forever to fill, a gap she closed by dreaming herself down the rocks and into the waiting *Coot*. Back inside, she filled the basin. Her mother passed close behind her, reaching a catalogue down from the kitchen shelf. Lighting a second lamp, she sat on the chesterfield to turn the pages. Time for Frank to rise and make his way to the cottage for a game. Kit waited. In the window, she watched him fill his glass.

Her father was the one yelling. It was her mother's voice, though, that first reached Kit through her sleep.

"Frank, you're not thinking right."

"Don't fucking tell me how I'm thinking!"

"Christ, I give up."

"Where do you think you're going?"

"I need some air."

"You meeting him?"

"What?"

"Get the old man pissed and meet up for a fuck in the bush?"

Her mother laughed, a sound like something tearing. *"Get* you pissed? Last time I looked, you didn't need any help."

"You watch it. I mean it, Bobbie, watch your mouth."

"Frank, listen to me—"

"You're meeting him."

"Frank! He's not even here, he's gone out to the island again for squid."

"Oh yeah? And how do you know that?"

They were the last words Kit heard clearly after she dropped down onto the moss. The sound followed her along the night path, though, both of them shouting now.

◊

Lo Yim had borrowed the cannery rowboat again. As fortune had it, your father did not come by for a game. I made myself sit up reading until midnight, then rose to change into my trunks.

Lys heard boots on the boardwalk before I did—she barked as though it was a stranger's fist at the door.

"Andy!" Knox shouted. "Open up!"

I pulled on my trousers and crossed to take hold of her by the scruff. "Hush, Lys. *Hush.*"

I opened up to find Knox in his nightshirt.

"It's Orpha," he said. "I need help."

I left Lys inside and followed him down the boardwalk. "Should you fetch Bobbie?" I said as we reached their front door.

He looked round. "She won't have her. Some quarrel or other, I don't know."

How long since I had set foot in the manager's house? There was a smell of camphor about the place, and mould, and something nameless. The windows shut tight as ever against the bay.

"This way." He led me past the polished staircase, down the lamplit hall. I could hear the wheezing long before we reached the end.

The air in the back bedroom was oppressive, the fire stoked up hot. Orpha Knox scarcely made a ripple under the covers. Her face was pale with a greasy shine, two troubling dabs of pink at her cheeks. Her eyes, too, were bright. She looked at me as though I had come to deliver her, or perhaps to do her in.

"Heeeee. Heeeee." That breathing of hers, a sound to upset the soul.

I thought of your mother, the times she had talked of sitting with Orpha, her tricks for soothing the manager's wife. "Bring the kettle," I told Knox, and off he went. I sat down on the bedside chair. "Now, Mrs. Knox, Orpha. You cannot seem to catch your breath."

She tucked her chin, initiating a violent cough. Without thinking, I did as my own mother would, laying my hand at Orpha's breastbone, a touch both light and firm. Holding her gaze, I made a slow, soft show of breathing. *In. Out.* The fit was over by the time Knox returned.

"Hang it over the fire," I told him.

"Right you are."

"Steam helps," I said to Orpha. "Is that right?" This time she nodded with no ill effect.

The bedside table bristled with bottles and jars. "Anything here for you?" I asked, gesturing to the collection. "Anything help?"

She watched me. "Heeeee."

I reached for the nearest bottle, a cloudy, yellowish mixture that smelled strongly of pitch.

"Dr. Pollock gave her that one," Knox said.

A slight shake of her head. Was it my imagination, or was her breathing a little quieter? She held up a finger and thumb, two inches apart. I picked up one of the jars and showed her. No. I chose another. Yes, almost a smile.

Most often a rub'll do the trick. I might have directed Knox, but I doubted he would have the touch. Besides, there was no time to waste in trying—Lo Yim was probably already out bobbing over Deep Cut Cove.

Strange to draw down the covers in front of a woman's husband, undo her nightdress at the neck. Steam billowing from the kettle, I twisted off the lid, scooped out a fingerful of peppery-smelling salve and rubbed it across the top of her chest.

She closed her eyes. *"Heeeeeeee."*

Knox watched, intent and wordless, as her breathing softened to a hiss. After a time I met his gaze and nodded. Stilled my hand and stood. Orpha's eyes flew open, the cough erupting again. She snatched at my wrist.

"There now," Knox said. "We're not going anywhere."

There was no clock in the room, no way to watch the time dissolve. I closed my eyes and saw Lo Yim draw up the jig, the squid all arms and eye-light, shooting ink against the hull. Time and again Orpha quieted, only to start like an infant when I withdrew my hand. That barking cough. Knox smoked his pipe and fed the fire and dozed, jolting awake now and then to offer reassurance from his chair. Finally, she slept.

Knox rose to pad after me down the hall. In the entryway, I wasted a moment more. "You cannot keep bringing her here."

How to read the look he gave me? He drew open the door. "Night, Andy."

"Good night."

Back at the cottage, Lys smelled me over, pushing fretfully at the fingers still greasy with salve. I crossed to my pocket watch on the bedside table—a quarter to three. A sensible man would have forgone the long swim to find his love had come and gone. But Kit, I was not tired. Not until I had run along the path and churned across the current to round the island's rocky shore. Until I had floated on my back in Deep Cut Cove, counting to one hundred in my head. Never mind, I told myself, righting my body in the swell. I would explain, Lo Yim would understand. We would arrange to meet again.

◗

It's their best morning yet, the sky mussel-shell blue, a fish for every yard of net they bring in. In his dark apron and boots, Jimmy has the look of something shaped by the sea. He works the pick like she taught him, gripping the mesh close to a twisting sockeye, loosing it where it's snagged about the fins. When the fish drops to the boards, he catches her watching. No smile, no frown, he simply holds her gaze. A tail slaps against the roller, and she looks away.

Later, with the catch off-loaded and the skiff riding high, she lies down while Jimmy rows. The sun wakes her, her feet sweltering in their boots. She sits up, blinking. He stands with his back to her in the bow.

"What is it?"

He turns, one hand shielding his eyes. "You ever go ashore just for the hell of it?"

Behind him, gulls surf the updraft along a staggered series of cliffs.

"Here?" she says.

"I don't know. Anywhere."

"The towboat'll be around this afternoon. You'll be on shore two whole days."

"I know."

"—I thought you liked being in the boat."

"I do." He stands there, rocking on the swell. "I just feel like stretching my legs."

Kit is quiet. In her mind, red light spills along a lengthening beach. "Okay," she says. "I know a place."

◑

Your father looked bad the next morning—worse even than the time I found him wide-eyed and silent in the loft. Not so quiet now. He threw the door open, the bell jerking on its wire.

"You seen her?"

"Bobbie?"

"Yes, Bobbie, who the fuck else?"

"Shut the door," I said, and to my surprise he did.

"She went walking." He came to stand at the counter. "I don't know what time." Then, "I'd had a few."

I nodded, saying nothing.

"We had it out," he said.

"Had what out?"

"Her and that fucking Chink."

"—What?"

"The cook. Ling Long, whatever the fuck."

"Lo Yim?" I almost laughed. "Frank, you have it wrong."

"You think so?"

Lys came shambling, nosing the stockroom curtain aside. Still alive to the sound of anger in her master's store.

"All right, girl," I said, and then the curtain moved again. You stepped out and stood watching.

"You seen your mother?" Frank demanded.

You shook your head, a motion that seemed to make the shop bell ring. Of course, it was the door. Knuckles Knox, looking like a man with a mess to clean up. "Anybody seen the cook?"

◗

Like his father before him, Jimmy is first out of the boat at Burntwood Bay. If he thinks to hand Kit out into the shallows, the look on her face has him think again.

Barefoot, trousers rolled, they drag the skiff up on shore. The fallen cedar is still there, stripped of much of its bark, shoved by winter storms to lie alongside the others above the tide. They walk some yards apart. In time Jimmy branches off onto dry sand. He slows a little, reaching the shifting slope of sea-worn stones. At the top he climbs over the great cedar and two or three lesser logs, progressing into thigh-high grass. Around him, blue-headed lupines sway.

Gone to relieve himself, more than like. He's been decent about that from the start, standing with his back to her when she's taken up with some task. As for the other, he waits, as she does, until his boat-mate is asleep. Only once did the rocking of the skiff rouse her as he hung his backside overboard.

As he moves out of sight, Kit turns to face the inlet, the clam-packed reaches of mud. There are tracks on the flats; a family of deer has moved through. He's right, Jimmy, it's good to stretch your legs. So why is she standing here? Why is she sitting down?

One year gone. Mother and daughter laughing their guts out, stomping down into the sucking mud. A good day, no matter where it led.

Her father was out front of the cabin when they got home, his chair tilted back against the wall.

"Geez," Bobbie said, "we got some haul."

He tipped forward, four chair legs on the hardpack now, elbows on his knees. Kit set down the heavy bucket alongside her mother's pail, the two of them standing as though for inspection, him staring at their mucky boots. Did Bobbie know then? Had she already made up her mind?

What if Kit hadn't climbed out the window that final night? What if she'd plugged her ears and waited through whatever it took for the trouble to die down, then come out to find her mother sitting at the table in her nightdress. She might have found the right words. She might at least have put the kettle on and made tea.

She hears Jimmy walking back, pebbles like rain, then the shush of his footsteps on sand. When he crosses the strip of sun-crisped seaweed, bladderwrack pops beneath his heels. She looks round, her mind taking a moment to catch up. He comes carrying lupines, a proper armful. Kit's known them all her life; she can remember picking the fuzzy pods as she'd been taught to pick her mother's peas. *Nuh-uh, Kitty-cat, you eat those, you die.*

He draws up before her, his face serious, the line in his forehead like a cut.

"Can't bring those on board," she says.

"No?"

"Bad luck on a boat, flowers."

"Right." He nods. "Guess I'll give them to you here."

She stares up at him. She knows this is something men do—was it her father, tearing up a fistful of violets from beside the lake? Or was it one of her mother's stories from the life before? Nothing Kit can be sure of, nothing she can quite recall. She looks at the flowers in Jimmy's hands. When he bends to kiss her, she turns up her mouth.

28

I could not believe it. To begin with, no one but your father did. Still, the cannery rowboat was missing, along with the man who had borrowed it and the woman who had been seen talking—seen *laughing*—with that man. Seen by more people, it seemed, with every day the pair of them remained gone. *Oh, Bobbie Starratt was friendly with the cook, all right. Maybe the two of them were old friends.*

Men laughed the way they had when your mother first came to Far Cry, and again they learned not to do so around Frank. Women, too, stifled their talk when he was near. I suppose I was spared the worst of the gossip as well—left to think the matter through, or try not to, on my own.

What if something bad had happened between Bobbie and Frank, something . . . worse? But why talk to Lo Yim? Could she not have come to me? Of course, she had. She had come down to the little beach to tell me about the comb, the anger they couldn't resolve. *Nowadays he can't even manage it half the time.* Perhaps Lo Yim had done more than listen. Perhaps he had offered to help. None of which meant he would not be back—would not at least send word.

They had been gone four days when I opened the side door to throw out the mop water, and heard a woman's voice.

" . . . worming her way into the office, and poor Orpha too ill to keep an eye." Agneta Jensen, holding forth on the boardwalk outside the store. "And now it looks as though Ed Knox wasn't enough for her."

A quieter voice now—Gladys Winslow, perhaps, or Janet Potts. "Poor Frank."

"Poor Frank? That man got what was coming to him. You don't bring home a goat and hope for wool."

I stepped back softly, closing the door and setting the bucket down. The idea might have been ugly in Agneta Jensen's mouth, but it was true—they were goats together, Bobbie and Frank, they had been from the start. Again I remembered his trouble in the bedroom—no way left for the pair of them to get close.

Even so. Even if she had seen a way out in Lo Yim, it was me he wanted. It was.

I had told myself he had married out of duty—his brother's wife, his brother's son. But what of the child that followed? Born lifeless, yes, but nonetheless born. There was a cold, clear sense to it. He would not be the first man to want it both ways.

I thought Knox would have the sense to leave us be. It was mid-week when he came knocking, your father and I partway through a game. I got up to fetch the watered bottle and another glass.

Knox had a cake tin with him, the first and only time he did not arrive empty-handed. Woodley's Best Ginger Loaf, a bear in a bonnet on the lid, sitting down with her cubs to tea. He placed it on the table alongside the board, took up his peg and stuck it in the third track halfway between Frank's peg and mine. *Law of averages*, he liked to say. What did it matter when I had been helping the fool win for years.

An hour passed peaceably enough, perhaps two. Neither Frank nor I made mention of the cake tin, though from time to time I found my eye drawn to the family of bears. Knox tried tapping a finger on the lid. When that raised no comment, he gave up and pried it off, releasing a smell of molasses and spice. I brought a butter knife to the table and cut wedges from the sticky wheel. Frank took the first and pushed it into his mouth.

"Good, huh?" Knox reached for a piece of his own. "The missus sent it along."

Frank nodded, chewing.

"She's in a bit of a state, truth be told. Has been ever since . . . well." Knox shook his head. "Leaving like that, without a word."

Frank had a finger in his mouth. He drew it out, scraping it clean against his teeth. "Yeah, well, she's a hard little bitch."

Knox's eyes widened. I set my drink down, making a sound.

Frank looked at me. "Gotta face facts, Andy. Folks were right around here—once a whore, always a whore."

The lid lay on the table, silver side up. I thought to turn it over and look again at the picture there.

"You think that's it?" Knox said. "She's gone back to work?"

Your father gathered up the cards. "When else you see a white woman shacked up with a Chinaman?"

"Vancouver, you think?"

"Fucked if I know." Frank began to shuffle. "San Francisco, maybe."

Knox had his nose down in his glass. "Least you got your money's worth."

Frank's head swivelled. "What'd you say?"

"Bobbie. She was . . . warm, you know. The two of you, anybody could see."

I watched your father. I was used to reading his face, but there was nothing there. "Frank," I said. "Frank."

"—What."

"Your deal."

Your father and I kept well enough on course while the cannery was running—it was only after Far Cry shut down for the season that things got bad again. I remember one night when we ran out of whiskey, and I came next door for more. I unlocked the cabinet beneath the counter, reaching for the last remaining bottle of the best. Something scratched at my hand. I recognized the comb by feel—one piece, two. I drew them out, half a sailboat on each. Just like the woman, I thought in my bitterness. A hiding place and not.

How often did you sleep in the stockroom during those months? I can say only that I woke some mornings to find Lys gone. For all I know, life may have been more peaceful with Frank crashing back to the cabin to pass out alone.

There were times when I should have made him stay, like that night in early February after days of sodden snow. He must have been lying there for hours—the dripping boughs had frozen a glaze over his coat. Thank God I took the shorter path on my way to swim. Not as much to intrude upon, I suppose, with just you and your father at home.

I carried him to the cabin, knocked with my boot until you came running in your nightdress. You were a diligent nurse. No matter how many cloths your father heated on his forehead, you had another cooling in the bowl. The cabin smelled of broth whenever I stopped by—chicken for the first pot, then the kelpy smell of boiling fish. Between visits I made a virtue of working like two men, tearing up softened sections of boardwalk and dock.

There were days of raving, much of it about his time lost at sea. Then that terrible hacking when the fever finally broke. I wonder, did you know how dangerous it was? All those years of listening to Orpha Knox's holey lungs, you could be forgiven for thinking a cough would not kill. You saw how it hurt him, though, how the violence of it wore him out. I knew he had had his fill of doctors overseas, but when Archie Paul motored into the bay for a sack of flour, I sent him on to Wardell's with a message for Dan Pike to relay. Four days passed before Dr. Pollock tied up at the long dock, and by then Frank was sitting up in bed.

The day my friend showed up at the cottage again, I got a shock. Leaning in the doorway, he looked like a man who had been a decade gone—his eyes large and dark, his cheekbones showing. A different man. More handsome, even, than before.

I was boiling coffee. I held up a mug.

"Fuck that," he said, crossing to the table. "I been three weeks without a drink."

I told myself it was all right. We had had our scare. I had managed things before.

◗

Back in the skiff, Kit and Jimmy sit together on the forward thwart. His expression is hard. She should never have told him about Knox.

"Are you mad at me?" she says.

"What? No. I'm mad at him."

She meets his gaze. "I can't stay here." And before she can think better of it, "I don't want to."

She's surprised when he lays his hand on hers. This time the kiss is careful. Blood flushes through her, until the problem comes clear. She draws back. "You want to live in the city."

"I do?"

"Your father—"

"He's gone, Kit. They both are. They chose another life." He takes hold of her hand and squeezes, the hundred smarting cracks. She squeezes back. "When?" he says.

"Soon. Tomorrow, maybe, or tonight."

"Really?"

"Really. Bugger the season."

He grins. "Wait, what about your place?"

Her mind moves over the cabin, everything it holds. "That won't take long." She turns her gaze down-inlet, Far Cry marked by a twist of smoke. A thought for the waterline, the trail up to her father's grave. She could be free of the place by day's end.

Except. She looks at Jimmy. "My uncle."

He nods. Somehow he understands. "Would he come?"

"I don't know," she tells him. "I can ask."

29

I suppose we got used to playing cribbage at the cabin while Frank was ill. Knox had been back a couple of weeks, and this time he had not dragged Orpha along. I cannot say if he came knocking at the cottage and found it empty, only that he did not brave the headland path to intrude upon a game.

Now it was my turn to carry over the bread. You are no more a natural baker than your mother was—you know that, Kit—but you fry a nice fillet. You seemed glad enough to have us there, and Lys liked the cabin's rug just as well as mine. Of course, you would take yourself off to bed when we sat up late—your own little cot or the pallet in the stockroom, depending on whether your father drank himself quiet or loud.

The night I am thinking of, he had found his way to the subject of your mother—how he was better off, he could see that now. With a slut like her it was only a matter of time.

I cut a glance toward your room.

"Don't worry," he said. "Sleeps like the dead, that one."

Even so, I stood and moved as quietly as my state allowed. Holding the curtain aside, I let in enough lamplight to find your bed made up tight. I remembered then, the knowledge lurching into view—you had taken Lys out some time before. Already judging it to be a night for the stockroom, you had not returned.

"All right?" said Frank.

"All right."

"Told you. You wouldn't believe what that kid's slept through."

I returned to the table and took up my cards. He made a smacking sound, lips against his teeth. "Can't trust the noisy ones, that's what the old man used to say. They holler for you, they'll do it for the next bugger too."

I shut my eyes. It was the first time I let myself see it—Lo Yim and Bobbie, Bobbie and Lo Yim.

"Fights, too," Frank said. "She never cared how loud she yelled."

I nodded, reaching for my glass.

"I never hit her," Frank added.

"Of course not."

"It's just, that night, she was fighting me, you know? I mean, what the hell more proof do you need? Never said no in her life, and all of a sudden she's fighting me off."

Where does the drink go, I wonder, when a body suddenly sobers up? It felt as though a door had blown open in the back of my skull.

"I didn't push her," Frank said. "I didn't." His gaze found the stove and fixed on it. For a moment I saw Bobbie sitting in the sun with her polishing rag and a bit of the brightwork, arms resting on her belly's mound. "Jesus, Andy," he said. "It wasn't even that hard a knock."

Was I numb, Kit? I could not seem to speak.

"I thought she was out cold at first. But then I knew." He nodded to himself. "And I knew whose fucking fault it was, too.

"Next thing I know, I've got her slung over my shoulder and I'm out the door. I even think to grab the axe. No sense chancing the rocks—I pushed through the scrub up top, down to where the back path comes out.

"I didn't like to put her down on the beach, but I had to. I had to flip over the boat. I laid her in the stern, and the axe alongside her. There's that oilskin you keep tucked under the thwart. I covered her up.

"Christ, I was shitting myself when we got out deep. My heart was going like a train. I couldn't look at the water, you know? I'm just rowing, watching the shape of her under the oilskin, looking round to the island now and then.

"It got a bit better when I could row in close, bring her round the far shore. The bastard was anchored in Deep Cut Cove. 'Hey, Lo!' I call out to him. You can see he's surprised, worried even. I'm not the one he's expecting, that's for damn sure. But that's all right, because by then I've got an idea.

"I row in fast. 'We need you back at the store,' I tell him. 'Andy, Mr. Viken, his shoulder's gone again.'

"'Anders Viken?' he says. I nod, and he says, 'Okay, I come.' Just like that. He bends to haul up the anchor and I reach under the oilskin for the axe."

I must have flinched, some hint of feeling on my face. Your father looked hurt.

"Christ, Andy, I used the butt. I'm not gonna cut the fucker's head off." He took up his glass and drained it. "Anyhow, he went down. Knocked the bucket over, too, squid and ink everywhere, filthy things." He shook his head. "I thought about taking her back with me, you believe that? Like, it's all right, the sonofabitch is dead, I can take her home. But it was him she wanted, so I tied up alongside him and folded back the oilskin, and there she was. Took a minute to get my balance once I picked her up, then I heaved her over into the other boat. They want to be together? All right, they're together.

"I gotta climb across then—Christ, I just about went in. I tie them up together with the painter line, and I drag up the anchor and wind that line around them too. Then I reach back for the axe. It's a trick keeping my footing in all those squid, but I swear, it only takes two cuts to scuttle that piece of shit. I barely had time to jump back into the *Coot*. There was this hissing sound, I remember, the jacklights going out. And then it was dark."

He left off, looking at his hands. It was some comfort, the idea of them sinking together into the silt, each with the other to hold. It came to me then—they had been down there when I had swum out hours late to find an empty cove. The heart so hungry. He had loved me. Lo Yim had loved me after all.

I took a breath. "What then?"

"Then?" Your father looked up. "Then I rowed back. I kept my eyes shut half the time—I even had to stop and puke over the side, but I made it. I hauled the boat up and flipped her over, made it back to the cabin, even stuck the axe back in the stump. I listened for Kit when I got in. Nothing. All I wanted was to take a bottle to bed, but the job wasn't done. Bobbie had that old grip, you know, the one she brought with her when she came. I pulled it out from under the bed and shoved in a few of her dresses—that fucking blue one, that went, and her nightdress. I even remembered her hairbrush. Put the fry pan in there too—she'd want that with her wherever the hell they were going, right? Besides, it'd weigh the thing down.

"I threw it off the cliff, out over the kelp. I'm walking back to the cabin then, thinking that's it, that's everything—only it's not, because there's two of them, right, and the Chinaman would take his stuff too. Christ, I felt those stairs going up to the cookhouse. Piss-weak. I don't know what time it was—still dark, but okay, if anyone sees me, I just say I'm looking for my slut of a wife. It's all coming out now.

"Turns out the little fucker hardly had anything to pack. Pair of trousers, couple of shirts, some book in Chinese by his bed. I put it all in a basket and chucked it out back of the coop."

Again, he fell quiet. Nothing now but the sea-sound in my skull.

"You see how it happened," he said.

There came a voice very like my own. "Yes, I see."

"You're not," he said. "You wouldn't—?"

I made myself look at him. I shook my head. He dropped his face into his hands.

"Frank," I said, "there is something I must tell you." He looked up, and the story spun itself. "That comb Bobbie had. After you— After it was broken, she kept the pieces."

"Doesn't surprise me."

"She hid them, Frank."

"Yeah?"

"On the *Dogfish*."

He stared at me.

"She said if you ever got the balls up to go back in the boat—"

"What?"

"Forgive me," I said, "I should have told you—"

But he was already standing, lurching toward the door. I stood up after him. There was only a sliver of moon—what did your mother used to call it? A fingernail. From the cabin door, I watched him find the path, listing dangerously, snatching at branches to stay on his feet. A friend would have followed. I turned the other way.

Down the rocks by starlight, as sure-footed as I have ever been. I dropped my clothes on the stones, thrashed out into the shallows and dove. Out over the kelp bed now, Bobbie's fry pan and nightdress below me, down where the great stems find their hold. Round the headland, swift strokes into the reeking drift.

The harder I swam, the less air I seemed to need. A glance up the headland showed I was even with Knox's house, shut up dark as a sleeping eye. Underwater now, driving on to the black, barnacled legs of the pilings, the stinking underside of the dock. I bobbed up in the echo, breathing. Already his senseless step, thudding through wood into water, shivering in my skin. How many strokes to the *Dogfish* at its mooring? The gap between dock and gunwale was sufficient. I reached for his boot as he stepped aboard.

I suppose he took in a lungful on the drop—I might have heard half a shout. Still, you know how strong he was. He struggled up, but I dragged him back and held him under. I held him until he was quiet, and then I let him go.

Swimming back, I felt the inlet's cold. When the headland slipped past, I turned, reaching for the shallows, for shore. The stream gabbled. The beach seemed steeper, as though it would tip me back into the tide. I dragged my shirt and trousers on over my wet skin, forced my feet into their boots. The moon was scarcely there. Taking the back path home, I missed my footing and fell. I lay listening for injury, my face in the litter of needles and leaves. Some time passed before I rose.

◖

Riding in on the tow, Kit sits facing Jimmy, looking back the way they came. Let the others see them talking—those in the closest skiffs might even hear. She's telling him about the inlet, everything she knows. The Pauls' true home in the village at its head, the ruin of Glenelg Cannery, Far Cry and the other going concerns. Everyone follows the fish. Not just the salmon—the herring and the candlefish, the rockfish and the greenling, the sharp-toothed ling cod on the ocean floor. Eagles and murrelets, sea lions and seals. The blackfish move through in their packs, big whales appear and dissolve—humpbacks and greys, sometimes a solitary sperm. Sharks too, arm-length and body-length, baskers as long as the collector boat, stem to stern.

Jimmy looks and he listens. When they get in, she'll show him the *Dogfish*, the first time she's set foot aboard since her father missed his step. First, though, she'll take the stairs two at a time up to the boardwalk. Find her uncle and give him the news.

◖

A twitch of Lys's ear as the towboat enters the bay. Soon fishermen will be climbing the stairs in search of a bottle or a blanket, a lantern or a lure. I should finish scribbling and go next door.

I swam out to the island last night. The drift seemed broader, filthier than ever before. Then the tide's long leaning, the island's rocky shore. Its outer face went scudding past. Fast as a blackfish, I cut into the cove.

Who knows the actual spot? I chose the place where Lo Yim had anchored that first night, when he and I made our way ashore. I thought to upend myself and dive, but Deep Cut Cove honours its name, and in any case, what could I hope to find? Their flesh would be long gone, their bones tumbled by the silent underside of the winter's storms.

The sea felt slippery, the inlet's smallest life sifting up to the surface to feed. I cycled in the water, fanning my arms. It did not happen as I imagined it—your mother's hair rising on an upswell to swirl about my ankles, Lo Yim's hand reaching to caress my calf. If anything touched me, it was the fin of a ling cod, the fluttering mantle of a squid.

Oh, Kit, I was tired, the *søvngjenger* a *søvn-svømmer* now. I hung there a little longer, until the sleepswimmer carried me home.

———

It is all I can imagine now, the plan Lo Yim and I shared, the dream of a lonely cove. Of course, I am acquainted with that life already—smoked rockfish and rain, mink in the trap and the dark-finned basker moving open-mouthed across the swell. A beginning, it might have been for the two of us. Alone, I will make it my end.

I will go tonight. Carry what little I need across the back headland path, float the *Coot* and take up the oars. Lys will be here for you to find—she has been yours as much as mine from the start. It seems I will leave these pages as well. You will blame me, Kit, how could you not. But will you forsake me?

There now, your step on the boards, I would know it anywhere. Lys too, old dog. She turns in her dreaming. She raises her silver head.

ACKNOWLEDGEMENTS

My thanks to the following individuals for sharing their time and expertise: Ben York; Cynthia Toman; Sarah Glassford; Tim Cook and Mélanie Morin-Pelletier at the Canadian War Museum; Alexander Comber at Library and Archives Canada; Claire Gilbert at the Royal BC Museum.

There is no writing without reading. The following books fed this one: *The Good Hope Cannery: Life and Death at a Salmon Cannery* by W.B. MacDonald; *The Salmon People* by Hugh W. McKervill; *Living on the Edge: Nuu-Chah-Nulth History from an Ahousaht Chief's Perspective* by Chief Earl Maquinna George; *Salmon: Our Heritage* by Cicely Lyons; *Whistle up the Inlet: The Union Steamship Story* by Gerald A. Rushton; *Vancouver: The Way It Was* by Michael Kluckner; *Paper Shadows: A Chinatown Childhood* by Wayson Choy; *Saltwater City: An Illustrated History of the Chinese in Vancouver* by Paul Yee; *Tales from Gold Mountain* by Paul Yee; *Red Lights on the Prairies* by James H. Gray; *A Window on Whaling in British Columbia* by Joan Goddard; *On the Northwest: Commercial Whaling in the Pacific Northwest 1790–1967* by Robert Lloyd Webb; *British Columbia: A Natural History* by Richard

Cannings and Sydney Cannings; *The Promise of Paradise: Utopian Communities in British Columbia* by Andrew Scott; *Shark Drunk: The Art of Catching a Large Shark from a Tiny Rubber Dinghy in a Big Ocean* by Morten Strøksnes (translation by Tiina Nunnally); *Weird Tales from Northern Seas* by Jonas Lie (translation by R. Nisbet Bain); *The Sinking of the HMHS Llandovery Castle*, issued by Canada's Department of Public Information; *Sister Soldiers of the Great War: The Nurses of the Canadian Army Medical Corps* by Cynthia Toman; *War Story of the Canadian Army Medical Corps* by J. George Adami; *Seventy Years of Service: A History of the Royal Canadian Army Medical Corps* by Gerald W.L. Nicholson; *A Surgeon in Arms* by R.J. Manion; *Tapestry of War: A Private View of Canadians in the Great War* by Sandra Gwyn; *Hell's Corner: An Illustrated History of Canada's Great War, 1914–1918* by J.L. Granatstein; *When Your Number's Up: The Canadian Soldier in the First World War* by Desmond Morton; *A Nation in Conflict: Canada and the Two World Wars* by Andrew Iarocci and Jeffrey A. Keshen; *When the Boys Came Marching Home* by Ben Wicks; *A Dictionary of the English Language* by Samuel Johnson.

As ever, thanks to the beautiful book people at Penguin Random House Canada, especially Anne Collins, who sees (and loves) both forest and tree.

Thanks also to my agent, the kind but mighty Ellen Levine.

Family and friends, I owe you everything.

Clive, my heart, I owe you even more.

ALISSA YORK's internationally acclaimed novels include *Mercy*, *Effigy* (shortlisted for the Scotiabank Giller Prize), *Fauna* and, most recently, *The Naturalist*. She is also the author of the short fiction collection, *Any Given Power*, stories from which have won the Journey Prize and the Bronwen Wallace Award. Her essays and articles have appeared in such periodicals as *The Guardian*, *The Globe and Mail* and *Canadian Geographic*. York has lived all over Canada and now makes her home in Toronto with her husband, artist Clive Holden.

A NOTE ABOUT THE TYPE

This book is set in Garamond Premier Pro, a modern font family based on roman types cut by Jean Jannon in 1615 and adapted from earlier types by Francesco Griffo and Claude Garamond. Considered the culmination of French Renaissance type design, Garamond's elegant lines have been popular among book designers for centuries. Some distinctive characteristics include an "e" with a small eye, and an "a" with a sharp turn in the bowl of the letterform.